Zombies
of Byzantium

Zombies of Byzantium

Sean Munger

SAMHAIN
PUBLISHING

Samhain Publishing, Ltd.
11821 Mason Montgomery Rd., 4B
Cincinnati, OH 45249
www.samhainpublishing.com

Zombies of Byzantium
Copyright © 2013 by Sean Munger
Print ISBN: 978-1-61921-229-9
Digital ISBN: 978-1-61921-180-3

Editing by Don D'Auria
Cover by Angela Waters

First Samhain Publishing, Ltd. electronic publication: February 2013
First Samhain Publishing, Ltd. print publication: February 2013

Dedication

To Cody, with all my love.

It is the Byzantine year 6225 A.M. (Anno Mundi), on our calendar the year 717 A.D.

Byzantium—the Eastern Roman Empire—is in peril.

On one side of the Empire, the Islamic Caliph, Suleiman ibn Abd al-Malik, prepares to conquer the last Christian kingdom standing between the armies of Islam and the European continent. On the other, the Bulgarian Khan Tervel lies in wait to pick the carcass of the Empire clean.

In just four years, three Byzantine Emperors have been deposed violently. Barely five centuries after the Christianization of Rome by Constantine the Great, the Empire is on its last legs.

Chapter One

In the Village of Demons

The Monastery of Chenolakkos (Asia Minor, central Turkey)
Spring, 717 A.D.

I had just started painting a new icon when the summons came. One of the rich merchants in Nicaea had wanted to show off to his dinner guests how pious he was, so he commissioned the monastery for a nice triptych he could display in his dining room. It was going to be one of my better pictures—Christ hanging on the cross in the center, the Virgin Mary on the right panel and a couple of saints being hideously burned, mutilated and tortured on the left panel. I had the whole thing sketched out on parchment and I thought I could polish it off in a week or so. It was a beautiful spring day in late May and the sun was shining brightly on the snowy slopes of Mt. Olympus visible through the studio windows. I'd mixed my colors and I'd just cracked the egg for the tempera when Brother Asidenos hurried into the studio. He was a mousy little man with squinty eyes and a twitchy little nose. "Brother Stephen?" he said. "The *hegoumenos* wants to see you in his chambers."

I grunted. "Brother Asidenos, I just started this."

"The *hegoumenos* said it was urgent."

I wondered what I was being punished for now. I'd been in the monastic life long enough to curb my habit of cursing—one of the lingering sins of country folk like me—so I bit my tongue, put down the tempera bowl and drew my cowl up over my head. Asidenos led me down the steps and through the colonnade. In the chapel, the other monks were just coming back from prayers at matins. Asidenos showed me into the *hegoumenos*'s office. It was a dingy stone-walled chamber lit only by a tiny window up near the ceiling. A big blackened fireplace held a crackling blaze no matter the season. The place was mounded with thick books and parchments. A dim candle smoldered on a spike. A rat, carrying a piece of gnawed chicken bone, scurried across my path into the dusty corner as I approached. Old Father Eunomios was busy writing something on a parchment with a reed pen. I wasn't sure he saw me—the old fool was mostly blind—so I cleared my throat. When he still didn't answer, I said softly, "Father *Hegoumenos*, you wanted to see me?"

"Yes, Brother Stephen." Eunomios didn't look up from his parchment. "Your services have been called for. You'll be leaving Chenolakkos within the fortnight."

From his stony expression it was obvious this prospect didn't trouble the old coot, nor did it me. In the six years, since I first took my vows after the untimely deaths of my parents from fever, I'd come to regard joining the cloth in general, and the Monastery of Chenolakkos in particular, as a colossal misfortune. The food was dreadful, the discipline harsh, the endless hours of prayer boring to the point of stupefaction. The closest I'd ever gotten to a woman was seeing a peasant girl bathing in a stream three years ago, and she wasn't even fully naked. I didn't want to let on that I was elated by the thought of getting out of prison after all this time, so my face remained as immovable as Eunomios's when I replied, "Oh really? Where am I going?"

"The capital. I've had a dispatch from Father Rhetorios at the Monastery of St. Stoudios. It seems that one of their venerable old iconographers has died, and as they have several urgent commissions they're seeking a replacement wherever one can be found. Naturally, I thought of you."

On the one hand I didn't want to look a gift horse in the mouth, but on the other I smelled a rat, more than just the little beastie in the corner chowing down on the remnants of last night's dinner. "St. Stoudios?" I said, drawing in my breath. "In Constantinople?"

"Do I speak with a stutter, Brother Stephen?"

"Uh—no. No, Sir. I just wondered if you thought—I mean, I've only been out of apprenticeship for a year and a half, since old Rhangabé died—"

The head monk finally looked up from his parchment. Squinting to see me past the cataracts in his ghostly eyes, he said, "You think your work is not up to the standards of the most important monastery in the Byzantine Empire, is that it?"

Damn the old guy. He had a passion for tempting me to say something that would get me in trouble. It was one of the few pleasures Eunomios had left in life, given that he could barely walk and had about two teeth left in his head. "Er, no," I replied. "That's not exactly what I meant. But I've heard about St. Stoudios. They supply icons for the Emperor and his family. Don't you have to apprentice for many years to even get in the door there?"

"Aye. You do." With a hint of a smile—which, given the rarity of such an event, almost cracked the old buzzard's plaster-like face—he finished writing and set the pen in its holder. "Let us speak plainly, Brother Stephen."

"Okay, let's."

"You're a bad monk. Of that, no one who lives in this cloister has any doubt. You've not given up your affinity for earthly things, for sinful things. I trust you believe in God as deeply as any of us, but in your habits, your language and your general demeanor you're an embarrassment to the entire monastery." Eunomios gripped the arms of his wooden chair, drew a deep breath and began to hoist his ancient black-robed frame out of it. For a moment I thought his spindly legs would give out and he'd crash to the floor. I didn't particularly relish the prospect of trying to pick him up, considering he bathed even less often than most of the stinking mounds of sweaty flesh that passed for

11

monks around here. But, astoundingly, he remained on his feet.

He continued. "You are, however, an excellent artist. Your lines are strong, your colors bold. You still have much learning to do, but there is potential. It occurs to me that perhaps you can serve the Lord in a greater capacity outside the walls of this monastery."

"I see."

With a wizened clawlike hand, Eunomios groped for his gnarled walking stick, leaning up against the desk. "Father Rhetorios is desperate. The new Emperor has been on the throne barely two months. He's purging the palace of all trace of his predecessor, including the very icons that the prior Emperor Theodosius and his family venerated in their porphyry chambers. The unfortunate death of one of St. Stoudios's younger iconographers couldn't have come at a worse time for them. Iconographers are very important these days. With an attack on Constantinople by the Saracens expected daily, icons over which to pray for the deliverance of the city are at a premium. Rhetorios also owes me a favor. He'll accept anyone I send so long as I vouch for them. Since I now have this unique opportunity to be rid of you once and for all, I figured I shouldn't question the Lord's clear direction in this matter." Having secured his stick, Eunomios began hobbling right past me. "Please complete your present commission as quickly as possible. Then pack up your paints and your personal effects and be gone within the fortnight. I've dispatched a letter to St. Stoudios promising you by Midsummer's Day."

I could tell the interview was over. "Thank you, *Hegoumenos*."

Eunomios was almost to the doorway but he turned back, smiling for the second time in forty years. "Oh, one other thing. Don't think I'm fool enough to release a twenty-one-year-old whelp on the open road to indulge his sinful desires with impunity. I'm sending Brother Theophilus with you. He'll make sure you stay in line."

For the first time my joy at getting sprung from this hellhole dampened. "Brother *Theophilus*?" I gasped. "He's what, eighty? Can he even make the trip from here to Constantinople?"

"That is what *you*, Brother Stephen, will be tasked with ensuring. We can spare no horses, so you'll have to go on foot." Eunomios looked quite pleased with himself. Pausing at the doorway, he said, "Well, hop to it! Don't you have an icon to finish?"

So that was that. I was being transferred to Constantinople to slave away in an Imperial icon studio, my chaperone would be Chenolakkos's oldest, frailest, most silent and most disagreeable monk, and we wouldn't even have the luxury of riding a horse. Fine prospect! But there was nothing I could say. Once such a thing was decided, nothing short of the personal intercession of God Himself could change Eunomios's mind.

I'll skip over the details of my last weeks at Chenolakkos. I finished the icon, it was delivered to the fat old rich man in Nicaea, I packed up my stuff and Theophilus made ready to accompany me on the road to Constantinople. We left on a warm morning in mid-June. Our path would take us down out of the mountains, past Nicaea and northward toward Kios, where (I hoped) we could catch a boat to Constantinople. We traveled light. I brought only a small leather shoulder bag containing my paints and a Bible. Theophilus brought an extra cassock and one blanket. We had no food other than a few scraps of bread. Between us we had only a few gold *solidi* in a leather drawstring purse that Theophilus insisted on carrying. It would probably be a four-day journey to Kios and who knew how long after that. We'd be depending on the Christian kindness of strangers and innkeepers to sustain us along the way.

Theophilus was a perfectly humorless man. Dressed winter or summer in a long thick black cloak and hood, he had long snow-white hair and a scraggly beard reaching down to his chest. In the six years I'd been at Chenolakkos, I'd heard the old guy say three words, and "Amen" was two of them. Even that morning as we set off from the monastery he said nothing. At the start of the old cobbled road leading down from the hills we paused, looking up at the blocky building with

13

its bell tower and single gnarled turret, and I remarked, "You'll probably be back, Theophilus, but I doubt I'll see the place ever again. Makes you think, you know?"

He looked back at the monastery, but then turned his head, planted his walking stick (which was a foot taller than he was) and moved past me toward the road. Theophilus didn't strike me as the sentimental type, and surely he'd return after dropping me off at Constantinople, but I doubt he'd been outside the walls of the monastery in years and you'd think he'd have something to say about it. When he remained impassively silent, I realized that I was going to have to entertain myself on this trip.

The day grew stifling hot. It's a weird thing to be roasting to death in a woolen cowl on a rocky sun-drenched road and to see the desolate snows of the mountain off in the distance at the same time. There weren't even many trees along the route so there was no shelter from the beating sun. There were no other travelers going our direction or the opposite on the road, which was a little strange, considering the profusion of monasteries in the area and the many monks and pilgrims who made the rounds among them. I did my best to get Theophilus to talk. "So, when was the last time you were in Constantinople?" was greeted with a shrug of the shoulders that suggested he was damned if he knew. "Anything in particular you want to do there?" met with a one-word answer, "Pray."

I shook my head. "Real life of the party, aren't you, Theophilus?"

Despite the heat and the taciturn company, I was excited. I'd never seen the capital before. Being a monk, it probably wasn't realistic to expect I'd get a chance to take in a show or even a chariot race at the Hippodrome, but I thought a nice bath and a tour of St. Sofia weren't out of the question—that was, if Rhetorios of St. Stoudios didn't chain me to a desk in the icon studio the moment I set foot in the monastery.

In the late afternoon we spotted a faint smudge on the horizon. After another turn or three on the stone road, we saw it was a plume of smoke. Theophilus stopped, planted his stick and shaded his eyes with his hand. "Village," he said.

"Ah, good." I wiped sweat off my forehead with the sleeve of my robe. "Maybe we can get some fresh water there. I'm parched."

"Strange," Theophilus remarked. "So many chimney smokes for such a hot day."

"Hopefully that means they're cooking up a feast for us."

As we drew closer, it became obvious from the amount of smoke and its black color that these were no chimney fires. A couple of miles away Theophilus paused again. "I think something's wrong," he said. You had to know something unusual was up; Theophilus had said more words to me today already than he probably had to anyone in the last ten years at the monastery.

"Do you think it could be a raid?" I said. "By the Saracens, maybe?"

Theophilus shook his head. "If the Saracen army was in these parts, we would have heard. There would have been a mass exodus." He planted his stick for another pace and continued walking.

The village nestled in a little valley near a small stream. The fields surrounding it were strangely deserted; there were no farmers or workmen in sight. From a ridge above the town we could see a cluster of shabby peasants' houses and a larger building that looked like a storehouse or granary of some kind. That building wasn't on fire, which told me this wasn't a raid because Saracens or other brigands seeking loot would have cleaned it out and burned it behind them the first thing. Several of the houses were aflame, however. We could see no activity in the town itself. I looked at Theophilus. "Should we go down there?"

"Do we have a choice?" he replied. "There may be people in need of help."

"It could be dangerous. We have no idea how this happened. If it was bandits or outlaws, they might still be down there waiting to pick off anyone who comes to investigate."

His cold gray eyes stared at me with an almost sarcastic look. "*You* are the young one, and I'm old," he said, "and yet *you're* the one

15

shrinking from danger?" He shook his head. Starting down the road, he muttered, "The youth of Byzantium is not as hardy as it once was."

Down in the valley, closer to the smoldering village, the mystery deepened. The deserted fields were filled with ripening crops. We passed a plow abandoned in a field of rye. The horse who had pulled it grazed lazily some distance away. That was telling. Anyone who had come to sack this village would surely have taken the horses, oxen and any donkeys with them to carry off their loot, and they probably would have burned the crops too. Then we started to see bodies. Theophilus noticed them before I did. He suddenly stopped, crossed himself and murmured a little prayer. Peering through the smoke of one of the nearby farmhouses, reduced to a cluster of charred timbers, I could see three human figures lying motionless in the dust. Buzzards were already circling. A mangy dog with bloody whiskers barked at our approach. Theophilus paused, and then ran (as best he could on his thin wobbly legs) toward the victims. As he neared them, he suddenly recoiled. "Dear God, preserve us!" he gasped.

Two women and a man were lying on the ground before us. Their clothes—the plain rough garb of country peasants—were covered in blood. The man's arm had been torn brutally from its socket, the arm itself missing. The corpses looked as if they had been feasted upon by ravenous wolves. One woman's stomach was torn open, her guts oozing into the dust, already attracting flies. I could see what looked like teeth marks in the neck of the other woman. I've seen death before, but I'd never seen anything like this. I backed away from the corpses, crossing myself. The stench of death in the village was like the breath of the Devil himself.

"Who could have done such a thing?" said Theophilus.

"Somebody with some *very* serious issues," I replied. I looked ahead through the village at the smoldering houses. "Come on, let's see if there's anyone left alive."

In our search, we found several more corpses. They, like the three at the entrance to the village, were also violently torn. One, heartbreakingly, was a little girl. "Could it have been wolves or some

16

other wild beast?" I asked Theophilus.

"I don't think so," he said. "The horses and oxen haven't been touched. Only the people."

"But why? Who would want to attack this village? Doesn't look like these people would have anything of value. If it wasn't raiders—"

Theophilus silenced me with a wave of his hand. He looked off to his left, hearing something. I heard it too. Above the crackle of burning wood there was a low moaning sound, the lowing of indeterminate voices. With his walking stick, Theophilus motioned toward the church at the end of the dusty village street. It had been set on fire, its thatch roof already burned away. The thick packed-mud walls were charred and scorched. The strange moaning seemed to be coming from there.

Hesitantly we approached. There were many bloody footprints in the dust before the doors of the church, and carnage, including a severed human hand. We paused perhaps fifteen feet from the doors. They were partially burned, but I could see, charred and blackened, the links of a great chain that had been drawn across the portal.

"Dear Lord!" I gasped. "They herded the villagers inside the church and set fire to it!" I sprang toward the doors, but Theophilus held me back with an outstretched hand.

"No," he cautioned. "Don't touch it. The fire is too hot."

We then saw the most curious—and the most horrible—of the sights upon which we'd laid eyes that day. The church had been burning for a while and a section of its exterior wall had collapsed. Through an aperture in the ruined wall a shambling figure emerged. It was impossible to tell whether it was a man or woman, for all the clothes had long since been burned off its frame. Indeed the person's skin itself was on fire. The figure, stumbling over the wreckage of the wall and lurching awkwardly toward us, was but one vast human-shaped torch. The figure did not scream in pain nor thrash about in utter panic as one would expect if he (or she) were engulfed in flame from head to toe. Instead it emitted a low mindless moan, very much like the other strange sounds emanating from inside the church.

17

Shocked, horrified, Theophilus and I both sprang backwards. The flaming figure did not move quickly. It shambled, as if unsure of its steps. Flailing its arms, one of them, burnt through at the shoulder, crumbled into chunks of flaming flesh, but the figure did not stop. It continued its approach toward us.

Theophilus and I glanced at each other. His eyes, wide and staring, must have looked like mine. "*Run!*" we both cried, and bolted for the road that led down out of the village.

The old man was not very quick. After only a few steps he stumbled. He managed to catch himself with the walking stick before we went down, but the flaming ghoul was able to gain on him. I ran back to Theophilus. Shifting the leather bag containing my paints to the other shoulder, I knelt down. "Get up on my back," I demanded. He did so as best he could, and I began to run. With Theophilus on my back, I was slower than I would have been otherwise, but together we were still faster than the torch pursuing us. Every half-minute or so I paused to look over my shoulder. The incendiary specter continued to pursue us, but it had not increased its pace. It was as dumb and unyielding as it was terrifying.

"What *is* it?" I whispered to Theophilus, watching the flaming ghoul stumble on the stones of the road across which we'd just come.

"The Devil," the old man said. "We must run!"

The flaming figure that came from the ruined village continued to trail us, as inexorable a follower as a faithful dog. I would sprint down the road a distance as far as I could carry Theophilus without resting and then stop for a time. The shambling torch never paused but we were able to stay well ahead of it. Eventually it was slowed down by virtue of losing a leg, which, like the arm we'd seen upon its escape from the church, burned clean through and crumbled into ashes. After that, the figure moved with sort of a limping crawl, walking on its stump and dragging its still-good leg behind it. Perhaps half an hour later as the road passed near a creek and a scrubby forest I noticed that most of the flames seemed to be dying, yet the ghoulish creature continued its approach. It was slow enough now where I no longer needed to carry Theophilus to guarantee our escape. Indeed we stopped and rested, both of us panting, and we occasionally glanced back up the road to check on the progress of our pursuer.

"It *must* be the Devil," I said. "No human being could have survived those flames. It doesn't even appear to be hurt."

"I don't think it's human," said Theophilus. "Not anymore, anyway."

The moaning made by the ghoul was especially unnerving. As it drew closer, I straightened up, shifted my leather knapsack and wiped sweat from my brow. "What are we going to do? It's obvious that monster is going to keep pursuing us until we give out."

Theophilus looked up and down the road. "The forest," he said, motioning.

So we left the road and entered the scrubby thicket. The trees here were small but at least there was shade, merciful shelter from the burning afternoon sun. The crawling, lurching ghoul pursued us right into the forest. "We must put this soul out of its misery and deliver it to God," Theophilus pronounced. "Find a heavy branch."

"Now you're making sense." I looked about and found a fallen bough with a thick knot on its end. Feeling its heft I could see its use as a weapon, but the prospect of going near enough to the monster to wield it was unsavory. I confess I felt a twinge of conscience as I looked back at Theophilus. "Do you suppose killing a thing like that is a sin?" I asked him.

"It would be a sin *not* to kill it," he assured me.

I swallowed. "All right. Here goes." The creature was perhaps thirty feet behind me. Holding the branch over my head, I ran at it, my heart pounding. One charred arm motioned toward me and its moaning seemed to reach a crescendo. I swung the branch. It knocked off the ghoul's burnt arm with scarcely more resistance than brushing away a

19

leaf or blade of grass. I swung again, this time connecting with the beast's head. Immediately its whole body—what was left of it—fell limp. I brought the branch down several more times but it was like hacking apart logs that were little more than charcoal. A cloud of foul-smelling ash rose from the thing. I coughed. Finally I tossed the branch aside and trudged my way back toward Theophilus. He held out a small jeweled cross on a chain about his neck and repeated the prayers for the Eucharist. When he was done, we both stared back at the smoldering remains of the monster. Theophilus found a stump to sit on and brought his thin body down upon it with a sigh.

"Now we know what happened in that village," I said. "Those people must have been possessed by demons. They went wild, killing those victims we saw on the ground. The survivors locked the demons in the church and set it on fire to destroy them, and then they fled."

"But they didn't smite the demons well enough. This wasn't the only one to survive the burning. There were others in the church—you heard their moans. Any one of them might escape as well."

"But *why* is this happening? What could have caused it?"

Theophilus hauled himself up off the stump and stepped through the brush in the direction of the road. "Brother Stephen, we can't know the plans of God in this world. Perhaps the people in that village were wicked in one way or another, and He sent a plague of demons to punish them."

"He couldn't have used a plague of locusts or something that wouldn't come after *us*?" I muttered. Theophilus had no answer to this, and I didn't expect one. There was nothing to do now but continue on. We still needed food and shelter for the night. If the wickedness that God had tried to punish in that unfortunate village was still afoot in the countryside, I rather hoped we would manage to avoid it. Being chased by a flaming formerly human demon, even at low speed, was not precisely the way I'd hoped to begin my new life as an iconographer in Constantinople, but, as Theophilus said, I guess we can't know God's plans.

As the sun sank we came upon a *xenodocheion,* an inn for public travelers. It was a low ramshackle stone building with a thatched roof and a couple of stinking stables behind it for horses and oxen. In fact, that was the first thing we noticed—the stables were awfully crowded, and one ass was even wandering loose in the street in front of the place, browsing along the dusty lane between a couple of flapping chickens. I could see smoke, thankfully white instead of black, spiraling from the portals in the roof. "Well, they've got soup on, at least," I told Theophilus. "I wonder if they know anything about what happened back there."

Judging by the din of voices we could hear all the way from outside, chattering excitedly in Greek, it appeared that there was definitely some excitement afoot. Before Theophilus and I had even reached the doorway the voices hushed. The heavy wooden door burst open and at once a foul-faced man with a rusty sword had sprung out of it, leveling the weapon at our throats. He might've been the innkeeper, might not have been; he wore shabby clothes and his boots were splitting at their seams. "Speak!" he cried. He waited only a moment before roaring, "*Speak now, or I'll smite you!*"

"What do you want me to say?" I gasped.

Theophilus seemed to catch on immediately. "We're men!" he cried. "We're not those mindless drones. We're friendly."

"They're monks, Onophrios," said a woman's voice from inside the building.

"She's right," I said. "My name is Stephen Diabetenos of the Chenolakkos Monastery. This is Brother Theophilus of Antioch, also lately from Chenolakkos. We require food, water and accommodation for the night."

Onophrios did not lower the sword but suddenly looked as if he wasn't so inclined to use it as he'd been a moment before. Judging us with a skeptical gaze, he asked, "You've come from Mt. Olympus?"

"Aye. We've been travelling all day."

"And you came through Domelium, the village?"

"Aye."

The sword finally drooped. "You must be stouter than you look, you men of God," Onophrios muttered. "Well, come inside. Good luck finding a place to sit, much less sleep. We're full up."

He wasn't kidding. The large single room we found ourselves in was quite crowded. There were scraggly peasant farmers, women in rough-spun clothes, ragged children, even a man in a well-tailored tunic who I guessed to be an official of some type, perhaps a tax collector. There were rough wooden benches and a few stools before the fire pits where cauldrons bubbled over with the stench of some unappetizing stew. Everyone stared at Theophilus and me as if our skin were green and we'd sprouted antennae. After shuffling about, looking for somewhere to sit, I finally approached a young man of about twenty sitting on the end of a bench. "Excuse me. Would you be so good as to let Brother Theophilus have your seat? He's quite aged, and we've been walking all day."

The young man yielded, as did the woman next to him. We sat down. Within a few moments some of the peasants had passed us rough wooden bowls of the watery meat stew, and I saw two tin beakers of fresh water making their way from hand to hand toward us. A middle-aged man in a dirty brown tunic stood before us. Perhaps he was the (former) mayor of the hell-village. As I took my bowl and beaker, he said, "Were there any left in Domelium? Any survivors?"

I opened my mouth but realized this was a trick question. "Well," I finally said, "that depends on what you consider a 'survivor'." I drew from my leather satchel a silver spoon with which to eat my stew.

"We're glad you were not harmed," said a woman.

"Not for lack of trying." I took a spoonful of the foul stew and looked up at the mayor. "What happened in the village?"

He looked puzzled at the question. Glancing between Theophilus and me, he said, "We were hoping *you* could tell *us*."

"How would *we* know what happened? All we saw were the bodies and the burning buildings."

"But you're men of God," said the woman who had stepped aside to make room for Theophilus. "Surely you must be able to make sense of these dreadful things. Why were we punished? We weren't wicked or sinful."

Theophilus and I glanced at each other with the same puzzled expression. Suddenly I felt out of my depth. I'm an icon painter. Sure, I've read the Bible, but I can't pronounce sentence on an entire village or diagnose why God chose to screw with them in whatever particularly ghastly way He had done so today. Meekly I asked the mayor, "What did you see? How did it start?"

The story came out in hesitant little bits, some from the mayor, some from the woman, parts from others of the villagers. Evidently the ordeal had begun with a mysterious traveler who arrived on horseback the night before last, seeking shelter in the village. He was a Byzantine, but the clothing he wore and the weapon he carried suggested he had spent considerable time among the Saracens, perhaps in Syria beyond the Empire's borders. He was very sick and nursing what he claimed was a wolf bite, and he said he was on his way to Constantinople to warn the Emperor of the latest intelligence of the Saracen armies that were encamped to the southeast. Within a few hours of bedding down with a local family the traveler died. When the man and his wife who owned the house tried to swaddle him for burial the stranger suddenly sprang up and attacked them with a murderous look in his eyes. He was ravenous, biting the flesh from their bodies, killing them in the most horrible fashion. The visitor was smitten with a sword blow to the neck, but a few hours later the man and woman whom he had killed rose from their rough-hewn biers, attacking everyone in sight in exactly the same manner. By nightfall ten in the village were dead and many of those resurrected to wreak bloody havoc. Early in the morning, after considerable toil and several more casualties, the men of the village had herded the flesh-seeking fiends into the church, bolted the doors with chains and set it afire. The survivors had time only to grab what

23

was closest at hand and they fled the village, vowing never to return.

"Let me get this straight," I said. "These people were *dead*, and yet they rose up again to attack others?"

"Stone-cold dead," said an old man, evidently the former apothecary for the town. "I examined them myself."

"The rising of the dead is a curse of damnation," Theophilus muttered.

"Is it a sign of the end times?" asked a woman meekly.

I shook my head. "Let's not go there just yet. You're *sure* they were dead? They weren't just knocked out or something? I mean, a lot of things could make you think someone was dead."

"I'm sure," swore the apothecary. "They didn't breathe. They were quite dead, and they remained so, even after they rose. Their eyes were glazed and blank. They felt no pain. They recognized none of their families or their comrades. They could not speak, only moan like the damned. I've lived a long life, young friar. I know a dead man when I see one."

"All right, all right, no need to take it personally." I picked up my bowl and my spoon again but the cold stew had suddenly become dreadfully unappetizing. "Well, I don't know what it's all about. I've never heard of anything like this before."

"A curse!" said a woman.

My brow furrowed. "Gee, you think?" I scoffed. "Of *course* it's a curse."

Theophilus put a cautioning hand on my arm. "We will pray for the dead, and for the deliverance of your village," he said to the townspeople, and rose from the bench. "Brother Stephen, will you join me?"

No sooner had we stood up and Theophilus produced his little jeweled cross than there was a commotion outside, a clatter of hooves and the excited shouting of a male voice. Onophrios, the innkeeper, bolted for the door, sword drawn. The door burst open. A young man rushed inside, panting from hard riding. He was a bit older than me, but still in his twenties. He had flowing blond hair and a close-trimmed beard. His blue eyes had a very piercing stare. From his chain mail shirt, armored skirt and boots I could tell he was a soldier, but he did not appear to be of the regular army. He carried a sword but no shield of any kind. Onophrios lowered his sword. The young man, before he said a word, seized a flagon of wine that one of the women had handed him. He drank down several swallows, passed back the flagon and then burst out, "A force of shambling demons approaches up the road from the northeast. We must make ready!"

This news was followed by another blast of alarm and excitement from the villagers, which again the mayor shushed. "From the *northeast*?" he said.

"Yes," replied the soldier. "The northeast—the opposite direction from Domelium."

"How many?" said the apothecary.

"I didn't stop to count. At least twenty, perhaps as many as fifty. I was scouting, came upon a hill, and when I saw them approaching, I rode back here as fast as I could. We must get the women and children to safety." The steely-eyed soldier finally noticed Theophilus and myself. "Who is this?"

"Travelers from Chenolakkos," I said. "I'm Brother Stephen. This is Brother Theophilus."

The soldier made a grunting little scoff. "We need soldiers, and the Lord sends us monks," he muttered, shaking his head. "Well, no matter. Every man who can wield a sword, club or pitchfork must make ready to defend this inn. Women, children, elderly, those unable to fight, will gather in the stables behind the building. I'll need two able-bodied men to guard them. These are the wishes of Lord Camytzes." All were frozen, rooted on their spots for a long dreadful moment, but the soldier wasted no time. "Let's *go*!" he shouted, and the villagers, perhaps fearing him more than the ghouls, at last began to move.

"Great," I said to Theophilus. "Just what I wanted to be doing after hiking all day—fighting off the walking dead." I pulled the strap of the paint bag from over my shoulder and handed it to him. "Here, you'd better take this with you to the stables to keep it safe."

Theophilus glared at me as if I'd told him *he* were the walking dead. "I'm not going to the stables," he said sharply. "I'll not be pushed aside like an old woman with the horses and cattle while the minions of the Devil run free!" He turned to the room. "Who will give me a weapon?" When a rough-hewn pitchfork, tossed by one of the villagers, sailed through the air and Theophilus caught it one-handed, as effortlessly as if he'd practiced it a thousand times, I willed myself to close my gaping mouth. For being a humorless old fossil who barely said a word, Theophilus couldn't have surprised me more.

Chapter Two

The Battle of the Xenodocheion

There were, alas, only a handful of swords to be had. The soldier—Camytzes, if I'd heard the name correctly—had one, Onophrios had another, and some of the villagers managed to produce a few other badly rusted and brittle blades. There were pitchforks, several scythes and a hammer that had evidently been taken from the village blacksmith (who had become a ghoul), plus the fireplace tools, and Onophrios's wife gave one of the younger men a large cleaver with which she had cut the meat for our indigestible dinner. The mayor of Domelium handed me a shovel, and I wasn't quite sure exactly of what use it might ultimately be. In the lengthening golden-red light of sunset, the women took their children and the elderly toward the stables, and we men, perhaps twenty-five in all, filed out of the front door of the *xenodocheion* with our makeshift weapons. Standing there in the dust before the road, we could hear or see nothing but the gentle rustling of the evening breeze in the trees and the cheerful chirp of birds. One of the men even commented, "I don't see anything," but Camytzes, at the front of the congregation, set his mouth in a terse line and replied, "They're definitely coming."

"How do you know?" I asked him.

"I was among the first to observe them in the village last night," the soldier replied. "They're attracted to any living person like moths to a flame. They mean to make food of us." To all the men he cried, "Do *not* let one of the demons bite you! Any man whose flesh is bitten by one of them is doomed to become a ghoul himself."

"Preposterous," scoffed Theophilus.

"Oh? Why don't you offer your own hand to one of them as a snack, old man, and prove me wrong?" Theophilus recoiled at this retort and was silent. "I need not say this to the men who fought with me in the village this morning," said Camytzes. "But for the innkeeper and the monks I advise that you aim for their heads. A quick blow to the head will bring them down. Almost nothing else will. These ghouls are utterly relentless. Sever one's arm and it will still claw at your flesh. They feel no pain, so they won't recoil from—"

"I hear them!" cried the apothecary. "They're coming!"

A hush fell over us. Indeed, behind the gentle rustle of the tree branches and the song of birds, I could barely discern the shuffling of many clumsy feet and a chorus of the same strange moans that Theophilus and I had heard emanating from the church earlier. The *xenodocheion* was situated at the bottom of a small hill, which hid from our view whatever was coming up the road from the northwest. We might not see the ghouls until almost the last second.

"There they are!" shouted a young man.

At last the ghouls crested the hill. Just looking at them almost made me sick. Their clothes hung in rags and tatters, and most were splattered with blood. One middle-aged woman was naked but her mottled grayish skin was smeared with carmine. Blood dripped and streamed from the mouths of the fiends and often from their clawlike fingers. Their eyes were clouded and blank. A young boy in the front of the procession was missing both hands. Whether he had lost them in life or they had been torn off since his transformation into a demon-ghoul was impossible to tell. The throng of ghouls staggered toward us, moaning incoherently. My grip on the shovel tightened. There were at least thirty of them, possibly more—were we supposed to smite them *all*?

Camytzes did not wait for a cue. With a roar of battle lust, he sprang toward the mob of ghouls, swinging his sword in a broad arc that beheaded two of them (including the naked woman) almost instantly. The other men lunged after him in one furious body, and I found myself being swept along with them. For a dizzying moment as the crowd crushed around me I could not tell friend from foe. Then a grayish head with blank eyes—a balding man with rotted teeth and blood dripping down his chin—popped up in front of me. I swung the shovel down on its head with all my might. It split like a gourd, sending a shower of blood in an arc, splattering my cassock. Instinctively I recoiled. "Ugh!" No sooner had this ghoul gone down than another one took its place, a woman, reaching her arm toward me. I swatted the arm with the shovel and took aim at her head. One blow was not sufficient to destroy her, but I had no chance to strike again. A scythe wielded by a swarthy young farmer split the ghoul's upper torso in two. Her head remained alive, moaning, still attached to a clutching arm, but it fell into the mêlée of lurching demons and thrashing villagers and was lost.

For the first two minutes of the battle we living souls held our own quite admirably. Camytzes stationed himself in front of all of us as a sort of vanguard, and with his sword and his warrior's skill, he dispatched more ghouls than any of the rest of us. Those that shambled around his flanks, or that he could not annihilate with one or at most two sweeps of his sword, were left for us to deal with. I had never seen such carnage. The crushing of heads, the brutal stabbing with pitchforks and the messy sweep of bloody scythes soon made a more or less constant shower of blood in the air, mixing with the dust of the road and forming a foul-smelling brownish cloud that hovered over the battle. At one point, after the young man next to me destroyed a demon-ghoul by splitting its skull with the innkeeper's wife's meat cleaver, I looked down at the gore-drenched sleeve of my cassock and saw an eyeball lodged in its fold. I flicked it away as my stomach heaved. I staggered, bile spewing from my mouth. I simply couldn't help myself.

Unfortunately the instinctive reaction was nearly fatal. The young

29

handless ghoul I'd noticed at the front of the throng had somehow managed to slip by Camytzes and the others. His mouth was open, snarling in demonic famishment; I could see tatters of human flesh hanging from his teeth. The child-ghoul propelled himself toward me much faster than I would've thought possible. As I struggled to regain my footing, my stomach still heaving, his little jaws nearly clamped themselves down on my hand. But in an instant the bloody head of a pitchfork shot forward, spearing the ghoul gruesomely in the forehead. The child-demon twitched once and went limp. A foot shod in a blood-slick monastic slipper planted itself on the ghoul's little chest and shoved, withdrawing the pitchfork. Wiping effluvium from my lips with the back of my hand, I looked and saw Theophilus, the wielder of the pitchfork. He paused only a moment to cross himself and whisper a little prayer.

After the first two minutes—during which I thought we were doing quite well—things became much more difficult. The ghouls were senseless, moved slowly and utilized no form of strategy or cunning to defeat us; they merely kept up their inexorable assault, lurching ever forward, lunging for the nearest human to satiate their dreadful hunger. But their numbers and their imperviousness to pain or fear made them a formidable enemy. Suddenly it seemed they were right upon us. I seemed to be surrounded by a solid wall of writhing arms and legs, some human, others demonic. A ghoul's head popped up in front of me and I stabbed upward with the shovel, driving its blade under the demon's jaw and into its head. When I raised my own head, gasping for breath against the cloud of blood and dust, I realized the ghouls had driven all of us back against the front of the inn. I watched the mayor of Domelium, inches away from me, screaming in pain and horror as two of the ghouls, a man and a woman, bit down on his arm simultaneously. A moment later the ghouls' heads were split by Camytzes's sword—together with the mayor's arm—and that was followed, swiftly and horrifically, by the beheading of the mayor himself. His face bore a surprised expression as his head toppled to the dust. At least he did not suffer.

It seemed the battle dragged on for hours, but in reality I doubt it was more than a few minutes. During those few minutes I saw sights of deep and profound horror. It occurred to me that this terrible paroxysm of fear, brutality and shock was what warriors such as Camytzes experienced every time they went into battle, and I pitied the soldiery of the Empire. I lost count of the ghouls that I myself dispatched. I merely swung and lunged with the shovel indiscriminately and with every ounce of strength I could muster. At one point I fell to the dust, where amidst the thundering, squirming feet of the villagers and the lurching legs of the ghouls I beheld a perfectly ghastly sight—the severed head of a woman demon, still quite animate, inching along the ground through the dirt by opening and closing her jaw. The head was advancing toward my leg. I brought my shovel down on it, crushing the horrid thing, and I retched again.

For several moments I couldn't rise. Then the crush of the crowd seemed suddenly to lighten. More heads fell to the dust, and more grisly arcs of blood sprayed into the air; but it seemed the villagers were at last gaining the upper hand. I looked up and witnessed Camytzes strike two ghouls at once with his blade. At that instant they happened to be in perfect alignment, one ahead of the other, and he was thus able to split both of their skulls with his sword, cleaving their heads neatly in two. They slumped and fell in opposite directions. "Don't neglect the stragglers!" he cried to the villagers who still clutched their weapons. "There, and there! Don't let them get closer!"

The main body of demons was mostly destroyed, but a few still staggered pell-mell up the road. Camytzes and two of the young men with the scythes—which had proved almost more effective as weapons than swords—ran to meet them head-on. Theophilus, shockingly, seemed affected by bloodlust. He leaped over a pile of dead ghouls, pitchfork in hand, roaring like a lion at the top of his lungs. A demon obliged him by lunging at him. He stabbed it first in the gut with his pitchfork, then in the head. Another turned toward him and received the same treatment. "Blast ye, Satan!" Theophilus cried. "Is that *all* you have to send? Has your dark power reached its pitiful limit? Come forward and receive the wrath of the Lord!" A third ghoul staggered out of the trees, moaning horribly. The old monk swung the pitchfork so forcefully that the demon's head crushed like an egg and its body collapsed like a sack of grain. "Anyone else?" Theophilus roared.

I surveyed the bloody ground in front of the *xenodocheion.* The carcasses of the ghouls lay in bloody heaps. The dirt was saturated with blood in a broad crescent-shaped swath thirty or forty feet out from the front of the building. Severed arms and legs of ghouls still twitched. A few continued to inch forward, blindly seeking prey. It was impossible to tell at first how many villagers had been wounded. A portly man who I remember seeing inside the inn staggered on his knees, wailing, clutching his hands to his neck that was spurting blood. Camytzes caught sight of him. The soldier bounded over the piles of corpses, swung his sword and beheaded the man cleanly and almost effortlessly. Instinctively I raised my arms—"No! Stop! *Don't!*"—but before the cries died on my lips Camytzes had beheaded another of the villagers who had obviously been bitten. Camytzes glanced up at me, lowering the sword, its tip dripping with blood. *"Don't!"* I shouted.

"We must stop this devilish pestilence," Camytzes replied. He turned his head and saw another ghoul approaching up the hill. He ran, beheaded it, and bounded back toward the inn. "You two!" he said, motioning toward the young farmers with the scythes. "Guard the door. Only those who have not been bitten by demons will be allowed back into the *xenodocheion.* We must make sure and examine everyone."

The villagers began to shuffle into a rough queue toward the front door of the inn. As Camytzes turned, he saw the apothecary standing amidst a pile of ghoulish bodies. The man, tears streaming down his face, handed the fireplace poker he'd been using to one of the other villagers. He limped toward Camytzes; it was obvious his knee had been injured. I could see the bloody bite through the tear in his clothing. He stopped before the soldier, and then glanced at me. "Brother—will you bless me?" he said.

It took me a moment to react but finally I spurred myself to action. I made the sign of the cross in the air and murmured the prayer of the

Eucharist. The apothecary knelt down, wincing at the pain in his knee. He put his hands together, prayed one last time and then looked up at Camytzes and nodded. A moment later his head fell to the dust and his body slumped forwards.

"Monstrous," said Theophilus.

"No doubt," I echoed. "At least it's over."

Camytzes moved a few steps toward me. "You're going to wish it was," he said, his low voice seeming all the more menacing considering his face and hair were covered in blood. "We have no idea how many more of them there may be out there. This could be just the beginning."

With this unsavory thought, Camytzes appointed himself inspector general of the inn, standing guard at the door and searching the villagers for wounds and injuries. Considering that most of us were drenched in gore from head to foot, it was not an easy task. I was relieved that both Theophilus and I were unharmed. Once admitted inside the building, we sat heavily on a bench. The women had been admitted through the rear door, and several of them were fanning out with buckets and cauldrons of water to clean our bloody bodies. "Let's hope the soldier is wrong," I said to Theophilus. "I'd rather not see anything like that again as long as I live."

Theophilus, using a wet rag passed to him by one of the women to mop blood from his long white locks, replied, "You did well, Brother Stephen. Sometimes being in the service of the Lord means praying in the cloister. Other times it gets a little more—*intense.*" An eighty-year-old monk wringing ghoul blood out of his hair was the last sight I had expected to see when I rose from bed this morning. But God's paths for us sometimes take very sharp detours.

The cleanup from the battle took several hours and in many respects was as grisly as the struggle itself. We learned that fourteen of our number were casualties, five killed directly by the ghouls themselves and nine more bitten and subsequently executed by

Camytzes. One young man, barely seventeen, had been slightly bitten on the finger and tried to conceal the wound; he'd made it through the cordon at the door but a young woman noticed his condition and gave alarm. The boy protested, shouting that it was just a scratch and he was sure God would protect him. It did no good, and Camytzes beheaded him as he had done the others. The boy's mother wailed and cursed and had to be dragged away. To his credit, the soldier seemed truly pained by the experience. Clearly he didn't relish these horrors. His gruff manner and endless shouts of orders seemed disagreeable to many of the villagers, but none openly defied him. The fact that not a single woman or child had been harmed by the ghouls—who, thanks to us, had never come close to the stables—attested that many in the crowd owed Camytzes their lives.

When the pile of ghoul corpses (and our own dead) was assembled behind the building, Camytzes and Onophrios emptied the inn's entire supply of lamp oil over and around it, pouring and shaking it from big earthenware jugs. Then we all stood back. "I suggest the friars lead us in prayer," said Camytzes somberly. "Not merely for ourselves, but also for the souls of the poor wretches that have been dispatched from this earth by God's hand and by our own." Theophilus and I prayed. A torch was lit and Camytzes himself tossed it on the pyre. It was dark now and the foul-smelling smoke made the nearly full moon glow ruddy red. We lingered only a few moments due to the stench and then we returned to the inn.

Camytzes had posted guards; we had no idea where the ghouls had come from and if there might be more of them on the way. But in the absence of any evidence of an imminent attack the cauldrons were fired again and at last we exhausted defenders of the *xenodocheion* were given food and drink—at least those of us who still had appetites. As Theophilus and I ate, this time not minding the horrid taste of the dreadful stew, Camytzes invited himself to sit among us, carrying a soup bowl and half a circle of bread. He'd by now doffed his mail shirt and washed his hair and beard. He looked quite different, almost normal, a young man not much older than I and considerably less fearsome-looking without his armor on and his sword in hand. "We haven't been properly introduced," he said. "My name is Michael Camytzes."

"Stephen Diabetenos. You're the lord of these lands?"

For the first time since he'd been in our presence Camytzes laughed. His teeth were crooked and jumbled, but he looked totally different when he smiled than the fierce warrior he had been a few hours ago, now mirthful and gentle. "Oh, no. I'm no lord."

"I heard you say 'Lord Camytzes wishes it' earlier," said Theophilus.

"I was speaking for my father." Camytzes bit off some bread. His mouth full he said, "He's a colonel in the thematic army. Owns a lot of the land around here. Most of the villagers of Domelium pay rent to him—well, *paid*, past tense. I'm pledged to the peoples' defense."

I knew of the themes, the estates that were also military commissions. A hundred or so years ago the Emperor had granted military men lands and hereditary titles in exchange for the pledge that they and their families would defend those lands against all invaders, most likely Persians or Saracens. "Where's your father now?" I asked Camytzes.

"He's in Ancyra with the regular army. They're assembling to oppose the invasion by the Saracens."

"Invasion?" said Theophilus. "You mean it's begun already?"

"Oh, yes," Camytzes replied. "The Saracens took Sardis and Pergamum last fall and have been wintering there ever since. The Caliph Suleiman has his sights fixed firmly on Constantinople, and our new Emperor seems to have run out of hollow promises of territory or tribute with which to buy him off." With his crooked teeth, the soldier tore off more bread. "You two are headed to Constantinople, aren't you?"

"Yes," I said. "I have a commission awaiting me at the Monastery of St. Stoudios. Theophilus here is my chaperone."

"What would you think if I came with you?" said Camytzes.

35

"I don't need a second chaperone. I can't get into *that* much trouble between here and Constantinople."

"No, I didn't mean that. Somebody has to tell the Emperor about what happened here. We must convince him to send regular army troops here to scour the villages and destroy what ghouls remain. If so many as one of those things remains at large, the whole Empire could be at risk." He bit off another piece of bread.

"You really think it's that bad?" said Theophilus.

"Aye. Some of the villagers think I'm arbitrary and cruel, executing those who were bitten by demons. I have no wish to destroy the people I'm pledged to protect. But we must stop the pestilence from spreading further."

Theophilus said, "This evil is a judgment by God. He sent the demons to punish your village. There must have been some wickedness afoot."

Camytzes grunted. "Wickedness has not a thing to do with it, and neither does God," he shot back. "This is a plague. The evil is spread from person to person through the bites of ghouls. The apothecary I beheaded this evening was as good a man as you could find in Domelium. There was nothing wicked about him. He submitted passively to my sword, bravely thinking of the welfare of the others before himself. No—we must make clear to the Emperor that this is a plague that must be controlled quickly. I'll come with you to Constantinople. There you will help me bear my witness to the Emperor of what happened here, and to impress on him the gravity of the situation. You want to serve God? That's how you can best be of service."

We were quickly learning that it was impossible to argue with Michael Camytzes. I didn't know Theophilus's feelings on the matter, but I for one was glad at the prospect of having an armed escort for the remainder of our journey. It occurred to me that the plague of ghouls might not necessarily have a theological cause after all. It was blasphemy for a monk to think that, yes, but Camytzes seemed to know what he was talking about. If there were more of those things out there on the road, at least we would have our own private bodyguard to protect us.

We spent a restless night at the *xenodocheion*. At every shudder of the trees in the wind outside or the snort of one of the sleeping villagers in the big dirt-floored room I jerked awake, thinking that the ghouls were attacking again. I wasn't in very good shape when we set out in the morning but at least we hadn't been attacked. Fortunately for us, Camytzes managed to convince one of the villagers to lend him two donkeys so Theophilus and I wouldn't have to walk the whole way to Kios. "Aye, if you can sell them in Kios or Constantinople, please do so," said the farmer. "And if you can subtract a few *solidi* from your father's bill for them, I'd be very grateful."

After we set out on the road, I asked Camytzes, "Your father's bill? What did he mean?"

"All the villagers of Domelium rent their homes and farms from my father, who is a *droungarios* of the theme," he explained. "When he is taxed by the Emperor on his lands, my father must pass on the cost of the taxes in the form of rents. The harvest has been poor the past few years and most of the villagers are indebted to him."

"What's going to happen to them now that their village is in ruins?" Theophilus asked.

Camytzes shrugged. "No idea. Some will probably make homes in other villages. Likely many will end up destitute, begging for charity at the monasteries."

I said, "Surely with their village destroyed your father will forgive their debts, or at least make it possible for them to rebuild and return to their homes."

Camytzes replied with a sad shake of his head. "You don't know my father."

"Hard-ass, eh?"

"He'll probably say that so long as the Emperor taxes him, he must collect his rents. I confess this is one of my aims in seeking an audience with the Emperor—to see if he'll forgive my father's taxes on Domelium—but I don't expect much success."

The Emperor. As we rode that long and uncomfortably hot day, I began to wonder if we might actually meet him. There was no telling whether we had a real chance of getting in to see him; Camytzes and his family seemed to be big shots out here in the country, but they were probably small fry in Constantinople. I confess I was curious to see what sort of man our new ruler really was. At Chenolakkos I kept up with politics more closely than did most of the monks, who considered earthly affairs sinful. Leo III was something of an unknown quantity. That in itself was nothing new. The last three emperors had been pitiful nonentities. It was difficult to decide which of them among Philippicus Bardanes, Anastasius II or Theodosius III had been worse; they were all deposed in turn by ambitious army officers, and Leo came from that class too. But it was said that Leo, in contrast to his predecessors, was even a more ruthless, cold-blooded ass-kicker than any of the others could have dreamed of being. He had come to the throne through the ingenious strategy of taking Theodosius's son hostage, and the old emperor had thus "decided" that perhaps stepping down in favor of Leo would be a prudent thing to do. You have to admit you'd need brass balls to even attempt something so brazen, and considering the prospect of a Saracen invasion didn't seem to spook Leo in the slightest, I thought he might be just the sort of emperor we needed right now. Whether he'd sit still for wild tales of undead ghouls rampaging through the provinces, though, was another matter.

It was three more days to Kios, and because our borrowed donkeys were much slower on the trail than Camytzes's horse, we didn't make as much daily progress as the soldier had hoped. On the second night we found another *xenodocheion* that took us in, but after that, when we were in the brushy hill country far from the nearest villages, we had to camp for a night. Being a soldier, Camytzes at least had some gear—a blanket, some tins for cooking and some flour he kept in a leather sack. "You brought *nothing* with you at all?" he scoffed. He had asked what wares we had to contribute to our supper. "Well, I guess that's the difference between monks and soldiers. A monk can usually expect to find a friendly place to bed down for the night. Not so for soldiers."

With the flour and his tins, Camytzes made a sort of hardtack bread called *paximadion*, which I actually found quite filling, if tasteless. We kept watch for ghouls, one of us awake and with our hand on the hilt of the sword at all times. Camytzes spent the most time on watch of all of us, probably figuring that neither Theophilus nor I would be very effective in fending off a gaggle of the fiends if they ambushed us in the middle of the night. Fortunately we saw no demons. We spent another night in much the same circumstance, and then shortly after noon on the next day our road snaked around a high ridge that offered us a view of Kios—an expanse of stone houses, bell towers and church domes carpeting the olive-green hillside down to the water cluttered with the sails of vessels, one of which would hopefully take us to the capital.

We descended to the city. In the bustling marketplace of Kios we found a merchant who was bringing a hold full of wines to Constantinople, and he agreed to take us in exchange for one of the two borrowed donkeys. The ship was not due to sail until the morning. Since the only inns about were *pandocheia*, for which you had to pay—as opposed to *xenodocheia* which were free—we decided to save what few gold sovereigns we had left and sleep on the deck of the ship.

With the hard plank deck under my back, it took a long time for me to get to sleep. Unfortunately I dreamt of undead ghouls, their cold clawing fingers digging into my flesh and tearing the life from my body. The horrors I'd seen at the *xenodocheion* were enough to give me nightmares for the rest of my life. The bad dreams wasted no time in getting started.

Chapter Three

Constantinople

Three Days Later

"Okay, I'm confused," said the Emperor of Byzantium, God's Vice-Regent on Earth, as he nibbled at the trout in *gakos* sauce on the elegant silver plate in front of him. "*Living* dead? What does that mean exactly, *living* dead? Isn't that something of an oxymoron?" With an elegant gilded fork, held by fingers bejeweled with gold rings, he took another bite of the fish.

"Ghouls," replied Michael Camytzes. "Demons. Corpses of dead people that were possessed by some terrible evil. They can move and walk and attack. They feel no pain. They cannot communicate and possess only the instincts of mute animals. Yet they are relentless. They seek only one thing—human flesh. Any living person who is bitten by them will die, and will subsequently reanimate and become one of them."

We'd been in the presence of the Emperor for barely five minutes and I could already tell that the interview, for which we'd waited, pleaded, bargained and implored for the better part of three days, wasn't going well. After waiting nearly all morning in an antechamber of the Great Palace, one of the Emperor's eunuchs—an unpleasant bald man called Eutropius—had finally ushered us into a minor room of the palace, where he said the Emperor would entertain us for exactly seven minutes while he ate lunch. I have to admit the palace was as dazzling as anything I'd seen in Constantinople in the past three days. Though this was a minor room, far from the grand *triklinos* reception hall with gold-inlaid mosaics on his floor that the Emperor supposedly used to entertain persons on state business, it was still pretty posh. There were carpets on the floors and hanging along the stone walls. The one behind the Emperor's small marble-topped lunch table bore a rich depiction of a hunting scene. An elegant rosewood table in the corner was mounded with books, parchments, golden scales, half-drained flagons of wine and a gilded candelabrum. If this was a little-used workroom where the Emperor paused in his busy day for a bite of lunch, I wondered what the rest of his place looked like.

The Emperor himself surprised me. With all the stately marble busts of previous Roman emperors studding the palace in various well-dusted niches, you wondered why anybody in their right mind would give the crown to *this* weird-looking guy. Leo was short, five-foot-six at the maximum. He was in his early thirties, quite chubby and so ugly I almost winced to think of what he'd look like at sixty. Just looking at him I could see the basis of the rumors that he was half Saracen, for he was swarthy and of dark complexion. He bore a shock of long curly black hair and his scraggly beard looked like nothing so much as overgrown pubic hair coating his chin. His eyes, narrow slits of dark brown, were impossibly far apart and covered with thick brush-stroke brows balanced precariously over a wide pug nose. His lips were full and thick, almost feminine. Leo was extremely stocky with broad shoulders and when he'd come into the room, his purple cloak billowing about his thick legs, he'd walked with an awkward gait I can only describe as an elegant waddle. The most powerful man in Byzantium, and possibly the world, looked more like an awkward country peasant who'd snuck into the palace to try on the Emperor's clothes to see what they looked like on him. Yet the way he cut his meat, handled his fork and spoon and reached daintily for the golden goblet of wine on the table next to him seemed very aristocratic in bearing. He was an Isaurian, like my own family, but spoke perfect Greek without a hint of a provincial accent. It was also said that he

41

spoke Arabic fluently. That he was very smart was obvious just by observing him, once you got past how ugly he was.

"Am I right in assuming," said Leo, between bites of fish, "that this condition, this sort of demonic possession of the dead, was God's punishment, brought on by some terrible wickedness of the people of that village—er, what did you say it was called?"

"Domelium," said Camytzes. "The churchmen may answer that more ably than I."

Leo's dark eyes turned to me and I suddenly felt terribly on the spot. Theophilus was standing next to me, clutching his walking stick with his white-knuckled hand, but he hadn't said a single word during the interview and I didn't expect him to break his silence now. My mouth opened and closed a few times before any words came out. My instinct was to say *Yes, Sire*, but I recalled the conversation Camytzes and I had had at the inn after the ghoul attack. I realized I had to choose my words carefully.

Camytzes said we need to convince the Emperor to send troops to wipe out the ghouls before they get out of control, I reminded myself. *If I tell him that the undead plague was punishment from God for Domelium's sins, that'll be the end of it. He'll just say it was God's will and only those who continue to do wicked deeds have anything to fear.*

Evidently I didn't answer fast enough because the white-robed official, the *kouropalates* standing next to the Emperor's table—he too was dark and swarthy, though much taller than his liege—said sharply, "The Emperor asked you a question! He expects an answer!"

"No, Sire," I finally replied. "That isn't correct."

One of Leo's dark brush-stroke eyebrows went up. "No?" he said.

At last some words seemed to come to me. "While I have no doubt that God sent this evil upon us, I don't believe it afflicts only the wicked. It's more in the nature of a plague. Fresh ghouls are not made by God alone, but by being bitten by another ghoul. Once someone is bitten, they themselves—"

"Yes, yes, they themselves become a ghoul. I think I got that part."

Leo drank some wine. "And you killed *how* many of them?"

"Thirty-six in the village," Camytzes replied, "and another forty-one who attacked us at the inn the following evening. That doesn't count the nine of our own number we had to slay in order to prevent their own transformation into ghouls."

"So we had seventy-seven of these 'living dead' ravaging the countryside," said Leo, "all of whom were slain by you and the surviving villagers, is that right?"

"Yes, Sire."

"But if they're truly living dead, how do you know you killed them? I mean, if according to you they're already dead, won't they just get up and walk away after a while? Is it necessary to just keep killing them over and over again? Sounds exhausting." Leo said this with a little chuckle that told me he wasn't taking any of this seriously.

"They can be destroyed with strong blows to the head. Crush their brains, Sire, and they'll go down for good. We learned this process by trial and error, very much to our peril, during the first outbreak in Domelium."

With his chubby fingers Leo picked up the fish bone and licked the remaining shreds of meat from it with a knobby tongue. "How charming to be speaking of crushing brains while I'm eating lunch." He tossed the fish skeleton back on his plate, which in seconds was whisked away by one of the robed eunuchs who'd been hovering to clear his table. A moment later the fish plate was replaced with a gilded dish of pistachio nuts. Cracking one open, the Emperor said, "I still don't understand the point of your visit. Assuming for the sake of argument that these ghouls exist, you just told me you defeated them, crushing their heads to the last man. Congratulations. Good work. Are you here seeking recognition for your heroic deeds? Decorations, perhaps? A promotion into the regular army? You two monks, do you wish to be released from your monastic oaths so you can follow your friend here into the crushing-ghouls'-heads business? If that's what you seek, you certainly have my leave to do so, as well as my enthusiastic encouragement of your future ghoul-crushing activities."

It was obvious the Emperor liked pistachios. In the course of this little speech he had cracked open no less than six of them, popping them into his mouth and devouring them without skipping a word. He tossed the shells casually onto the polished porphyry floor. He continued eating as he listened to Camytzes's somewhat flustered reply.

"Nay, Sire. We can't be sure that we destroyed all the ghouls. Even if we did, the ultimate source of the pestilence remains unknown, which means that sooner or later someone else will be bitten and the cycle will begin again. I'm convinced that there are more ghouls out there. What I think is required—if I may beg the Emperor's pardon—is for several regular army units of heavy troops to be sent to the Olympus area to scour the countryside in a wide swath and positively ensure that all the ghouls are destroyed. Only then can we be certain that the plague won't strike again."

Leo, his mouth full of pistachios, laughed. His giggle was airy and annoying. As more pistachio shells fell to the floor, he scoffed, "You want me to send *heavy troops* to the provinces in search of undead ghouls? Is that what you're asking me for?"

Camytzes swallowed. "Aye, my liege. I am."

"You wish to command these troops, I take it?"

"No. I'm just a foot soldier. My father is a *droungarios*. My job is to patrol his lands to keep order and fend off raids by bandits and brigands. I'm not fit to command large bodies of men."

"Ah, *but*—" said Leo, raising a green-stained finger, "—how would these regular army troops recognize these ghouls when they see them, and how would they know the best way to annihilate them most efficiently? You would naturally have to go along to advise them, wouldn't you? And you would need special imperial orders to ensure that the regular army commanders would take your advice, which is tantamount to command in every way that matters. I see your game, Camytzes. Convince me that some obscure and exotic threat exists and that you're the Empire's sole expert at combating it. Then you convince me to give you a couple of divisions of heavy troops to do with as you please, and you become the big cheese on the slopes of Mt. Olympus. Fancy your own little fiefdom down there in Anatolia, do you? Or is it more personal than that—perhaps you want the troops to overthrow your father and take over as *droungarios* of the Anatolikon theme?"

Camytzes looked shocked and wounded by these accusations. "No, Sire," he stammered. "It's not like that at all—"

"Oh, no worries," chirped the Emperor cheerfully, tossing nutmeats into his mouth. "In fact, I commend you for such a unique and original form of intrigue. I could use a man with your gumption. Most of my military commanders are whimpering idiots. And honestly, I wouldn't care if you *did* take over the Anatolikon theme, so long as your troops wouldn't eventually raise you up on a shield and proclaim you Emperor to supplant me, which they probably would. Then I'd have to go down there with *more* troops and kick your ass. Such are the weary burdens of office. But none of that's going to happen anyway because sending heavy troops to the provinces to smite imaginary ghouls is quite out of the question. If we were at peace, we had money to burn and I had, say, a hundred-thousand infantry and cavalry sitting around playing with themselves for lack of something to do, I might be inclined to grant your request just for the sheer novelty of it. As you know, however, that's not the situation. We happen to have two colossal Saracen armies camped this very moment at Sardis and Pergamum, and the Saracen navy is about to come out of their winter rest at Cilicia. If you really want to go ghoul-crushing with my troops, perhaps you ought to saunter on down to Damascus and convince Caliph Suleiman to withdraw his troops so your grand project can be given a chance. Then you'll have to zip right up to Ochrid and get Khan Tervel's assent as well since he's hovering on our border like a spider to duke it out with whichever one of us, Emperor or Caliph, is left alive when it's over. Such a diplomatic mission would be a great help to me. Pull it off and I'll make you commander of anything you want. I'll proclaim you Grand God-Emperor Messiah with the Biggest Cock in the Universe and I'll give you a golden ghoul-crushing sword blessed by the Patriarch of Constantinople and the Pope in Rome. Come back to me when you've secured the kind cooperation of the Caliph and the Khan, and then you can claim your rewards."

It was obvious that Leo considered the interview over, but because there were still six or eight pistachios left in the golden bowl he didn't dismiss us immediately. Camytzes boldly seized the delay. "Sire, I understand that the Saracens have invaded us," he spoke up. "That's exactly *why* I urge you to take this step. The plague of undead could become a mortal threat festering in our rear, demanding military attention when all our effort is needed to resist the Saracens. You must send troops to wipe out the ghouls now, before the Saracens get here. Eliminate the threat as quickly as possible. Otherwise we risk enlisting hordes of living dead as *de facto* allies of the Caliph."

"Oh, so you're a grand strategist now too?" Leo retorted. "Okay, great. When the Caliph's army of 80,000 troops draws up against the walls of Constantinople, which could happen at any moment, I'll seek your expert advice on how to repel them. *Kouropalates* Artabasdos! Draw up an edict immediately relieving all senior military personnel of their offices. Foot soldier Camytzes here is promoted to Grand Domestic of the Army. We'll all be following his orders from now on. Oh, and don't forget to send our best legions down to the Mt. Olympus region with orders to exterminate all undead ghouls on sight. Our new Grand Domestic informs us that this move is crucial to the survival of the Empire, as well as the preservation of holy Christendom against the Mohammedan hordes."

Camytzes looked stunned, and I can't say I was ready with a reply that wouldn't get me beheaded. At that precise moment, however, the necessity of a response evaporated, for a feminine voice boomed into the chamber. "Leo! Are you in here?"

From one of the elegant arched doorways at the rear of the room a woman suddenly swept inside, and instantly all attention was on her. "Oh, you are. Good." She wore a very brightly colored gown, brocaded in gold, and her neck, wrists and earlobes dripped with jewelry. She had very long, silky dark hair and vivid sea-green eyes. Her nose was slightly aquiline but it didn't detract from the geometric perfection of her face. She moved so quickly that she'd planted herself next to the Emperor's lunch table before I realized that I was staring open-mouthed at the Empress of Byzantium. I'd heard very little about the Empress Maria, and given the way she looked at the moment, I was surprised that word of her beauty hadn't spread far and wide across the Empire.

Now face-to-face with her husband—the Empress was taller than he was—she drew a little breath and then blasted, as if Theophilus, Camytzes and I weren't even there, "You absolutely *must* speak to Anna. She's being perfectly *impossible*. We just got that whole new crate of gowns from Cilicia and she refuses to try on a single one of them. She threw her hairdresser out again this morning, and says she won't even go to the reception for the senators this evening. I told her that if she persisted in being ornery, the Emperor would have to speak with her, and so she says, 'Fine, let him'—I mean, the *insolence* of that child! You really must speak with her right now—I know you're busy, but..." Her voice trailed into a cataract of recriminations. The way she emphasized certain words, with a kind of ostentatious flutter, was really unusual. After a while I couldn't even follow what she was saying, and then I realized she'd lapsed into another language, Arabic perhaps, which she spoke even faster.

For his part, Leo kept cracking pistachios, popping the nutmeats into his mouth and flicking the shells onto the floor. At an arbitrary point he interrupted his wife and said in Greek, "Maria, dear, I fully understand your predicament, and I sympathize. What you don't seem to have gotten through your head, though, is that she's totally beyond us now. The girl turned twelve and became Princess of Byzantium on the same day. Now, I can do one of two things. I can be Emperor, or I can control Anna. I can't do both. Which would you rather have me do, with the Saracens about to batter down our doors at any moment?"

The Empress looked up at the *kouropalates* hovering above her husband's chair as if expecting help from him. "Well, how about *you* talk to her?" she said insistently. "You're only her future husband, Artabasdos. You're going to have to deal with her sooner or later."

"Madame," replied the *kouropalates*, "I know better than to venture into the den of the lioness so much as one moment before my duty calls me to."

The Empress rolled her eyes. Shaking her head, she said, "You two are pathetic. Fine. If you want to parade the Princess of Byzantium in front of the Senate in her old Isaurian rags, what skin is it off *my* nose?" With this, Maria drew her skirts up around her and started to make her exit. As she did, she finally threw a glance at Theophilus, Camytzes and myself. "Sorry to interrupt your business," she said. Instead of looking at her husband as she said this, however, her eyes were fixated firmly on me.

"Oh, no bother, dear," said the Emperor in a patronizing tone. "We're finished." Having eaten the last of the pistachios, he brushed shell fragments off his hands and rose from his chair. "Well! This has been very entertaining. I enjoy comic theater while eating my lunch. I'm told that a jester hasn't been employed at the court since the time of Justinian the First. If I decide to revive the office, I'll give careful consideration to you three for the position." Leo paused to flick a fragment of pistachio shell from his purple robe, and then said sharply, "High Chamberlain, please show our guests out. Maria, if you insist on me speaking to Anna, I'll reluctantly agree to try to change her mind about the reception, but I don't know why you expect her to mind me any more than she does you."

The interview was over.

The eunuch Eutropius looked positively incensed as he guided us through the colonnaded corridor back toward the antechamber. "You three should be horsewhipped for wasting the Emperor's time in such a manner," he grumbled. "How dare you come here at this busy time and distract our venerated ruler with such childish trifles?"

I'd remained reluctantly silent in Leo's presence, but being dressed down by this nutless lackey got my hackles up. "He didn't listen!" I protested. "We saw these things with our own eyes! If you'd seen what they did to that village—"

"Brother Stephen, quiet," said Theophilus, his first words since entering the palace.

"Heed your elder," the eunuch growled. When we came to the main door leading to the gardens, flanked by two soldiers, Eutropius merely motioned to them and then outside. He turned on his heel and walked back toward the palace complex, and Camytzes, Theophilus and I were jostled roughly by the sentries until we stood outside the main gate in front of the Great Palace, back on the bustling streets of Constantinople.

"That could have gone better," said Theophilus.

"Well, I didn't hear *you* jumping to our defense!" Camytzes roared. "We didn't even get a chance to ask him about the taxes!"

"You heard him," I replied. "His daughter's dresses are more important to him than anything *we* had to say."

Camytzes shook his head. "It's so unfortunate. Sooner or later the Emperor is going to have to deal with this problem. I only fear that by the time he takes it seriously it may be too late to defeat the ghouls."

Theophilus grasped his walking stick and looked out over the busy street, teeming with horse carts, merchant stands, donkeys laden with cargo and hordes of people rushing to and fro. "We must trust that the Emperor knows best," he said. "Even if he doesn't, we have nothing to say about it. Let us return to our humble professions and hope that God will look after us."

Camytzes looked for a moment as if he was going to argue. I felt for him. He obviously cared about the people of his father's lands, and his argument about the ghouls potentially distracting the military from the very important job of defending us against the Saracens seemed very logical to me, even if it was comical to the Emperor. But Camytzes seemed to be thinking the same thing I was—*We took our story to the highest level possible. Nothing came of it, but there's nothing more we can do.* Finally he nodded, and as Theophilus stepped in the direction of the Monastery of St. Stoudios, Camytzes and I followed him. The episode involving the Undead Ghouls of Domelium was, for all intents and purposes, over.

I was staying at St. Stoudios permanently, but I expected Theophilus and Michael Camytzes to be leaving shortly. I would be sorry to see them go. Their stay was not an uncomfortable one. The huge complex, built as all monumental structures in the capital of gray brick striped with reddish-brown, easily put Chenolakkos to shame. In addition to the lovely gardens, colonnaded cloisters and tall arched windows it had a vast library tower and a colossal and well-appointed church. The cell which *Hegoumenos* Rhetorios assigned to me was three times as large as my quarters at Chenolakkos and had a real bed as opposed to a pallet of straw. The arched windows and elegant pavilions offered stunning views of the city, which glittered like jewels spilled on the jumbled grassy hillsides. I could see the domes of St. Sofia—the Church of the Holy Wisdom, which I had not yet visited—and the vast white horseshoe-shaped edifice with four glinting gold specks on its front that was the Hippodrome. Constantinople was dazzling, vibrant, opulent and lavish. It was also, as I was to discover, intensely boring.

"Yes, well, this is where you *would* be working," said Father Rhetorios, showing me around the long cluttered room that was the iconographers' studio. It was a busy jumble of easels, tables and desks, and I marveled at the many shelves filled with brightly colored powders and roots. "That is, if we had any work for you. Our studio has been virtually shut down since Emperor Leo's coronation last March. Most of the monks who worked here have since been put to operating the wine presses, or to copying manuscripts in the scriptorium." Rhetorios, a paunchy middle-aged fellow who was far more agreeable than Eunomios, smiled and patted me on the shoulder. "Don't worry, Brother Stephen of Chenolakkos. I'm sure we'll find a job for you."

I was overawed as I looked about the room. No paints were mixed, no half-finished icons were propped up on the easels, and Rhetorios and I were the only monks in the entire place. "*Hegoumenos*, I'm afraid I don't understand," I said. "Father Eunomios told me that you'd written to him begging for another iconographer. He said the new Emperor threw away all the old icons in the imperial chambers, and you couldn't keep up with the demand to replace them with the new ones he ordered."

"I did write to Father Eunomios, on the very day of Leo's coronation in St. Sofia," Rhetorios replied. "And yes, we were told that one of his first commands was to strip the Great Palace bare of all icons, which is a very unusual and curious order—I don't think any previous Emperor has ever done that. Since Brother Isaac died in February, I feared we'd be unable to keep up with the demand of restocking the entire palace with new icons, which is what I assumed would be the result of the Emperor's housecleaning. But we didn't anticipate that Leo wouldn't order new icons *at all*. He threw away all the imperial icons because he doesn't *believe* in icons. He wanted them all out of his sight. After we learned this, I wrote a second letter to Eunomios, telling him we had no need of one of his iconographers after all, but the letter evidently never reached Chenolakkos. Nonetheless, since he sent you in good faith, I will not refuse you a place in this order."

We withdrew from the silent studio and made our way through a stone corridor, brightly lit by the late June sun. I was very disappointed. "How can the Emperor not believe in icons?" I asked, shaking my head. "I've never heard of that before. Is it some new teaching?"

"I think it's based on the Ten Commandments," Rhetorios replies. "'Thou shalt not make any graven images.' We've never interpreted that to prohibit icons, but evidently the Emperor does. It is not yet Church doctrine, but perhaps someday it may be."

"But that would put iconographers out of business forever," I protested.

Rhetorios turned on his heel and fixed me with a disarming stare. I

51

immediately fell silent. He paused a moment, and then started down the stairs.

After the midday meal and spending much of the afternoon at prayer—a boring but necessary task that I'd neglected sorely during our adventures with the undead—Father Rhetorios came to look me up. "I bring good tidings, Brother Stephen!" he said. "We've found a position for you. You can start right away."

The position was in the tannery. By dinner time I was stripped to the waist with a rag tied around my nose and mouth, my body covered in blood, cow hair and fat, scraping stretched hides with a piece of bone and walking on sand sprinkled on the floor to avoid slipping in the shit and rotting cow entrails that littered the place. The other monks who worked there kept up a constant chorus of holy chants as they went about their grisly tasks. The chanting fortunately drowned out the curses I muttered under my breath. First ghouls, now this. I was an artist trained by the great Rhangabé, and now I was splashing buckets of human piss over stretched hides and picking moldering bits of cow intestines out of my hair. I wished God would let me know what I'd done to deserve this.

Camytzes and Theophilus remained guests of the Monastery of St. Stoudios for nearly two weeks. Theophilus didn't want to stay that long, but Camytzes refused to let him go back to Chenolakkos unescorted, for fear of the ghouls that were (presumably) still out there. Camytzes's father had told him that he was on his way to the capital and Michael was not to leave Constantinople until he arrived. Unfortunately I saw little of my friends during this period, and frankly, given the way I smelled after working in the tannery, I would have been embarrassed to be in their company. But one evening in mid-July Camytzes sent me a note stating that he and Theophilus were departing for Chenolakkos in the morning. Camytzes had met his father and received new orders. Brother John, who headed the tannery, graciously released me from my duties after supper that day so I could say goodbye. I took a very long bath, washing myself thoroughly with lye soap, but embarrassingly I could still smell cow guts and piss in my hair and on my cassock. Hopefully Camytzes and Theophilus wouldn't notice.

As it turned out, Camytzes was my only companion; Theophilus was at prayer. We strolled in the lavish gardens that filled the courtyard of St. Stoudios. Many flowers were then in bloom, and the evening was beautiful, with the setting sun painting the sky over Constantinople orange pink. "So, I suppose your father is accompanying you back to the country?" I asked Camytzes. "That'll be good for Theophilus to have two experienced warriors escorting him instead of just one."

"No, my father's staying here in Constantinople," the soldier replied. "The Emperor has ordered all the thematic commanders to remain in the city to help defend against the Saracens. I'd be staying too except there's nobody left in our district for local defense."

I felt my stomach sink a little bit. "So the Saracens are coming, then?"

Camytzes nodded. "Oh, yes. They're coming. They crossed the Dardanelles from Abydos just a few days ago. Eighty thousand strong, marching this way. I'm a little worried about running into Saracen raiding parties on the roads back toward Domelium. I'm going to try to stick to the back roads, the less-traveled ones, for Theophilus's safety."

"Why hasn't the Emperor sent an army out to defeat them? He could destroy them before they even get here."

"Evidently he feels more confident of taking on the Saracens here, against the walls of Constantinople, than he does out in the open country." Camytzes looked at the ground as we walked. "The truth is, Stephen, he doesn't have much of an army. As angry as I was when he refused my request to do something about the ghouls, I understand his position. My father is now under the command of regular army officers. He tells me the regular army's been totally demoralized by all these revolts over the past few years. Leo keeps his loyal troops here in the capital, to protect his crown against usurpers as much as to defend the Empire from the Saracens. He can't count on many more troops than the ones he has here. If he tried to call up every available man in the Empire outside the capital, maybe a third at best would actually show up. The Caliph's army has met with virtually no resistance. They've marched all the way from Syria and into Thrace, and to almost the gates of Constantinople, without having to unsheathe their swords."

"I don't know much about military matters, but that sounds pretty pathetic to me."

"It is." We walked a distance farther. Sounding a bit sheepish, Camytzes said, "It may be blasphemy to utter this within the walls of a monastery, but, if it comes down to it, I would probably convert to Islam."

I was shocked. "It *is* blasphemy," I said. "I'm not a very good monk—I think everybody agrees on that—but if they conquer us, I hope they kill me quick because I couldn't live under the swords of heathens."

"Oh, it wouldn't be so bad. You can't eat pork or drink wine, but life among the Saracens isn't so awful. They're a very advanced and interesting people. Their art, their music, science—every bit as good as ours. I'm told Baghdad is even more beautiful and magnificent than Constantinople. Probably in many ways they're more like us than they are different. I never understood why this God business is worth so much blood. I'm a soldier out in the frontier. I can understand fighting for grain, for water, for livestock or other resources, or to hold a border. But which God you worship? That just doesn't seem worth fighting over." He wore a little smile. "There, now you'll have to denounce me as a heretic."

I smiled. "I wouldn't think of it. I owe you my life." I patted his arm. "God bless you, Michael Camytzes. Be careful. Watch out for those ghouls."

"You too, Stephen. We'll probably never meet again in this life. Good luck to you."

I went to bed that night feeling very uneasy about everything. With his quiet contemplations on life under the Saracens, it seemed that Camytzes had pronounced the epitaph for the Empire. The news that the Caliph's army was on its way, soon to besiege Constantinople, filled me with dread. I remember hearing stories about the last siege, forty years ago when the Persians tried to conquer the Empire. It had lasted five years and caused untold amounts of suffering among besiegers and besieged alike. Was that my future? Years upon end of enduring battles, battering rams, projectiles, siege engines, possibly eating rats and straw in order to stay alive? That night I said a private little prayer in my chambers, begging God for the deliverance of Constantinople and the salvation of Christendom. I wondered which would be worse, Constantinople being conquered by the Caliph or being overrun by undead ghouls. It'd be hard to choose between those fates.

After a long time I finally settled down to sleep. It didn't seem like I had slept very long when I was awakened by the sharp voice of a monk proceeding down the hallways, calling everyone to prayer in the chapel. There was no timepiece in my cell of course, but glancing out the window—just a narrow vertical slot in the stone wall—I could see that the waning moon hadn't moved very much from when I went to bed. Instantly I knew something was wrong. I put on my cassock and proceeded out into the hallway, thronged with monks heading toward the chapel.

"What is it?" I asked Gennadios, a young colleague who'd also been an iconographer before they set him to work on the wine press. He was probably the closest thing to a friend I had at St. Stoudios. "It's not even matins yet—why are they getting us up so early?"

"We are to pray urgently for Constantinople," Gennadios replied.

"Oh?"

Gennadios's mouth was a grim line as he told me, "The Saracen army appeared outside the walls just tonight. The siege has begun."

Chapter Four

The Secret Icon

The first days of the siege were very strange. The news that the Saracens had camped outside the Land Walls of Constantinople—and the sight of their army in all its vastness—was more terrifying than anything they did. From the windows and parapets of St. Stoudios we could see a long sea of white tents dotted with little campfires that twinkled at night, the whole scene crowned by many majestic banners, bearing the star and crescent, fluttering in the warm July breeze. But for several days the Saracens did nothing. The Emperor had ordered the gates of the city closed and locked, and the guards on the walls increased their patrols, but so far as I know there was no actual fighting. At the monastery we were at first very concerned that our foodstuffs wouldn't hold out, but Rhetorios addressed us before supper one evening and explained that we needn't fear. "The harbors of Constantinople are open and operating quite normally," he told us. "Ships are moving in and out the same as they always have. The Emperor assured me personally that not a man, woman or child in the city will have a single mouthful less of bread than he or she had before."

Given what had happened, I wasn't surprised to see Theophilus at our supper table, his usual silent self. After the meal he and I walked toward the chapel together, where the candles were just being lit for vespers. "So, looks like you'll be staying at Stoudios for a while," I said. "I'm sorry. I know you really wanted to get back to Chenolakkos."

"Perhaps it is for the best," sighed Theophilus. "At least I can keep an eye on *you*."

"Have you heard from Michael? I guess with the city gates sealed up he wasn't able to leave either, but I haven't seen him around the monastery."

"Yes, he left the monastery, but he's still in the city. The last I heard, his father called for him to join their military camp. Perhaps he'll come visit us, or send word." Theophilus crossed himself. "I pray for all our brave soldiers. They'll need all the fortitude and luck God can bring them."

"Yeah, well, it doesn't seem like the Saracens are so tough. They've just been sitting out there for four days and nights, doing nothing."

"I'm quite sure that won't last. The battle will be joined soon enough."

Theophilus's words were prophetic. That very night I was awakened in my cell by a commotion from somewhere beyond the monastery. It was not terribly loud, for it was far away, but it was unusual enough to wake me. I shrugged into my cassock and crept to the small window to have a look. What I'd heard sounded like the distant shouting of many voices. My window faced west, toward the Land Walls, not far from the Golden Gate. Through the narrow portal, across the moonlit tile rooftops of the buildings between the monastery and the walls, I saw many dark figures crawling like ants. I saw the twinkle of their torch fires—the normal patrols of the wall guards—but there were also small arcs of some burning material, catapult projectiles most likely, dancing up and over the walls. Some were fired from inside, some from without. It didn't appear to be a large fracas but it was the first fighting I had seen. I watched for perhaps twenty minutes. The little fire arcs, two or three each minute, didn't seem to be doing much damage. Maybe it was just a small attack intended to harass more than anything else. I whispered a little prayer for the victory of our forces and went back to bed.

The onset of the siege greatly increased our workload at the tannery. As I learned within twenty-four hours of the Saracens' arrival, we and many tanners at monasteries and private compounds all over Constantinople had been co-opted into the war effort by order of the Emperor. The large hides we were making were to be draped over the wooden breastworks atop the walls as a sort of shock absorber for the Saracens' fireballs. The theory was that if they were kept stiff, they could serve as extra shields for our troops, and if they were kept wet, any fireballs that landed on them would fizzle out. Every moment of every day that we weren't eating or in prayer, those of us who manned the tannery were scraping hides and pounding pigeon shit furiously, with all the disgusting side effects that resulted. I'd soon gotten inured to the stink of the place, but I was rudely reintroduced to the humiliation of it all when I slipped on a wet cow's eyeball left on the floor and knocked over a vat of urine that subsequently splashed all over me. Brother Thomas, one of my compatriots, was kind enough to douse me with a bucket of water, not that it helped that much. "Things like that happen to the best of us," he shrugged, and we kept on working.

Because of the pace of our work, I was quite relieved—though understandably puzzled—when, on the seventh day of the siege, Rhetorios's assistant Henoch appeared at the door of the tannery and said, "Brother Stephen of Chenolakkos, you have a visitor."

I looked up from the frame across which a hide, almost denuded of cow hair, had been stretched. "I do?" I said, pausing to wipe my bloodstained brow with my elbow.

Henoch cupped a hand over his mouth to dampen the stench. "Aye. A sister of God. She says she must speak to you urgently. She's waiting in the cloister."

For the life of me I couldn't think of any nuns who would want to talk to me. "Did she give her name?" I asked.

"She didn't. She said she could speak only to you. Will you see her?"

I glanced at Thomas, who shrugged. I tossed him my bone scraper. "Give me a quarter of an hour to get cleaned up," I told Henoch.

When you work with dead animals, piss, shit and lye for twelve hours a day, fifteen minutes isn't enough to do more than wash the grossest layer off of you. I still stank heartily as Henoch led me into the cloister, but at least I had a clean cassock (borrowed from Gennadios) and I somewhat resembled a normal monk. Beyond the columns of the cloister I could see smoke rising from parts of the wall, indicating a skirmish in progress, but the situation didn't look much changed from what it had been the past few days. A figure as black as midnight stood near one of the columns looking out at the battle. She was about as tall as me, totally robed in black, her head covered with a hood. "Sister?" I said, after stopping short of her. I still had no idea who this could be or what her business was. "You wanted to see me?"

The nun turned. Her face was totally covered by a black kerchief, leaving only her eyes showing, in the manner of Mohammedan women. Her eyes looked vaguely familiar but I still couldn't place her. She said something, but her words were totally lost by the muffling of her kerchief. "*What?*" I said. "I can't understand you."

She spoke louder. "I *said*, you are Brother Stephen Diabetenos, the iconographer from Chenolakkos?"

"Yes. Do I know you?"

The nun's eyes—they were a lovely shade of sea green—flicked over toward Henoch. "My business with Brother Stephen is private," she said. "Would you mind leaving us?" Henoch bowed and took his leave. Finally the nun unfastened the veil across her face. The eyes *were* familiar, but I could scarcely believe it. I was alone in the cloister face-to-face with the wife of Emperor Leo III.

"Empress!" I gushed. I had no idea what protocol was expected in this situation, but I thought it prudent to bow.

"No, no, please don't bow," she whispered loudly. "I disguised myself as a nun so I could get in here without attracting attention." Her nose wrinkled. "Eww, what's that *smell?*"

"It's me, I'm afraid. They have me working in the tannery."

"An iconographer, working in a tannery?" The Empress shook her head. "I suppose that's my husband's doing."

"More the Saracens' doing. We're making hides to hang over the tops of the walls to absorb their fire arrows." I was intensely curious why she'd come to see me. "I'm sorry, Your Majesty, but—how do you even know who I am?"

"I remembered you from last week," she replied. "You, the elder monk and that soldier came to the palace to see my husband. Later I asked him who those people were. When he told me you were an iconographer, I remembered your name and later wrote it down." Maria looked about nervously. "Walk with me, Brother. Nod and occasionally cross yourself as if we're discussing religious matters."

I began to walk slowly and she kept pace. "How can I help you, Your Majesty?"

"You must keep this very quiet. You're not to tell *anyone*. I could be in very serious trouble if anyone knows I've come here to see you." Softer, almost a whisper, she said, "I want to commission *work* from you."

"You want me to paint an icon?"

"Yes."

"I was told the Emperor hates icons."

"He does. He won't have one in the palace. He believes they're sinful, an offense against God. That's why this must be kept secret. Leo and I don't agree on the subject of icons. It caused a great deal of *strife* between us when he ordered all the religious images banished from the palace. But we need an icon. I hate to go behind his back, but the preservation of Constantinople from those Saracen hordes out there may depend on it."

"Why is that?"

She paused for a few moments. Still walking, she said, "Do you remember hearing of the great siege of Constantinople by the Avars and the Persians, ninety years ago?"

"Yes. I've heard of it."

"I'm told it was every bit as fearsome as the present siege promises to be. In fact the city almost fell. But the blessed Virgin Mary saved it. The Patriarch toured the walls of the city every day carrying an icon of the Virgin. Later, at the height of the siege, soldiers saw a woman robed in purple, believed to be the Virgin herself, walking atop the walls. The sight of her caused *panic* in the hearts of the besiegers. They gave up and were soon defeated. That was how the Virgin Mary became the traditional protector of Constantinople."

"I think everybody in the Empire has heard that story at one time or another."

"Don't get me *wrong*, Brother Stephen. I'm not a superstitious woman. But if there is any truth in the story, I'm willing to enlist the aid of the Virgin Mary in defense of our city, even if my husband isn't. Therefore, I want you to paint me an icon—the Virgin Mary, robed in purple, looking over Constantinople and keeping it safe. I'll make sure you're well paid. I know you must work in secret, and it'll be a double burden for you because of your normal work in the tannery. But please keep it *quiet*. My husband can't find out. Will you do that?"

I was overwhelmed. Never in a million years would I have dreamed that the Empress of Byzantium herself would be commissioning an icon from me, and a secret one at that. "Why me?" I asked her. "I'm far from the best iconographer here. I only just got here, in fact. I'm a last-minute replacement for another artist who died. If you talk to Father Rhetorios, I'm sure he can find you a top-notch artist who—"

"No," Maria interrupted. "I don't feel I can trust anyone in authority. Sooner or later they'd just go blabbing to the Emperor, or else word would get out some other way. Besides, I don't know any iconographers. Since the day I got to the palace and knew that the Saracens were coming I'd hoped that I might come across one, if only by chance. You came to the palace last week, so you were in the right place at the right time. And, you also saw my husband in person. You *know* how strong-willed he can be."

Something told me instinctively that I didn't want this assignment. "I don't know," I said skeptically. "Sneaking around behind the Emperor's back is a dangerous business. If he's so touchy on this subject of icons, who knows what he might do if he finds out? I doubt he'd do anything to you since you're his wife, but he probably wouldn't think twice about blinding me or throwing me in a dungeon or something."

"Don't worry. If there is any trouble, you can get word to me and I'll make sure it's smoothed out. After all, I am the Empress." She looked over at me with her sea-green eyes. "Will you do it?"

"When do you want it, this icon?"

"As soon as you can possibly manage it."

"Well, I can guarantee it'll take awhile. I'm going to have to work secretly in my cell at night. I'll have to sneak paints and materials out of the studio at odd hours. And with all the work they're making me do at the tannery, I have to sleep now and again: So it could be some time before I finish it."

A smile broke her lovely face. "You'll do it, then?"

I'm going to regret this, I thought. *But damn, she's beautiful.* And I had to admit the whole thing was kind of flattering. Someone of importance was finally asking me to do my job, and for a very crucial cause. "Against my better judgment," I said.

"Oh, *wonderful!* Thank you so much." The Empress replaced the black scarf across the lower part of her face. "I'd better get out of here before someone recognizes me. Thank you, Brother Stephen. I promise I'll get word to you very soon. Start the icon as soon as you can. Remember--Virgin Mary, clothed in purple—"

"Yes, yes, clothed in purple and keeping watch over Constantinople. Just like in the siege ninety years ago."

Maria glanced over to either side. "Better cross as though you're giving me absolution," she said.

I did so. "Good afternoon, Your Majesty."

"Good afternoon."

I went back to the tannery, bewildered. I honestly had no idea what to think. It occurred to me that maybe I was being set up somehow. After all, I didn't know the Empress, and the small dose I'd had of her at the palace wasn't particularly positive; could I trust her that this thing wasn't going to come back to haunt me somehow? But, it seemed like she'd taken some risks to come see me, sneaking out of the palace and all, and surely if the Emperor hated icons as much as she said he did Leo would be enraged to find out she'd commissioned one. Maybe I could give her the benefit of the doubt. As I returned to my scraping and dung pounding, I started sketching out the icon in my mind. I'd painted the Virgin Mary countless times of course, but always under some master's direction. This would be the first time I'd do one according to my own plan with my own ideas. Immediately I decided I would give her piercing sea-green eyes. I wondered if the Empress would appreciate that.

Within a few days the idea in my mind became a sketch on parchment, a ragged fragment that I kept folded up and hidden under the bed in my cell. Although the Empress hadn't asked for a diptych, I decided that was what I would do. The central panel would be the Virgin Mary robed in purple with the city of Constantinople behind her. She would be holding out her right arm, and the second panel would open on the left, showing the Virgin's hand holding down the Saracen hordes. The design certainly wouldn't be subtle but I doubted the Empress was interested in subtlety.

The hardest thing would be to get the wood on which to paint the icon. There were plenty of blank icons in all formats in the studio, but they were all carefully inventoried, and if one went missing, it would certainly be noticed. Thus I'd have to build one myself. It was this task I set myself to the next few evenings, when after working in the tannery

I would find one reason or another to hang around outside the carpentry shop, browsing through the scraps and remnants that wound up there.

In the meantime, all of us at St. Stoudios watched the progress of the siege with apprehension. There was a hospital at the monastery, and, being the nearest one to the far corner of the walls where fighting with the Saracens had begun, eventually it began to fill with casualties from the skirmishes. They weren't very bad at first, reflecting the halfhearted nature of the fighting—a few scrapes and some burns from flaming projectiles. I was told that the fighting was mainly a ruse to keep the troops busy while Emperor Leo tried to negotiate with the Saracen commander, Maslama, believed to be the Caliph's own brother.

Not long after, though, the fighting took an upturn in intensity. The shouting and fire arcs over the walls near the Golden Gate were both much more pronounced, and in the morning, columns of smoke rose not merely from that spot but from several other places along the Land Walls. Sure enough, I heard after chapel that nearly a hundred wounded wall guards had been brought to the infirmary during the night and in the early morning. We could also see with our own eyes that the Saracens' siege towers had been moved much closer to the wall. Presumably this meant that negotiations had broken down. If there had ever been a chance that Emperor Leo could buy the Saracens into withdrawing, it seemed to be over now.

Still, almost no one at the monastery ever directly mentioned the siege. A prayer for "the deliverance of Constantinople" was now standard at vespers, but aside from that the subject was taboo. I decided I'd rather not know how the battle was progressing. If the Saracens managed to breach the walls and storm the city, we'd know all about it in short order. In my own private prayers I dared to ask God to watch over Michael Camytzes and his father. "Dear Lord, they're probably right in the middle of the fighting down by the Golden Gate. Give strength to their swords and protect them from the Saracens. We're all depending on them." Each night I peered through my little slot window at the fracas going on in that area of the wall, day after day—that was, until one Tuesday morning when it abruptly stopped. There was no telling for sure what had happened, but I guessed the Saracens must have moved their focus to another part of the walls, for the columns of smoke during the day and the distant twinkles of fires at night seemed to center thereafter around the Second Military Gate. Maybe Camytzes was out of danger.

That very evening, however, our generalized troubles suddenly became a lot more specific. It was in the first week of August and very hot. We gathered for supper in our usual hall, the monks sitting down at the very long wooden table with Rhetorios at its head. He led us in the typical evening prayers, adding tonight, "We pray for the souls of those warriors, both Byzantine and Saracen, who have met thee, Lord, in the recent fighting." There was seldom any conversation at supper and the hall was filled with only the sounds of the monks' utensils clunking against their wooden bowls as we consumed our soup, bread and watered-down wine. Tonight, though, was different. I jumped, startled, as nearly everyone did, when the heavy door to the mess chamber burst open suddenly. Henoch stood there, his eyes wide, his face nearly white. "*Hegoumenos*, and Brothers!" he cried. "We must beat a hasty retreat from these quarters! Fighting has broken out inside the walls of the monastery!"

Instantly the mess hall was in an uproar. Several bowls of soup and tankards of wine crashed to the stone floor and a burst of excited conversation was muted by Rhetorios who bolted from his chair and shouted, "*Silence!*" In the next empty seconds we could hear some sort of commotion coming distantly from elsewhere in the compound, much panicked shouting and screaming. "The Saracens have breached the walls of the monastery?" said Rhetorios.

"Nay, *Hegoumenos*," Henoch replied. "It's not Saracens. The fighting is in the infirmary. No one's sure what happened. Several of the soldiers went crazy or something. Brother Ignatius and two others are dead. The berserkers are mauling everyone who comes near them. I ran to warn you all that we must get to safety—they're overrunning the infirmary!"

My stomach sank. Theophilus, seated four chairs down and across the table from me, glanced at me and I at him.

"Maintain order!" the *hegoumenos* shouted. "Everyone, please go out the west door there, through the cloister. Move quickly but don't crowd. Henoch, take a horse. Ride down to the wall and bring back some men-at-arms. Everyone, stay *calm!*"

The monks of the Monastery of St. John Stoudios moved as one body toward the west door of the dining hall as Rhetorios had decreed—except for two, Theophilus and myself. We both dashed toward the door through which Henoch had entered. "Wait, Brother Stephen, Brother Theophilus!" Rhetorios cried.

"What did they look like?" Theophilus shouted, grabbing Henoch by the shoulders. "Did they have dead eyes, these berserkers? Impervious to pain? Were there bites on their bodies?"

"I—I don't know!" Henoch replied, seeming as terrified by Theophilus's questions as by the danger we faced. "I only saw one—a man, a soldier, he—"

"He what?" I said. "He *what?*"

Henoch made a pained, disgusted face. "He sprang from his bed and tore off Brother Ignatius's arm," he replied.

Theophilus let go of him. I could feel adrenaline rushing through my veins.

"Go, Henoch," said Rhetorios. "You must bring back the men-at-arms. There is a garrison at the Gate of Christ, but half a mile from here—"

"No," I said firmly. "Ride to the Golden Gate instead. Find a soldier named Michael Camytzes. You'll recognize him, he stayed here a few weeks ago. Bring him a message. The message is—'They're back. Come quickly.' You can remember that?"

Henoch was still quaking, but he nodded. "Yes. I can remember that."

"You know something of this, Brother Stephen?" said Rhetorios.

"It takes too long to explain. Go, Henoch! In the meantime we have to defend ourselves." I looked around at the jumbled chairs, the messes of bowls and wooden spoons littering the table and the floor. "We need weapons. What can we use?"

"The kitchen!" Theophilus cried.

We both sprang toward the other door, the *hegoumenos* shouting after us in bewilderment. There was no time to stop and explain it to him. My legs propelled me almost independently of my brain. All I could think about was—*I hope Camytzes can get here in time to stop them. If he can't, he may find a monastery full of living dead to contend with.*

Chapter Five

The Ghouls' Incubator

The implements that we found in the monastery kitchen were only marginally better than the makeshift weapons we'd had on hand at the *xenodocheion*. There were some large knives, a few cleavers and a colossal wooden fork, but as these were tools for cooking, not fighting, they wouldn't be very effective except at uncomfortably close range. Theophilus, however, discovered a cache of huge iron skewers, as tall as a man and sharpened at both ends, standing in the corner near the fireplace. They were probably intended to roast pigs or other large animals over the fire. "These will do until the soldiers come," said Theophilus, grabbing one of the spits.

"They'd better come fast," I said, taking a shank. It was quite heavy and unwieldy, but at least it was better than a meat cleaver.

"Brothers, what is this madness?" cried Rhetorios, who had followed us into the kitchen. "We must get out of the way. If the berserkers are so fierce, you must not risk your lives—"

I whirled, holding the spit like a spear. "Listen, Father," I said. "You don't know what you're dealing with. Theophilus and I ran into these ghouls out in the country on the way here. We have to destroy every last one of them. Every time a ghoul bites a man, the victim becomes a ghoul himself. If we don't stop them now, we'll have dozens, maybe hundreds of them running around by tomorrow."

"We need to know where they are," said Theophilus, peering out the doorway of the kitchen into the monastery's courtyard. "And which direction they're coming from."

"Father, do as I say, please. We have several of these long spits. Go to the congregation and bring back eight or ten brave monks. Gennadios, Thomas, people like that, young people, strong people. Have someone go to the blacksmith's shop and see if there are any weapons there—swords, spears, fireplace pokers, anything. We've got to hold back the ghouls until Henoch can come back with reinforcements." The *hegoumenos* stood dumbstruck, certainly not accustomed to being ordered about by a young monk a third of his age, but he jumped when I cried, "Please, Father, *now!*"

"I hear them!" Theophilus shouted. He readied his own spear. "They must be moving toward the courtyard."

As Rhetorios bolted back through the dining hall, Theophilus and I made our way cautiously out the other kitchen door that communicated with the monastery's courtyard. It was dusk and the shadows were long; the darkness would make our task harder. The well-sculpted gardens were full of neatly trimmed trees, long rows of hedges, rosebushes and banks of flowers and a few vegetable crops in rows of soil among the stone passageways. Across the courtyard was the wing of the monastery that contained the infirmary. There were screams and cries coming from that direction. As we stood in the garden, our long pig spits at the ready, we saw a monk come staggering out of the cloister, screaming horribly. *"God preserve us!"* he cried. *"The Devil is afoot!"* He slumped against a column, leaving a bloody handprint upon it. His cassock was drenched in carmine. As he stumbled closer to us, I could see that his right hand was gone, ending in a blood-dripping stump that had clearly been torn from him by ravenous teeth.

"Lord, forgive me," I whispered with a glance toward the darkening sky. I lunged forward with the spike. The end of the metal rod crunched into the wounded monk's skull like a stick poking through the shell of an egg. His horrified scream ended abruptly. I pulled the spike from his head, only to see three other monks, who looked to be unscathed, sprinting as fast as they could away from the infirmary. "They're coming!" one of them shouted. "Run!"

Another still-human victim staggered from the direction of the infirmary. It was, horribly, a nun. Her black robe was torn and her neck had been bitten by a ghoul. She wailed and wept as she flung herself toward Theophilus. "Brother, bless me," she stammered as she grabbed at Theophilus's robes with her bloody hands. "The Devil has come for me!" Theophilus winced. He closed his eyes, made the sign of the cross over her and then plunged his spit into her head. Soon the nun was a lifeless pile of flesh and black robes lying on the stone pathway.

We saw no more living victims, but the characteristic wail of the ghouls emanating from the infirmary wing told us that they were there and heading this way. As we crept into the cloister connecting the courtyard to the infirmary wing—its stone floor covered with the bloody footprints of those who'd fled the horror—I heard voices and motion behind me. Gennadios, Thomas and one other monk, a lad of barely seventeen called Alexius, had come from the chapel to lend their aid. "Go to the kitchen and arm yourselves with spears such as these," I called to them. "They're stacked in the corner next to the fireplace. Come quickly! The ghouls will be upon us soon." The other monks did as I bade them. Alexius stopped short of the body of the nun, gaping upon her in horror; Gennadios took his arm and led him away.

"Only three," said Theophilus. "We have no idea how many ghouls there are."

"We'd better hope Camytzes gets here soon."

"He may not come at all. Suppose the Saracens chose this precise moment to attack his sector of the wall? He can't well tear himself away." Theophilus jumped. "There they are!"

Three ghouls shambled down the cloister toward us. Two of them were dressed as soldiers, in shirts of mail, armored skirts and boots. One's arm had evidently been wounded, probably in battle; it hung limply at his side. The third ghoul was mostly naked, clad only in the torn bloodstained shreds of what was a burial shroud. He must have been a casualty of the Saracens. His skin was mottled and horribly burned. Probably he had died, or at least been thought dead, and then reanimated as a ghoul after his body had been set aside for burial. All three were drenched in blood from head to foot. One of the armored ghouls was gnawing on a human hand, perhaps belonging to the monk I'd killed. They approached, emitting their mindless soul-splitting wails. Gennadios, Thomas and Alexius drew up behind me, carrying their spits. All three looked to be in shock. At least I didn't have to convince them the ghouls were real; they could see what was happening with their own eyes.

"We must destroy them," I said to my brethren. "The only way to bring them down is to destroy their brains. They feel no pain and won't react to wounds as living men do. Whatever you do, *don't let them bite you*. We're now five against three, so we ought to do well."

"We go together on three," said Theophilus. "Take that one first, the one with the hand. Then the one behind him, then the naked one. One...two...*three!*"

Five iron spears shot forward at the lead ghoul. The mindless thing could not feel fear, so it did not recoil, but a moment later its head was thoroughly perforated. It twitched, emitted a rattling sound and slumped to the floor. Thomas's and Alexius's spikes were difficult to dislodge. Gennadios, seeing his spike withdraw from the ghoul's head with one of its eyeballs stuck to its end, dropped his spear and staggered backwards, vomit exploding from his mouth.

"Again!" Theophilus roared, and he and I struck at the second ghoul. A few moments later Alexius had freed his spike and it joined ours stabbing into the ghoul's brain that disintegrated like a crushed melon. Blood and brain matter splashed backwards onto the naked ghoul, who lurched at us unusually fast. I'd only just withdrawn my spike and had no chance to rear back and lunge again, so I swung my spit like a club. It connected with the ghoul's head, dashing him against the stone wall opposite the colonnaded side of the cloister. The thing roared and gasped. Theophilus sprang forward, piercing the ghoul's ear with his spike. He drove it in so hard and fast that it went all the way through him and I heard it *chink!* against the stone wall. The demon twitched and fell still. Theophilus pulled back his spit and the thing collapsed in a bloody heap.

Thomas and Alexius stood near me, panting hard, their bloody spears ready. Both looked positively mortified. In the courtyard, poor Gennadios was on his hands and knees, still retching copiously. "This can't be all," said Theophilus. "There *must* be more of them."

"Wait," I said. "Here comes one." Another ghoul staggered from the direction of the infirmary. It was not a soldier or a monk, but dressed in a white tunic splashed with blood; perhaps it had been one of the surgeons. Someone had already tried to smite it, because the ghoul was missing one foot, cleaved neatly off as if by the blade of a sword. It was slower than the other three because it hobbled along on the stump of its ankle. "I'll take care of this one," I said. I jammed my spit into the center of its forehead. This was the easiest kill of the day, but it was still gruesome to see the thing collapse to the floor, its brains shattered. This had once been a human being, probably a man of God. I cursed this pestilence that turned holy men into mindless monsters.

No more ghouls approached and the infirmary was eerily quiet. "We have to go in there," said Theophilus. "See if there are more of them."

This was the part I dreaded. "There are probably casualties in there too. People who've been bitten and haven't reanimated yet. We must destroy them as well."

"This is madness," Thomas gasped.

"If we don't," Theophilus retorted, "the whole monastery, and probably the whole of Constantinople, is at risk."

"Maybe we should wait for the soldiers," I suggested. "Stake out a perimeter here, where the infirmary leads to the cloister and the other parts of the monastery. If they come out one by one, we should be able to take them, among the five of us."

Theophilus crept closer. Through a distant stone doorway,

illuminated like a cavern of Hell with the flicker of a torch, we could see or hear nothing from the direction of the infirmary. "Perhaps you're right," he said. "Okay. Stephen, Thomas, you two here on this side. Alexius and I will take the other. Gennadios! Get up off your knees. Go back and tell the others not to come this way, and that no one must enter the infirmary wing for any reason until the troops get here. Bring the spike with you in case a ghoul has gotten loose and ambushes you on the way."

All did as they were told, but as we stood there, spikes at the ready, Thomas began to weep. "I can't believe what we did," he blubbered. "God will surely damn us forever."

"He'll do nothing of the kind!" Theophilus retorted angrily. "Whatever is the source of this pestilence, the ghouls take the forms of our friends and loved ones so that we'll hesitate to destroy them. Any hesitation means *death*. Remember that."

For nearly an hour we stood as the sentinels at the door of the infirmary wing. During that time only one more ghoul delivered itself into our hands, and it was a plenty horrifying one. We heard ghoul moaning in the stone hallway and a long slow shuffling sound, but the demon didn't show itself right away. After a while it became evident why—the ghoul was *half* a man, a wounded soldier whose body simply did not exist from the waist down. It crawled along the ground with its arms, in the manner of a seal, making very slow progress toward the human meat it inexorably craved.

"Vile!" Theophilus gasped when he saw it. He quickly smote the ghoul with his own spike. Perhaps twenty minutes after that we heard the wailing of a human voice from the infirmary, a man's, *"Is anybody there? Help me, please help! I'm wounded! I can't move! Please, help!"* Theophilus forbade any of us to go to his assistance. "He may reanimate and become a ghoul at any moment," he said. It was heartbreaking listening to the man's incessant wail. *"I can hear you out there! Please, why won't you help me? God will damn you for not coming to my aid!"* Thomas couldn't take it anymore. He threw down his spit, crumpled against the wall and sobbed, crossing himself incessantly and murmuring unintelligible prayers.

We were all relieved when we heard a clatter of hoofbeats and considerable commotion outside the walls of the monastery. "They've come!" Alexius gasped. Theophilus warned us to remain on our guard; we could still be attacked at any moment. A few minutes later—it was now night, and only a few small torches illuminated the courtyard—a cadre of Byzantine soldiers armed with swords rushed among the trees and hedges, their chain mail clinking. I heaved a sigh of relief and nearly collapsed backwards as I lowered my spear.

"Brother Stephen and Brother Theophilus!" boomed a familiar voice across the courtyard. Michael Camytzes, now dressed in the uniform of a regular soldier, followed his men toward the cloister. "Why am I not surprised to see you on the forefront against the demons? And it seems you've been victorious too. If the ghouls of Byzantium had the sense of men, they would tremble at the mention of your names!"

Camytzes strode confidently up to the doorway leading from the cloister. To one of his men he said, "Post sentries to relieve the monks. Then assemble a detail to clean out those rooms back there. Everyone remains on their guard at all times."

"It's good to see you," I told him. Looking at his uniform, and his cloak bearing the mark of the Roman Legions, I said, "You've been promoted?"

"I've been appointed official aide-de-camp to my father. Our task is the defense of the Golden Gate and the Marble Tower."

"I've seen fighting in that quarter. Has it been heavy?"

Camytzes laughed. "Oh, the Saracens have just been toying with us, testing out their new siege towers and trebuchets. We've given as good as we've gotten, but the real fighting won't start until the Saracens' fleet gets here." He motioned toward the doorway. "So, what's the story in there?"

Theophilus and I told him what had happened. We assumed there were bodies in the infirmary who hadn't yet reanimated, but we couldn't be sure. Camytzes asked if there were any other exits, and if we knew of anyone who had been bitten and might have gotten away. We told him no.

"Do we have any idea how it started?" he asked. About this we knew nothing. It stood to reason that someone who had been bitten by a ghoul must have been taken to the infirmary as a casualty. That suggested that there were more ghouls out there in Constantinople somewhere.

"The Emperor should have listened to us," Camytzes muttered. "All right. You four stay here. You, soldier! Let's have that detail to go in and clean out the infirmary. We can't be certain of who is a threat and who is not. Everyone who's still alive must be quickly and cleanly killed. The heads of all corpses must be destroyed, preferably by crushing. Let's move!"

The soldier, a young man with olive skin who looked as if he had Saracen blood, was horrified by the order to slay everyone still alive. "I cannot carry out that order," he said. "There are innocent people in there. How can we destroy them?"

"You don't understand what we're up against. In that room are any number of bodies who will reanimate at any time and become ghouls. They must be completely annihilated. The safety of our Empire depends upon it!"

I can't say I blamed the young man, who had obviously stumbled into a situation he didn't understand. He and Camytzes argued for several minutes, but the bickering was cut short by another commotion—the shouting voices of monks and the loud clop of a horse's hooves on stone. A figure, clad in mail and a blue tunic, was riding his horse right up the cloister on the opposite side of the courtyard. I heard Henoch, pursuing the rider, shouting, "No! You'll ruin our gardens!" but the rider kept coming, heedless of any obstacle in his path. Several rosebushes and a vegetable patch were trampled in short order by the horse, which wore its own sheath of mail. The rider reared back and the horse whinnied as he stopped it just short of Camytzes and the small detail of soldiers. "What is this?" blasted the horse rider. "Why are you all standing about aimlessly? I was told there were Saracens inside the gate!"

The rider, obviously an officer, was imposing. Locks of long gray hair peeked out from under his chain mail hood. His features were rugged, as if weathered by many years on campaign. Just by glancing at him I could tell who he was, for his eyes looked familiar—they were exact duplicates of the piercing orbs that stared out of Camytzes's face. The elder Camytzes carried a silver goblet of something, wine perhaps. He took a swig from it and said, "Well? What *is* this dire emergency that required you deserting your post on the wall to come here?"

Before Michael could answer, the young soldier who had argued with him rushed up to the horse. "*Droungarios* Camytzes, Sir!" he said snappily. "Your son has given us a monstrous order. He wants us to slay the sick and fallen who may be in the infirmary, innocent people—"

"Father," said Michael, "this is of the utmost importance. You remember I told you about what happened to Domelium? Well, it's happened again, here, tonight. There are people in that infirmary who will become ghouls in a matter of hours. These brave monks destroyed the ones who already animated—"

"Ghouls?" blasted the elder officer. "What ghouls? All I see are a couple of dead monks and a nun."

I stepped forward. "Sir, your son is correct. All of us monks standing here before you saw the same thing tonight. These ghouls must be stopped. What your son recommends is the only way to be sure that no more are created."

"Oh? And who are *you* to give *me* orders? I'm Gabriel Camytzes, *droungarios* of the Anatolikon theme! You're just a monk. What do you know of these matters?"

"He knows what we're fighting," Michael said tersely. "If you don't believe us, why don't you go into that infirmary and see for yourself? I'll come with you—just in case one of those things tries to jump you from behind."

The officer looked stunned at this dressing-down by his son, but ultimately, as I guessed, he couldn't turn down the challenge. He drained the silver cup and stuck it into a pouch of the bag across the horse's saddle. Then, drawing his sword, he got down from the horse. "This is ridiculous," he muttered. He walked up to one of the ghouls we had slain, the naked man, and kicked the corpse over with his boot. Grunting, he stepped toward the door of the infirmary and stopped to listen. "Ghouls, eh?" he finally said. "I hear nothing."

"They probably haven't reanimated yet," said Michael.

"Well, let's take a look." I noticed that the elder Camytzes did not sheathe his sword before he started through the doorway. If he truly believed there was no danger, he probably would have.

Following his father, Michael said to the sentries, "We'll be right back, but stay on your guard. Kill anything that comes out of this doorway unless it's myself or the *droungarios*. Make sure no harm comes to the monks."

The two Camytzes were gone for perhaps five minutes. Theophilus, the other monks and I paced nervously in the cloister, awaiting their return; Gabriel's horse continued to ruin our gardening, eating several heads of cabbage and defecating into the rosebushes. We heard no sounds of battle coming from the infirmary. All we heard was the elder Camytzes's voice on two occasions. "Well, they're all dead," and a little later, tellingly, "That's the most disgusting thing I've ever seen." Finally they emerged. Gabriel's sword was sheathed, but Michael's was not. The son was nearly pale. His father looked completely nonplussed.

"Well, it is unfortunate," the older officer finally said. "Someone went berserk in the infirmary and killed eleven people, not counting the ones out here, in the most brutal and grotesque fashion imaginable. I grant you, it's quite a bloody spectacle in there—but what justifies you, my son, abandoning your post on the wall when the Saracens might renew their attack at any moment? Why is this not a case for the civil or ecclesiastical authorities?"

"Every single one of those eleven corpses will be a raging, ravenous ghoul by this time tomorrow," Michael replied. "If so much as one of them gets loose in Constantinople, the Saracens outside the wall will be the least of our worries."

"So you say." I couldn't believe it but Gabriel said this with a grin. "Nonetheless, since there's nothing happening here now, might I suggest we return to our posts at the Golden Gate? I believe these monks can clean up the mess."

I grunted. Michael's father was being as stubborn and closed-minded as the Emperor had been. Then, quite suddenly, I had an idea. Michael's mouth opened and he began to retort to his father—"*Droungarios—Sir*—I respectfully request that you allow a detail to remain—" when I stepped forward again.

"May I make a suggestion?" I said boldly.

"Oh, you wish to give me orders again, young monk?" said Gabriel.

"No, Sir. But I wish to impress upon you the danger of what we're facing here, and why I called for your son's help. If proof that the ghouls are real is what you want, I'll give it to you." I motioned back toward the doorway. "The door leading into the infirmary wing can be sealed up. Let's blockade it. We'll post guards. My brothers and I defended the monastery by ourselves before you rode in here, and we can do it again. Leave one or two of your men here for good measure, and also to prove that we're not tampering with anything. Then you and Michael return tomorrow and see what's inside that infirmary. By then we'll need your help to kill those eleven ghouls."

"Nonsense," Gabriel scoffed.

"It shouldn't be necessary," said Michael. "But if seeing these ghouls with your own eyes is the only thing that will convince you, Brother Stephen's suggestion is the best way to proceed—so long as we can be *sure* that once they reanimate none of them will escape."

The elder Camytzes suddenly seemed bored by the whole enterprise. "Fine," he said, vaulting back onto his horse. "Do whatever you want, so long as you, Michael, are back on the wall in one hour's time. If not, I will personally court martial you for desertion." He pulled back the reins of the horse, causing the animal to rear back and crush a hedge with its hoof. At the same moment several dollops of dung dropped from its rear onto the stone pathway. With a clatter of hooves the officer rode away, leaving our gardens ruined in his wake.

Michael Camytzes looked at me. "All right," he sighed. "Let's get to work on that barricade. I don't want any of those ghouls getting loose during the night and wreaking havoc in here."

"Your father is as thickheaded as the Emperor."

"Even more so, if that's possible." He patted my shoulder. "Don't worry. I'll bring back a large contingent of troops tomorrow afternoon. Assuming our barricade holds and those eleven don't get out of the infirmary, we shouldn't have too much trouble dispatching them."

I suddenly felt almost sorry that my plan was being implemented. "Yeah," I said. "*If* the barricade holds."

When Camytzes returned to his post near the Golden Gate, Theophilus and I took charge of the defense of St. Stoudios Monastery against the demons that were soon to ravage it from within. Michael left two guards with us, but was also kind enough to give us a few extra swords, figuring they would be more useful than our primitive pig-roasting spits. Since the ghouls were not yet reanimated, we had a rare and fortunate chance to prepare thoroughly. I ordered that dozens of new torches be lit and placed around the courtyard so we could be certain that no ghouls would creep upon us in the dark. The main door to the infirmary was blocked with many heavy timbers into which we drove huge iron spikes. Brother Honorius, the physically largest of the monks at St. Stoudios at almost seven feet tall, hurled his three-hundred-pound body against the door to test its strength. It did not give a millimeter. We posted sentries in all points around the infirmary, armed with pig spits (Theophilus and I took the swords). Plates of bread and flagons of watered-down wine were brought to the defenders in the courtyard. I admit that organizing the defense was diverting, and I relished the chance to finally be doing something useful. "You know," said Father Rhetorios to me as we patrolled the trampled gardens, "if you weren't an iconographer, you might have made a fair military man." I took this as a tremendous compliment.

I slept little that night, retiring to my cell only for an hour to catch a nap. Even then my sleep was interrupted. Henoch came to my cell shortly before dawn. "Excuse me, Brother Stephen?" he said. "We've begun to hear sounds from the infirmary. We thought you should be informed."

I went back down into the courtyard and accompanied the two soldiers to the barricaded door of the nightmare chamber. From behind it we could hear the moaning of ghouls and the scrabbling of fingernails. "I wouldn't have thought it possible!" one of the soldiers gasped. I listened carefully, pressing my ear against the door.

"How many?" Theophilus asked me.

"Sounds like one. There'll be more soon enough." I backed away from the door, sword in hand. "All right—everybody stay vigilant. I don't think these demons will get out of there, but we have to be ready in case they do."

As the light from the east spread into the sky, the moaning and scraping of one ghoul at the infirmary door soon multiplied. We couldn't tell just from listening if all eleven corpses in the infirmary had reanimated, or only some of them; but the exercise, nerve-racking as it was, at least illustrated in no uncertain terms the dangers posed by massed ghouls. By midmorning the door, braced so sturdily and tested by Brother Honorius's bulk, bowed outward and recoiled visibly when several ghouls smashed against it at the same time. I surmised that the ghouls probably could have knocked down the door with their combined strength if they had the wits to communicate or cooperate; clearly they had none. The sentries we had carefully posted in the cloisters and grounds surrounding the infirmary were thankfully not needed.

The vigil continued throughout the day. Due to the urgency of the situation, *Hegoumenos* Rhetorios released me from my duties in the tannery, but, as my presence at the door of the infirmary wasn't needed all the time, I was able to steal way to my cell a few times during the morning and early afternoon and work on the secret icon. I wasn't yet ready to begin painting, but I'd selected some boards to use as the diptych canvas, and I must say that my first attempt at carpentry turned out quite well. Every hour or so I'd return to the infirmary door to see if the situation had changed. Meanwhile, outside, the smoke rising from the wall told us that the skirmishing with the Saracens continued. Camytzes's casual explanation that the siege hadn't really started yet, and would not until the Saracens brought their ships, made me quite uneasy. Aside from stocking the warehouses with extra grain and draping our hides over the breastworks atop the walls it didn't seem like the Emperor was making a tremendous amount of effort to protect his capital.

In the middle of the afternoon, without any advance warning, a body of troops descended upon St. Stoudios. I happened to be in the courtyard listening to the moan and rasp of the ghouls behind the door when Henoch rushed from the cloister. "They're here!" he said excitedly. "They've come!" The two Camytzes rode mail-clad horses at the head of a phalanx of perhaps twenty-five infantry, bearing shields and carrying swords that glinted brilliantly in the hot August sun. This time they were kind enough not to ride their horses through our courtyard, but the detail of troops kept their formation impressively as they marched up to the infirmary door. Michael's father planted himself in front of me. His mouth opened as if to say something but then I saw his head swivel as he stared at the door, pounding outward with the press of the ghouls behind it. For the first time he seemed genuinely surprised.

"Well, Father?" said Michael. "Still ready to court martial me?"

Gabriel approached the door. "I don't believe it." With his gauntlet-sheathed hand he reached forward, but recoiled when the door pounded suddenly. He looked at me. "Is this some sort of trick?"

"No, Sir," I replied. "There are eleven ghouls behind that door. The first one reanimated toward dawn. Thankfully the barricade held."

"You give me your word, then, that this door was not opened since last night?"

"I'll swear an oath before God to that effect, if that's what will convince you."

It was clear to me that Gabriel Camytzes wasn't used to being addressed in any tone that wasn't totally obsequious. His eyes grew a shade colder and he stepped backwards from the door. "Not necessary," he said. He glanced at his son. "Well? What's your recommendation?"

"Recommend we break down the door and dispatch the ghouls, Sir."

Gabriel rolled his eyes. "Well, of *course*. How do we do it?"

"Quickly, and in force. Aim for the heads. Decapitate them first. The heads themselves must be crushed to be absolutely certain of their destruction, but that's much easier to do when it's just their heads lying around trying to bite you than whole bodies coming at you. Any man who is bitten must be destroyed immediately in the same manner."

Gabriel looked taken aback. "Execute our own wounded, is that your recommendation?"

"Yes, Sir. Any casualty of a ghoul attack will become a ghoul themselves, as this exercise has demonstrated."

I saw a few of the soldiers in the detail glance at each other uneasily from under their helmets. I wasn't unconcerned for them, but I thought the danger to the troops was far less than the peril we monks had faced last night. The troops, after all, were clad in heavy chain mail. A ghoul's teeth were no match for armor that deflected Saracen swords and arrows.

"Very well," said the *droungarios* with a sweep of his arm. "Take charge of the operation."

Michael did not hesitate. "Bring a battering ram!" he called to his troops. As four of them ran to retrieve it, Camytzes patted my shoulder. "I'll take it from here. Thank you for your industry and your vigilance, my friend."

So we, the monks of St. Stoudios, stood back and let the soldiers do their bloody work. Michael Camytzes, sword drawn, gave the order to batter down the door. It splintered in seconds under the military's heavy bronze-headed ram as if the door were nothing but a sheet of bark. The detail marched in, swords flashing. Within five seconds several of the ghouls had been decapitated. One hideous head, still chewing a mouthful of human flesh, bounced against the archway of the door and rolled out into the cloister. Arms and legs were cleaved and fell in bloody piles to the floor. Once the troops were far inside the infirmary, we couldn't see much of the slaughter from where we stood in the courtyard, but Theophilus, Thomas, Alexius and I stood back listening to the dreadful din. We were relieved that someone other than ourselves was making a stand against the demons. In the garden, Gabriel Camytzes paced, occasionally glancing at the ominous doorway, but never for very long.

The battle lasted less than three minutes. I didn't expect that eleven mindless ghouls would last long against a battalion of Byzantine troops. The soldiers emerged from the infirmary, their tunics and chain mail splashed with blood, their swords wet and dripping with gore. "Well done, men," said Michael as he stepped into the cloister, sheathing his sword. "Now we'll need a cleanup detail. I want all of these corpses, and all pieces of them, gathered together in a pile for burning."

At that moment Camytzes happened to be standing right over the severed ghoul's head, still animate, that had bounced out of the infirmary and rolled to a halt. Its jaw was opening and closing, its waxy gray eyes seeing nothing. It was the head of a middle-aged man with dark hair. Camytzes paused a moment, then reached down and picked up the head by its hair. Instantly the ghoul's teeth clamped down on the chain mail of his arm and tried to devour it. I thought at first that Camytzes would unsheathe his sword and pierce the head with it in front of all of us, a sight of gratuitous uneasiness that I didn't look forward to seeing. However it seemed he had other plans. "Brother

83

Stephen!" he called, looking over at me. "You work in the tannery, do you not? How about fetching me a large glass jar filled with some brine solution?"

"Why?" I asked, swallowing back my revulsion.

I couldn't believe it, but Camytzes smiled. He said, "I think maybe it's time for our friend here to meet the Emperor."

Chapter Six

The Emperor's Plan

This time—after an outbreak of ghouls not even three miles from his palace, attested to by the eyewitness of the *hegoumenos* of the most prestigious monastery in Constantinople, personal friend of the Patriarch—the Emperor couldn't brush off what had happened. I have no idea exactly what information actually reached him, except that he was told something extraordinary and troubling had occurred at St. Stoudios, requiring the prompt intercession of regular army troops. Two days after the battle in the infirmary Camytzes got word to me, a hastily scribbled note, that the Emperor himself was planning to visit his sector as part of a tour of the defensive walls. *You and Theophilus must be here*, he wrote. *I'm sending my father's personal guard to fetch you at noon today.*

Our trip to the Land Walls was at once dazzling and terrifying. A cadre of five soldiers brought Theophilus and me toward the Golden Gate on horseback. As we wound through the crowded sunlit streets of Constantinople, I was struck by how much grain I saw. Everywhere we looked there were carts full of bushels of wheat, barrels of flour and heaps of bread loaves being hauled and loaded into warehouses and even stacked in alleyways. "Must be rations for the siege," I commented to Theophilus. We passed several churches, their doors open in the afternoon heat, and they were completely full of parishioners praying for the deliverance of Constantinople. In an alleyway, I saw a group of children playing with wooden swords, pretending to attack the Saracen hordes.

The terrifying part of the journey came as we neared the walls. The columns of smoke were much closer today, and over the wall I could barely see the top of some wooden structure on the other side, probably a siege tower, burning. My blood chilled when I heard the high distant song of a male voice—one of the Saracens' muezzins calling for prayer. The soldiers brought their horses to a halt at the foot of one of the colossal towers, and Theophilus and I halted there too. Climbing down from the horse, still hearing the prayer call hovering on the wind, I said, "Wow, the Saracens really are on the other side, aren't they?"

"Let's hope they never get on *this* side," muttered one of the soldiers. "This way, please."

There was a large room inside the tower on the ground level. It was dark and gloomy, illuminated only by a few small notch windows in the thick walls of grayish-white stone and red brick. A few dying candles drooped on rusty brackets protruding from the walls. Inside the bunker there was much activity. Soldiers were rushing to and fro, stacking sacks of flour, moving barrels and otherwise making ready. We passed numerous iron racks filled with swords, spears and bows. In one part of the long room a few soldiers cooked some foul-smelling gruel in an enormous iron pot. Toward the end of the room there were tables and chairs arranged haphazardly. The two Camytzes stood over one of them, poring over a map of the walls and the encampments beyond. As we neared, I could hear snippets of their conversation. "Our scouts confirmed that the Saracens are cultivating fields in this area," said Michael to his father, motioning to a spot on the map. "They're also hitching up plows to horses in this part of the field, on the slopes of Maltepe Hill. Probably planning to divert the Lycus River to irrigate their crops."

"That's Bartusis's sector, isn't it?"

"Yes, Sir, I believe it is. He's defending from the Gate of St. Romanus up to the Fifth Military Gate. His flank is right about here."

The two of them noticed Theophilus and me. "Ah, our visitors," said the elder Camytzes. To his son, "You're sure we really need them here?"

"They fought the ghouls valiantly when we first encountered them outside of Domelium," Michael replied. "If they can help the Emperor understand our problem, their presence here is more than warranted."

"Problem?" scoffed Gabriel. He began to roll up the map on the table. "I was under the impression that there *was* no more problem. The ghouls have all been slain."

Almost immediately there was a great commotion in another part of the long room as troops hastened to stack away their provisions and snatch up their swords. An adjutant ran up to the Camytzes, breathlessly proclaiming, "Sir, the Emperor and his guard are just outside!"

"Very well," said Gabriel. "Let's make him welcome. All troops to attention! I want everybody in their ranks and not a hair out of place. We will impress the Emperor with our discipline."

Every one of the phalanx of well-dressed guards who accompanied Leo into the tower was taller than he was. Indeed, waddling about on his stubby legs, our ruler was not only unimpressive but almost comical. He wore an ornately inlaid breastplate of old Roman fashion over a mail shirt and he trailed a long purple cloak that matched his boots. The heavy gold rings on his fingers would have played havoc with his grip if he'd tried to handle a sword. He sauntered in casually as if he owned the place (which, technically, he did) and he walked entirely without ostentation or apparent hurry. By contrast, his guards were so stiff and formal in their movements that they might have been tin soldiers. We all bowed as he entered; Leo deflected the move with a casual sweep of his hand. He made a lazy inspection of the place, looking over the barrels of provisions, the racks of weapons and Camytzes's soldiers who stood at rapt attention before him. For a man defending his capital against a siege by the Saracens, Leo was positively languid. After a while he opened the drawstrings of the little leather pouch hanging from his armored skirt, shook a few pistachios into his palm and ate them casually, tossing the shells on the dirt floor. He sauntered coolly up to Gabriel Camytzes. Still chewing pistachios, the Emperor said, "You're the *Droungarios* Camytzes, in command of this detachment?"

Gabriel bowed his head. "I am, Your Majesty."

"Nice tower you've got here." He popped another nut into his mouth. "Those stacks of flour over there—how long do you think you can keep your men fed?"

"At least six months, Sire."

"Six months. Mmmm." Unshelling a nut, he added, "We could be detained here by the Saracens for longer than that. You're aware of the reports that the Saracens are planting crops around their camp outside the walls?"

"Yes, Sire. We were just discussing that intelligence."

"Oh, Maslama," said the Emperor flightily, smiling while he did so. "How vexing he is, bottling us up in our nice comfortable city where we can sleep with our heads on pillows of flour. It cost me a pretty penny to buy up all the grain in the Empire, but that's what money is for. So, without a stalk of wheat left standing anywhere in Byzantium, the Saracens will soon be reduced to eating their own shit!" The Emperor exploded in laughter at his own crude joke. Camytzes and the soldiers evidently felt compelled to laugh too. I cracked a grin but that was it. Theophilus, as usual, remained stony-faced.

It was to him and me that the Emperor next turned his attention. Standing before us, his thick eyebrows raised and he said, "Ah, and you two here as well? The venerated experts on ghoul killing. And how perfect is it that they should be monks? Well, they told me you had something extraordinary to show me, and when I heard I was to visit Camytzes's sector, I recalled the name and grinned in anticipation of further ghoul-related entertainment for my amusement. What, then, do you have for me?"

"This, Your Majesty," said Michael, who was already kneeling to pick up the bundle under the command table. He set the large glass jar, covered with a rough wool cloth, on the table. The Emperor, obviously thinking this a game, smiled and clasped his hands together. Camytzes whipped the covering from the jar. Inside the grayish brine the animate head of the ghoul thrashed and snapped like an angry fish. The Emperor's dark eyes widened. He crept toward the jar, leaning over as he did so. Studying the awful thing, he tapped on the glass. The head reacted, snarling and trying to propel itself toward him; the thing's forehead clunked against the side of the jar.

"Well!" Leo finally exclaimed. "You certainly don't see one of *these* every day." He reached toward the earthenware stopper that sealed the jar. "May I?"

"I strongly advise against it, Sire," said Michael. "The head is severed, but as you can see it's still dangerous. We wouldn't want you to be bitten. If you were, you would yourself transform into—"

"Yes, yes, I'd become a ghoul myself, I remember that part." He tapped the glass again. "How did you obtain this—er, specimen?"

"When Brother Stephen sent me an urgent message that the Monastery of St. Stoudios had been attacked by ghouls, I led a detachment of troops to vanquish them. There were eleven in all, not counting several dispatched by the monks themselves. This head was among the carnage. We incinerated the corpses, but I chose to preserve this head so you could see it—and perhaps understand the gravity of the situation."

Leo looked skeptical. He turned to Gabriel. "*Droungarios*, do you believe your son's story about these ghouls?"

"At first, Sire, no, I did not. However, I now know it to be true."

"And *how* do you know that, exactly?"

The elder Camytzes briefly described the experiment we conducted by sealing the demons in the infirmary. Leo listened, stroking his chin, occasionally glancing at the head in the jar. I dared to hope he might at last be convinced.

"This head," he said, tapping the jar, "if we let it out and allowed it to bite somebody, that person would become a ghoul, yes?"

"Correct," said Michael.

"Those eleven victims in the infirmary—how long did it take them to become ghouls?"

"The time varied," I answered. "The first reanimated shortly before dawn, the others after that."

"And *all* eleven transformed?"

"Yes, Your Majesty."

Leo nodded. He reached for a few more pistachio nuts, pacing slowly, never taking his eyes off the head in the jar. At last he turned to Michael and said, "Well, Camytzes, I have to congratulate you on your cleverness. Despite my natural skepticism, you've managed to convince me that you're useful. How fortunate for you that the demonic pestilence happened to infiltrate the Monastery of St. Stoudios! If it hadn't, you would never have had the chance to impress me with your friend in the jar there."

Camytzes didn't seem to catch on, and neither did I. "Useful?" he echoed. "If I may be of service to Your Majesty—"

"Well, of *course* you may be of service!" said Leo, as if this was the most elementary thing in the world. "I'm immediately detaching you from your father's garrison. And you two monks, I temporarily release you from your vows to serve as Captain Camytzes's aides-de-camp. Yes, *Captain* Camytzes—I'm promoting you. You'll have everything you need at your disposal. I'll need a working demonstration, of course, but considering you already conducted an impromptu one in the field, I don't expect that'll be too difficult. I'm thinking convicts would be the ideal subjects. We'll get you some. Shamefully, we don't have significant numbers of Saracen prisoners yet, so our own criminal refuse will have to suffice. I stress to you of course the utmost secrecy of this project. One whiff of this gets to the Saracens and we'll lose our advantage."

Michael, bewildered as I, shook his head. "Your Majesty?"

"Don't you understand?" boomed the Emperor. He strode over to the table and tapped the jar containing the snapping head. "You've discovered the perfect weapon against the Saracens! Once you've figured out the most efficient way to transform Maslama's soldiers into ghouls, we'll spread a little taste of this into his ranks and then I'll sue for peace. We might not even have to use the weapon in combat. A mere demonstration might be enough. Scare the turban right off his head! Captain Camytzes, as of this moment you're officially High Commissioner of Ghoul Warfare. This project has the highest priority. You'll report to the *kouropalates*, my soon-to-be son-in-law, General Artabasdos. No one else must know."

We all stood there staring at each other in disbelief. Even Gabriel Camytzes seemed astonished. Michael's mouth opened and closed a few times but no sound came out.

Finally I forced myself to speak. Choosing words that wouldn't send me to prison was difficult. "With all humility, Your Majesty," I said, "I think that approach might be—"

"Might be *what?*" Leo demanded. He spit a fragment of pistachio shell onto the floor.

Foolhardy was the word on the tip of my tongue, but of course I couldn't say that. Michael, fortunately, came to my rescue. "Your Majesty, these ghouls are extremely dangerous," he said. "Trying to multiply them would pose as much of a risk to us as to the Saracens. There'd be no way to ensure that they wouldn't get loose and ravage Constantinople. Once out there, this pestilence is extremely difficult to contain—"

"That's precisely *why* it makes such a perfect weapon," the Emperor replied. He patted Camytzes's shoulder. "Look, Captain, you have to be careful what you wish for, because you might get it. A month ago you came to me wanting to be in charge of all military matters in the Empire involving ghouls. Now you are! If you weren't ready to impress me with your prowess, you shouldn't have ventured to make the request. These are desperate times. I'm duty-bound to pursue any avenue that might even arguably give us an advantage over the Saracens. Surely you understand that."

"Yes, Sire, but you must understand—"

"Captain!" Gabriel had gotten over his astonishment and stepped forward to cut short his son's protestations. He bowed. "Your Majesty, my son fully understands his duty. You can count on him, I assure you."

"Excellent." The Emperor grinned, and tossed a pistachio nut into his mouth. To Michael he said, *"Kouropalates* Artabasdos will soon be in touch with you." Glancing around the tower room, he added flightily, "Good job preparing your tower for defense. Keep up the good work!" In less than twenty seconds he and his guards were gone.

"How *dare* you talk back to the Emperor!" Gabriel hissed at his son as soon as the royal and his entourage had left the room. "Are you mad?"

"No, *he's* mad!" Michael shot back. "Do you know what will happen if we let that thing loose?" He motioned to the head in the jar.

"I do—we may defeat the Saracens!"

"Michael's right," I spoke up. "This is madness. We've seen these ghouls in action. We know what happens to people who are bitten by them. If we start breeding ghouls purposely, and so much as one of them gets out, the entire Empire could be at risk."

Gabriel stiffened. He glanced at me, at Theophilus and at his son. I could see the gears turning in the old soldier's head. He stepped closer to me, and with a quieter and much more sinister tone in his voice he pronounced, "The Emperor is God's personal representative on this earth. Neither you nor my son have any business questioning the orders of the Emperor. They're not the orders of Leo III. They're the direct orders of *God.* As a monk, Brother Stephen, I would expect you to understand that. Are you not bound to serve God in any way He may see fit?"

I could see where this was going. I swallowed. "Yes, Sir."

"Well, then. You know what to do." Gabriel strode back to the table, snatched up the rough woolen cloth on the table and draped it back over the jar containing the severed ghoul's head. "I suggest you get started quickly. I have a defense to organize!" With that he strode away, barking orders at his men.

Michael Camytzes shook his head, staring at the lumpy jar on the table. "The things we do for this Empire," he muttered. "Well, I guess we'd better get started."

The three of us were all deeply troubled by this development, but it turned out to not be the only or even the worst occurrence on an already bad day. That very afternoon the Saracen fleet arrived.

Constantinople was soon hemmed in by land and sea. The nearly two thousand Saracen ships that took up their positions all along the three sides of the city—from the Sea of Marmara to the Golden Horn— cut off the capital from any and all hope of reinforcement or supply. On top of the tower, in the golden light of the coming dusk, Michael, Theophilus and I stood at the north parapet, looking out over the glittering domes and grand houses of our city, and beyond them the distant dark dots that were the Saracen ships moving to blockade the harbor. No one fired at the ships. What would be the point? The city was battened up, tight as a tick, and we all knew it.

"How long do you think this siege will last?" I asked Michael Camytzes, after I lost count of the number of dots slowly moving against the glinting horizon.

He was lost in thought for a moment, his eyes seeing what I saw, and he glanced back at the south parapet and the tent city of the Saracens with its fluttering star-crescent flags. Finally he said only one word, "Year."

"You mean we're going to be stuck here for a *year* without reinforcements and without fresh food?"

"Perhaps the end will come before that," said Camytzes.

Theophilus at last opened his mouth in an attempt to be helpful. "I've heard that the warehouses are filled to bursting with grain. The Emperor prepared for this eventuality, as did the emperors before him.

93

At least we'll have enough to eat."

A crackling sound diverted our attention. We turned to the south, toward the army, and saw some flaming projectiles flung half-heartedly from one of the Saracen siege towers against the wall. We could hear the Byzantine soldiers shouting taunts and epithets at their attackers below. I saw a man's sword glint in the sun as he raised it defiantly over his head.

"Somehow that doesn't make me feel better," I sighed.

Camytzes patted my shoulder and then started toward the dusty stone steps leading to the interior of the tower. His mute resignation spoke volumes. Our situation was now unchangeable. We were, all of us in Constantinople, in the same boat.

Chapter Seven

Tinkering with Death

For me the next six weeks were a strange mixture of gloom, exhilaration, dread and curiosity. Almost immediately the *kouropalates* Artabasdos sent word to Michael Camytzes that he was reserving several rooms of the Praetorium of the Eparch for use as our laboratory and headquarters. It wasn't an especially fun place to work. The Praetorium was Constantinople's largest prison, its gloomy stone cells crammed with murderers, thieves, child molesters and sodomites. That we found ourselves there was partially Michael's doing. He insisted to Artabasdos that no experiments involving the ghouls could be conducted with any modicum of safety unless the subjects—that's what he began to call them—could be kept pent-up behind impenetrable walls, separated from us and from their guards. The Emperor happily obliged. I also gained an insight into Leo's perverse and macabre sense of humor when I learned that he'd told the prisoners of the Praetorium, through their warden Bringas, that many of them were "about to perform a service for the Empire that, if successful, will result in the total repayment of your debts to society". Naturally he and Bringas neglected to mention that this service would involve their deaths. Perhaps it wouldn't have mattered much if they had said so; many of the prisoners were condemned to death, and those who weren't couldn't expect to live long anyway due to the bad food and terrible conditions of the prison.

Theophilus and I still lived at St. Stoudios. As grim as our task was, I have to admit that at least I was relieved to be absolved of working in the tannery. My skin, clothes and hair didn't reek like moldering intestines and day-old urine when I retired to the straw-covered pallet in my cell every night. I also found that my new job as a special servant of the Emperor offered me a certain amount of status at the monastery. No one knew precisely what we were doing, but word had spread among the monks that Theophilus and I enjoyed the favor of the Emperor and were tasked to carry out some special project for him. As a result, Rhetorios offered us permanent seats at the head of the table and we were constantly greeted in the hallways and courtyards, as no other monks were, with kind bows of the head and greetings such as, "Good morning, Brother Stephen." This may have been due as much to our new status as to gratitude at having slain the ghouls that had rampaged through the infirmary, which was still closed and sealed off indefinitely. Either way, it wasn't bad.

Our status came with one very good fringe benefit—privacy. Unlike most other monks I was not obliged to join prayers at specific hours and my time—what little there was of it when not in conference with Theophilus and Michael Camytzes at the Praetorium—was my own. Consequently, I began to make significant headway on the Empress's icon. By the end of September the diptych was fully constructed and I had prepared its surface for painting. At night, working by candlelight, I sketched the figures of the Virgin, the Saracens and the city of Constantinople. I even managed to secure a few paints and some brushes lifted from the art studio, which was still shuttered and idle. As hesitant and uneasy as I was about the project involving the ghouls, at least I could satisfy myself that I was spending an hour or two a day doing what I should have been doing all along in the service of God—even if no one but the Empress herself would ever know.

"If we're going to do this," said Michael Camytzes, "we need a definite plan. The Emperor is deluded if he thinks it's going to be as simple as simply creating a couple of ghouls and then sending them out to wreak havoc through the Saracens' lines. We have not only the safety of our own people to consider, but also we must determine how to make these ghouls an effective weapon against our enemies. This requires much thought and planning."

Camytzes uttered these words on our first day at the Praetorium. Michael, Theophilus and myself enjoyed an expansive office—formerly the chamber of the warden Bringas, who had relocated to a smaller room—fitted out with elegantly carved chairs, several large tables, candelabra and a fireplace. In the corner of the room was a colossal wooden trunk bound with bands of steel and held shut with a giant unbreakable padlock. Inside this chest, which had been built at Michael's direction by the prison carpenter, was the jar that contained the severed ghoul's head. I avoided that corner of the room. It wasn't because I was afraid the head might get loose, but if you listened closely, you could faintly hear the sound of the head snapping and thrashing in its preservative fluid, still fighting after many days to taste human flesh. The whole business made me shudder.

"How do we propose to introduce the ghouls into the Saracens' army?" I asked. "And how do we do it in a way that doesn't put our own troops at risk?"

"That's a very good question," Michael replied. He reached for a parchment and an inkpot. "We should brainstorm some ideas. The *kouropalates* told me the Emperor has taken a personal interest in this project, and we need to provide him with some evidence that we're at least doing something."

"How about catapults?" Theophilus suggested.

"Yes, that's good," I replied. "Once we have a suitable number of ghouls, we'll behead them and fire the heads as catapult projectiles over the wall into the Saracens' lines."

Michael scratched this idea on the parchment but I could tell he wasn't especially taken with it. "What of the risk to the men loading the catapults?" he said. "If so much as one of them is bitten by one of the heads, the pestilence will be loose in our lines."

"Put the heads in glass jars," I suggested. "They can be loaded safely by the artillerymen, and the jars will shatter on impact and let the heads loose."

"There's still the problem of the safety of those loading the heads into the jars in the first place. And what if one or two are broken in the process of loading the catapults, as surely they will be? We'll have hungry ghoul heads rolling around on top of the towers and inside the walls, hiding in dark recesses ready to bite some unsuspecting archer or infantryman. Additionally, we can't be sure of how many of the heads will survive the landing. Do you know the force that a catapult projectile packs when it lands on something? The act of firing them may crush the heads like eggshells, rendering them useless."

"Plus, we have no idea how many of the heads will actually succeed in biting Saracen troops," said Theophilus. "A disembodied head can't move. It could be easily crushed underfoot, even without weapons. We couldn't expect more than one in a hundred heads to actually be effective."

"One is enough," I pointed out.

"Not necessarily," said Camytzes. "In Domelium we slaughtered seventy-seven ghouls in an afternoon, and at St. Stoudios eleven. Yes, it was desperate and dangerous, and in each case the outbreak must have begun from a single ghoul, but we did succeed in smiting them. We can credit the Saracens with no less martial capabilities than our own. How could we be sure the ghoul weapon will be more than a temporary annoyance to the enemy?"

Such were the questions we dealt with in those first days. It was maddening because nearly every idea we hatched brought with it one or more complications that made it impractical or dangerous. For instance, to solve Theophilus's objection involving the limited usefulness of severed ghoul heads, we considered the notion of not beheading the ghouls but simply launching them whole over the walls. This would have been done by encasing each ghoul in a terra-cotta sphere, which would shatter upon impact. Of course this raised the very large question of how a thousand potters were supposed to craft human-sized spheres around their deadly cargoes and somehow avoid being bitten or torn to pieces by them. Plus this scheme would have required thousands of tons of raw clay, an army of potters and the use of precious cords of wood to fuel the furnaces needed to bake the pots—something rather impractical in the middle of a siege where firewood was at a premium for the coming winter. Nearly every permutation of catapult-fired ghouls had complications of this type, and so, a week or so into our deliberations, we abandoned the catapult idea and focused on other methods.

"How about sapping?" Michael Camytzes sighed one afternoon. He was pacing; I was doodling aimless forms on a parchment with a quill, and Theophilus was asleep in a chair. "We tunnel under the walls and introduce ghouls directly into the Saracens' camp. At the appropriate moment, they pop out and wreak havoc."

"Ghouls can't dig," I shrugged. "You'd need a living man with a shovel at the end of the tunnel to dig through the last break of earth at the right moment. We couldn't trust a slave or a convict to do that, and even if we could get a soldier to volunteer for a suicide mission, how could we make sure the ghouls don't simply tear him apart before he manages to finish the tunnel?"

Despite the objections, the sapping option received much consideration over the next few days. Theophilus had the idea of digging the tunnels ahead of time, ending in a large cavern just under the surface on the Saracens' side and protected from our side by a heavy door. The roof of the cavern would be supported by a wooden pillar that could be pulled down by means of a system of ropes. At the proper moment the pillar would be yanked away, causing the cavern to collapse into a sinkhole which the Saracens would naturally try to investigate; then the ghouls would be released in the tunnel and the door shut behind them. We liked this option and Camytzes was on the verge of writing down an official proposal to the Emperor in this regard, but he consulted one of the professional sappers working for the army who told him that it wouldn't work. Supporting the sinkhole cavern would not take *one* pillar, but an entire system of pillars and support structures which would consume vast amounts of lumber and ropes, not to mention the hundreds of men that would have to labor for months underground to dig the tunnels. This was how our deliberations went—when an option was logical, it turned out not to be practical; when an option was practical, it turned out that the limitations on materiel due to the siege made it impossible. We were stymied at every turn.

One evening in October I gave voice to our frustrations. The candles were burning down to nothing and as the faint clicking and thrashing from the as-yet unused ghoul head in the chest mocked our lack of progress. It was late and Theophilus had already gone to bed. "Catapults won't work," I said. "Tunnels won't work. Simply dumping the ghouls over the walls in wheel barrows won't work. *Why* won't they work? They're either too dangerous to our own troops, or we can't be sure the ghouls won't be more than a momentary annoyance to the enemy. The instant the ghouls get over the wall—however they do—the Saracens will slash them to pieces with their swords, just as they would if they were Byzantine troops instead of ghouls."

"The Emperor," sighed Camytzes, "is convinced the ghouls are a super-weapon. He doesn't understand the practical difficulties."

"All the methods we've been discussing aren't that much different than the methods any military commander would use to try to gain an advantage against the enemy. I mean, catapults, sapping, throwing stuff over the walls—you'd do that normally, right? Those are methods you'd try even if we weren't talking about using ghouls?"

"What's your point?"

"My point is that we can't use a method that the Saracens are already expecting. We can't introduce the ghouls into their lines by force. In order for this to work the Saracens are going to have to *want* to let them in. If they voluntarily let the ghouls into their lines, maybe without realizing what they are or how dangerous they are, we've succeeded."

"Let me guess--we have the Emperor trick Maslama into thinking he wants to make peace, and instead of a peace delegation we send a bunch of ghouls dressed like soldiers?"

"It's worth a try."

Michael shook his head. "They'd know it was a trick the moment the ghouls appear. A bunch of wailing, shambling men scattering mindlessly, tearing their own clothes off aren't likely to be mistaken for a surrender party. The Saracens would cut them down like grass in seconds."

"Yes, but we only need a very short window of time. Once they're in, they're in."

"The Saracens will be on their guard. Leo is the most treacherous man ever to sit on the throne of Byzantium. You don't think that even if he sent a cadre to Maslama under a white flag that the Saracens wouldn't have phalanxes of guards surrounding the cadre and watching their every move just in case it happened to be a trick? Maslama would be an idiot *not* to do that. The Saracen commander is many things, but stupid isn't one of them."

"If we *could* keep the ghouls in line for a few minutes, though— maybe we can use ropes or chains or something, maybe lash them together in formation, if we conceal it from the Saracens so at first glance it looks like—"

"That's *way* too complicated. The more complex a scheme is, the more can go wrong."

I grunted in protest, but I knew he was right. I sat back in my chair, staring at a map of the Theodosian walls that was draped over the edge of the table.

My eyes lingered on this image. The shape of the parchment in that position—the curl of the edge of the map over the wooden surface of the table—gave me an idea.

"What would the Emperor do," I asked Camytzes, "if the army happened to capture a few Saracens? Maybe some high-ranking ones, officers or something?"

"He'd torture them mercilessly and try to get all the information

101

out of them that he could about their plans," Michael replied, turning away from the window. He walked back to the table and reached for a flagon of wine sitting on it.

"After that. They'd certainly be killed, wouldn't they?"

"Obviously."

"*Then* what would he do with them? Their bodies, I mean."

Michael looked at me in a way that suggested he was catching on. "Most likely he'd behead them and throw their carcasses into the Bosporus to deny them a proper Mohammedan burial."

My finger traced the curve of the map lying over the edge of the table. "Might he hang their bodies on ropes over the walls to insult Maslama? I've heard of that being done during sieges."

"Yes, he might do that."

"And these soldiers who died heroically—the Saracens would be obligated to cut them down and bury them as heroes, right?"

"Yes."

I smiled. "The Saracens would have nothing to fear from dead men, would they? I mean, possibly Maslama himself would grieve over them."

Michael smiled back. He seemed to understand. "And then get a *hell* of a surprise."

It was fortunate that we came up with this idea when we did. The Emperor was growing very impatient. Artabasdos frequently inquired of Camytzes about what plans were afoot, how many convicts we had turned into ghouls, and when the weapon would be ready for deployment; Michael kissed him off with vague responses, but we had no illusions that this would work for long. In retrospect, I think we deliberately stretched out the planning process because we were understandably reluctant to begin the actual ugly work of creating demons, and the more ideas we hashed over, the more we postponed that inevitable future. But at the end of October the *kouropalates* paid our office in the Praetorium a visit. We found him in a foul mood, which grew worse when he pressed us again about how many ghouls were currently ready for combat and how many we could expect to have ready in a fortnight's time.

"*None?*" he roared. "You three have been sitting around for two months, gorging yourselves on chicken, wine, bread and olives at the Emperor's expense, and you haven't transformed a *single* ghoul?"

"Sir, you must understand this is a complicated matter!" Michael protested. "We must have very careful and precise plans, or this weapon will be useless—or worse, will backfire on us."

"The Emperor has bent over backwards for you!" Artabasdos blasted. "He's been dithering with Maslama since the fleet arrived. He's been mollifying him with false claims that he's negotiating with the Patriarch and the army for authority to surrender the city. The Emperor has been doing this precisely to buy time for you to create your army of ghouls with which to destroy the Saracens. Do you understand what will happen to you when I go back to the palace and tell him that there *is* no army—just a head in a jar and couple of sheets of parchment?"

I was tired of being dressed down by the Emperor and his minions, and I was finally ready to speak out. "We *can't* transform the ghouls yet," I said sharply. "In fact, we can't do it until literally hours before we strike. The plan we're working on involves delivering the ghouls to the Saracens while the men are still dead, during the period of dormancy before they reanimate. That has to be timed precisely."

For once Artabasdos held his tongue. He looked at Michael, at me and at Theophilus—who, characteristically, had been totally silent during the exchange—and finally the *kouropalates* snatched up one of the papers on the table. It was a drawing, done by me, of five bundled bodies hanging on ropes over the walls, with the Saracen army below.

"So, this is how you plan to introduce the ghouls into their lines?" he said. "Lowering them via ropes? That's something, at least. How many are you planning on deploying? Five hundred? A thousand?"

"It will depend," said Camytzes.

"On what?"

"On how many Saracens we can lure into the city and capture alive."

Artabasdos's eyes grew wide. *"What?"* he gasped.

"It's very simple," I replied, snatching the paper from the *kouropalates*'s hands. "Maslama sends a delegation of envoys into the gates of Constantinople under a flag of truce. We immediately take them prisoner. To taunt Maslama, the Emperor gives back the bodies of his friends by hanging them over the walls. Unbeknownst to the Saracens, however, we will have allowed the envoys to be bitten by ghouls, whereupon they'll be swiftly put to death. The bodies will be bundled up in sacks while still dead. The Saracens cut them down and prepare to give them heroes' funerals in full view of our troops. Then the ghouls reanimate and infect the Saracen army."

Artabasdos's features hardened. "That plan is absolutely unacceptable," he pronounced. "You plan to invite Saracens—heathens, Mohammedans—into the holy city?"

"It's the only reliable way to introduce the ghouls into their camp," Theophilus spoke up.

"We respectfully request His Majesty's coordination with our plan," said Michael. "This can work, Sir. If Maslama's sitting still waiting for the Emperor to surrender instead of launching a full-out attack on the walls, that means that Maslama thinks there's a chance the Emperor *will* surrender. Maslama believes the Emperor is weak, and from what you've said of His Majesty's activities, it seems that the Emperor has been actively promoting that impression. Maslama hasn't even used his navy. His ships are just sitting there blockading the harbors. If the Emperor says that he's ready to discuss terms, Maslama will jump at the chance. I'm sure of it. This plan will be successful. You can assure His Majesty of that."

"But a peace delegation would be small," said Artabasdos. "Ten people at most. I'd been under the impression that we were going to create hundreds of ghouls, transformed from the inmates in this prison."

"We don't need hundreds," I replied. "Ten is enough. And far less dangerous to our own people than packing dungeons with legions of ravenous ghouls."

"What if this attack fails, young monk? Your plan requires the Emperor to commit an act of treachery that will enrage the entire Mohammedan world beyond all measure. Your plan requires the Emperor to sue for peace and then slaughter a delegation of envoys, personal representatives of the Caliph, acting in good faith under a flag of truce. Suppose the Saracens quickly slaughter your ten ghouls, as you yourselves did at St. Stoudios. We'll be left with a powerful enemy who will be morally outraged at the Emperor's duplicity and even more determined to reduce Constantinople to ruins than they were before. At that point, all negotiation would be impossible regardless of circumstances. You would have the Emperor throw away *any* chance of a negotiated settlement on this speculative scheme."

"With all due respect, *Kouropalates*," said Michael Camytzes, "I don't believe the Emperor ever intends to negotiate. This war will end with one of two outcomes—either the Saracens are defeated and humiliated, or Constantinople falls and the entire Byzantine civilization is destroyed. He will never settle for any other result. I've met His Majesty but twice, and yet I know this. I'm surprised, Sir, that you do not."

Artabasdos seemed taken aback by this criticism. I thought the man fulsome and vague, and it baffled me why the Emperor would give his own fair daughter in marriage to him; but then again I wasn't one to understand the vagaries of politics.

Artabasdos finally responded by pointing a fat finger at Michael's face. "The Emperor is not one to leave such large questions open to resolution by mere underlings," he sneered. "I'm going to speak to His Majesty about your plan. I promise you I'll present it honestly, but I predict the Emperor will be no less enthusiastic about it than I am.

And when he rejects it, you'd better have another plan. A *practical* one. Is that understood, Captain Camytzes?"

"Yes, Sir. Clearly understood."

The *kouropalates* grabbed the parchment from my hands. "Good evening, then," he said bitterly, and left.

When the door closed, Theophilus rolled his eyes. "Will you two *ever* learn how to speak to persons of authority properly?" he moaned.

Camytzes walked over to the table to refill his flagon of wine. "Anyone want to lay odds whether our plan will even get to the Emperor?" he said casually.

"Gambling is a vice, and therefore sin," I replied. "But if I were a gambling man, I'd probably bet the same way you would."

We were all pessimistic, both that Artabasdos would keep his word to propose the plan fairly to the Emperor, and that Leo would even honor us with a reply. Therefore it was with some surprise that, two days later, we received at the Praetorium an official messenger from the palace bearing a scroll in a wooden tube decorated with gold leaf. Theophilus broke the seal, unrolled the note and laid it on the table. All three of us leaned over it with both curiosity and dread. The Emperor's handwriting was very poor, and the edges of the parchment were stained with smudged green fingerprints—from pistachio nuts, no doubt. The note read—

To Captain Camytzes and Brothers Stephen and Theophilus, c/o the Praetorium, Constantinople:

The kouropalates has told me your plan for employing the so-called 'ghouls' in the fight against the heathen Saracens. I must say I was quite pleasantly surprised by both your ingenuity and your duplicity! Such is a maneuver worthy of a Byzantine. You will do us much honor on the field of battle.

Plan approved. I will make the necessary overtures to Maslama and keep you informed of our progress. However, I cannot say that I'm entirely ready to stake the future of our civilization on such a small number of ghouls. If your plan fails, we'll need a new plan. Consequently, I suggest that we develop a contingency in case our aims are frustrated.

Please begin breeding ghouls at the earliest convenience. I expect the full spate of negotiations with Maslama to take a fortnight. I hereby direct you to have five hundred (500) ghouls transformed and ready to deploy by that time. Hopefully they will not be needed. But, it's always best to be prepared!

God be with you!

Basileus Imperator of Rome and Constantinople, God's Vice-Regent on Earth, His Majesty Leo III.

Chapter Eight

The Attack

The morning after we received the Emperor's note we began the grim process of transforming ghouls in the Praetorium dungeon. "God will provide," said Theophilus, standing back as Camytzes began to unlock the thick heavy padlock on the iron-banded chest in our office containing the severed ghoul's head. "Whatever happens, His will shall be done."

Camytzes, being the military man who had on occasion been required to carry out the dreadful duty of killing innocent people, thankfully spared Theophilus and me the horrors of having to create our first ghoul. He requested of Bringas that the most notorious murderer in the Praetorium be brought to a heavily fortified cell and chained, in a supine position, to a board with his hands and feet securely fastened. The man Bringas chose was a foul stinking brute of a man barely capable of speech, and who was said to have buggered children and murdered them. Nonetheless I crossed myself and whispered a little prayer when Michael told me that he tossed the severed ghoul's head into the cell—it landed on the wailing murderer's loins, right in his lap—and that the prisoner, helpless to defend himself, was bitten several times in the course of a few minutes. Camytzes said he returned to the cell an hour later and looked through the bars. The murderer was stone dead. The severed head had managed, even without a body, to tear open the man's abdomen and was happily munching on his oozing entrails. Having been preserved in the jar of brine for over two months had done the head no harm at all. The murderer's body was released from its bindings, while a guard stood with his boot on the severed head, still chewing and moaning.

Because our plan depended upon the introduction of ghouls into the Saracens' camp while the victims were still dead but before reanimation, it was very crucial to know how much time elapsed on average between the death of the infected person and their reanimation as a ghoul. Theophilus and I had a rough estimate of this time period, which we called the "Dead Zone", from our experiences at St. Stoudios, but this was an opportunity to measure it precisely. Camytzes posted a guard by the murderer's cell with instructions to tick off the hours (as measured on a sundial, whose results were shouted down in the dungeon by a messenger) until the murderer rose again. In his case it was slightly over six hours. After the word came to our offices that the transformation was complete, Theophilus, Michael Camytzes and myself, accompanied by the warden Bringas, descended into the torch-lit darkness of the dungeon to view our grim handiwork. I shuddered as I heard the insensate moaning coming from the murderer's cell. Camytzes, his sword drawn, held us back at a safe distance. Visible in the flickering torch light we could see a burly bald man—or what was left of him—dressed in filthy rags. His eyes were blank, his mouth hanging slackly open. His skin was ashen. A huge chunk had been taken out of his stomach and his entrails were shredded. As soon as the ghoul saw us he launched himself against the iron latticework of the cell door, stretching out with a blindly clawing hand. Even the severed head was attracted to us, inching along the dirty stone floor by opening and closing its jaw until it too was pressed up against the bars, moaning incoherently.

"Monstrous!" whispered Bringas, as we stared transfixed at the ghouls.

Camytzes turned toward him. "Warden, station a heavily armed guard down here at all times. Have your men begin bringing the prisoners down one by one and placing them in this cell. The process of opening the cell door and forcing them inside may be extremely hazardous, particularly when the ghouls begin to multiply in larger numbers. Instruct your men that they need not worry about killing ghouls—if they feel threatened enough that they must destroy one to prevent being bitten, that's perfectly acceptable. Any man who *is* bitten by a ghoul *must* himself be incarcerated in the cell, regardless of their protests. Is this clearly understood?"

Bringas, a man who had spent a lifetime guarding the most foul and dangerous men in society, looked as though this was almost too much even for him. He swallowed hard and nodded to Camytzes, but offered no protest.

"You should go," said Michael to Theophilus and myself. "Await word from the palace regarding the negotiations with Maslama."

We needed no prodding. Raising our cowls against the eerie wails of the ghouls, Theophilus and I ascended the stone steps back to the main level of the Praetorium. Distantly I could hear from other cells the clanging of chains and the defiant shouts of the prisoners. I shuddered to think that within the space of a few days all of those men would themselves be ghouls, and the Praetorium would be a charnel house of Satan's evil, right in the center of the Empire's capital city.

Three days later—by which time the ghoul population of the Praetorium had increased to approximately fifty—the Saracens launched a major attack against the walls. It began at daybreak with the wheeling of twenty new siege towers up to the Fifth Military Gate, where the River Lycus flowed under the Land Walls into the city. It was unseasonably warm for early November and the fighting raged furiously for many hours, with our men trading flaming arrows and projectiles with the Saracens until well into the late afternoon. Wounded men flooded the infirmaries of Constantinople's hospitals and a pall of smoke hung over the central part of the city.

At the Praetorium we were hushed and dejected. Camytzes had assumed that the Saracens' offensive meant that the Emperor's attempt to negotiate with Maslama had failed. "If they don't buy that the Emperor wants to surrender," he remarked, "there's no way Maslama will send a delegation into the city. Our plan will be useless." Above all things we dreaded having to use the ghouls who were now multiplying in the Praetorium's dungeons. No one was quite sure how they would be deployed into the Saracens' lines, and all of us feared that the result would be the infestation of Constantinople itself.

The fighting slackened at dusk but did not end, and the night the offensive began I returned to my cell at St. Stoudios, deeply troubled. I took a meal of gruel and watered-down wine and worked furtively on the secret icon until the candles burned almost to nothing. All night I heard the distant shouting and clanging from the battle out my window. I was just beginning the process of putting away the painting supplies when there was a knock at my cell door. "Brother Stephen!" It was Thomas, my old companion from the tannery. "Someone is here to visit you. He says his business is urgent."

"All right. Just a moment." I draped a cloth over the icon and stashed the paints in the wooden chest by my bed. I went to the door. As I opened it, a crack of orange light from the candle in the hallway illuminated my visitor. It was a monk I had never seen before. He was obese and wore a new cassock, bound at the waist with a straining rope, and a heavy hooded cloak. His hands were clasped together inside his sleeves. A long gray beard was the only part of the stranger's face protruding from his hood. My only thought was that this may have been some sort of official business from the Emperor, but it seemed strange he would have sent a monk to deliver a message.

"Can I help you?" I said.

"This monk has taken a vow of silence," said Thomas, who stood behind the visitor. "He presented these at the door." He handed me three notes scrawled on parchment. The first one read—

I am from the Monastery of the Christ Pantocrator.

The second—

I must see Brother Stephen Diabetenos immediately. It is most urgent.

The third—

I have taken a vow of silence, so I must communicate only through writing. I seek the Lord's forgiveness for the inconvenience.

"I beg your pardon," I said, handing the notes back to the monk. "If you've taken a vow of silence, how exactly are you supposed to tell me what it is you want?"

At this the fat monk immediately unclasped his hands and withdrew them from his sleeves. In one hand he held a quill pen; in the other, a roll of parchment.

"Oh. I see." I stood back from the door. "Well, you'd better come inside. Thank you, Brother Thomas."

The strange monk stepped inside and I closed the door to my cell. I stepped over to the candle on my desk. "Well, I guess I'll have to light a fresh candle, if you're going to be writing," I said, lifting the lid of the desk. "This one's almost out."

"No matter," said the monk softly, pulling back his cowl. "I'm sorry to have *deceived* you. I employed the ruse of the vow of silence so my *voice* wouldn't arouse suspicion."

If I had been surprised when the Empress came to see me before, you could have knocked me over with a feather this time. There she stood, dressed in a monk's cassock, untying the false beard from her chin. She'd added a pillow around her stomach to make herself look fat, thus disguising her ample bosom. Her sea-green eyes looked even more ravishing in the dying light of my candle. Instinctively I bowed. "Your Majesty," I breathed softly.

"I told you *last* time, forget all that ostentation." Maria immediately made for the shape of the easel underneath the cloth. "Is this the icon?"

"Yes, but please don't look at it! It's not even close to fin—"

The Empress had already whipped the cover off the diptych and was examining it. There was not much to see. I had sketched the outlines of all the images, but only the background color and a few buildings in Constantinople had yet been painted. I always hated having my work viewed by its patrons before it's finished. Invariably they suggest changes. If it's already done and you're on their doorstep demanding payment, it's much harder for them to insist that this or that be done differently.

"I don't *care* what shape it's in," said the Empress. "I had to come see it. This is the only place I know of where I can even find an icon. There are no icons at the palace, as you know, and my husband doesn't like for me to go to church without him—and there are never icons in his presence. When the attack started today, I became apprehensive. I felt I had to give my prayers to the Virgin for the strength of our men's arms in repelling this ghastly *attack*." With that, the Empress dropped to her knees and crossed herself. She lowered her head, but then looked up at me, her hands still clasped together. "Well," she said expectantly, "aren't you going to join me?"

"The icon's not finished yet," I said. "Praying with it before it's blessed wouldn't be—appropriate."

"Brother Stephen, our entire way of life is hanging in the balance. I think the Virgin will forgive us just this once."

It took a few moments for me to remind myself that it was the Empress of Byzantium—and not just a devastatingly pretty woman— who had asked me to pray with her. I said nothing more. I came and knelt on the stone floor next to her. I crossed myself. We bowed our heads and we both prayed, whispering, her in Greek and myself in Latin, beseeching the Virgin Mary to once more come to the aid of our beleaguered city. We both said "Amen" at almost the same time. The

Empress did not rise from her knees at once.

She was looking at me, and smiling.

"You don't smell like entrails this time," she observed.

"No, Your Majesty. Thankfully I haven't been employed in the tannery for some time."

"You needn't call me 'Your Majesty'. I have a name." She got up off her knees and began to untie the rope around her waist. "This disguise is dreadfully uncomfortable. I can't *bear* the thought of shuffling back through the streets toward the palace wearing it again so soon. You don't mind if I remain a few minutes, I hope?" The cassock fell to the floor of my cell. Underneath it the Empress Maria was wearing a ravishing dress, deep royal blue, its sleeves decorated with thin brocade. She wore a gold necklace with lapis inlays. The showy display of her wealth alone would have dazzled me, but the fact that her dress was considerably lower cut than any I'd seen her in before was enough to take my breath away. The Empress was *endowed*. Seeing that girl bathe in the stream three years ago had nothing on what I was seeing now.

"Um—of course not, Empress—er, I mean—Maria." My eyes were fixated on her bosom, but my mind reeled at the tortures her husband would inflict upon me if he knew she was here and that I'd allowed her to be so familiar with me. Yet I was very, *very* far from asking her to leave.

"So, this is how our monks live these days, is it?" said Maria, looking around the empty room. "Not very much comfort, is there? Look at that bed. You'll be hunched over with a twisted spine by the age of thirty, sleeping on that thing." She sighed. "I have a wonderful bed. It's six feet across. Rosewood imported from Egypt—before Egypt fell to the Saracens, that is. My husband doesn't share it. He says it hurts his back. When we have to 'do our patriotic duty', as he calls it, I of course have to go to *his* room. That's the price of living in the luxury of the purple chamber."

I admit I was intrigued by this talk, but horrified too. "Your Maj—

er, I mean, Maria—please, you mustn't talk about such things. I'm in the employ of the Emperor. I'm handling a special project for him that could be crucial to the survival of Byzantium. I wouldn't want any—er, *personal* things to interfere with that."

While I had been talking, the Empress moved closer to me. She ran her fingers along the rough wool of my monk's habit about my shoulders, as if feeling the coarseness of the fabric. Being so close to her was intoxicating, electric. I tried mightily to remind myself of my monastic oaths. *I've made an oath to God to renounce the pleasures of the flesh*, I repeated to myself. *And it's certainly a sin to think such lustful thoughts about the Emperor's wife!*

"Why shouldn't I talk of such things?" she replied. "The Emperor and I aren't marble gods, you know. We're human beings like any other. After all, it's not like a flock of *storks* leave royal heirs under bushes in the imperial garden, now is it?"

She was now full-on massaging my shoulders. Sin or not, my manhood was in a condition comparable to the bronze column that supported the giant statue of Justinian in the plaza outside St. Sofia. My mind begged her to stop, but my body cried out for her to continue.

"The Emperor may not be a god," I said, "but he was certainly *appointed* by God."

At this the Empress laughed. She stopped massaging but kept her hands on my shoulders. "You think so, do you? Your pious patriotism is admirable, Stephen. But it's not the truth. It was not God who appointed my husband Emperor of Byzantium. It was an army. Specifically, his army. That's how things work out there in the world. Don't you know that?"

"I know very little of the world. I'm a monk." This was as close as I got to telling her to stop. You have to give me credit for attempting even this much.

"What other things about the world don't you know?" She began kissing my neck.

"Er—many things."

"Do you know how things *are*—between a man and a woman?"

"Such knowledge is forbidden to a monk."

She smiled. "But not to an Empress."

As if what had already happened wouldn't have been enough to convince me that my resistance to the Empress Maria's charms was completely pointless, the deep kiss that she planted on my lips in the next moment ended all pretense of resistance in my mind. My monastic vows seemed so abstract and arbitrary at this moment.

Nevertheless, thoughts of God and the next world were not totally alien to me in that next sinful but glorious hour. The sight of the Empress's heaving breasts, her taut nipples pointed skyward as she helped me find in the enveloping comfort of her spirit the kind of rapture I had never before experienced in the company of God, reminded me that God made all beautiful things, and He had made this woman too. If to recognize beauty was holy, was to surrender to it such a mortal sin? God causes all things to happen for a reason. Perhaps it was He who brought the Empress to my little cell at St. Stoudios, and if it was, His will must be respected. But these thoughts too quickly evaporated from my head in the joy of my release. The Empress's love was all-encompassing.

It was only a few hours before matins, still in the middle of the night, when the Empress Maria, robed as a monk, her false beard reattached, slipped quietly from my chambers and made her way through the dying torchlight toward the stairs leading down to the rear doors of the monastery. I had decided that if she was observed by anyone and I was asked about how unusual it was to entertain a visitor so late, I'd just say that the monk who visited me wrote very slowly and took a great deal of time to inscribe his important and very holy message to me, so important and top secret that he insisted the parchments it was written upon be burned upon his departure. But I didn't think I'd have any problem, and I didn't. Outside, the battle was still going on at the Fifth Military Gate, having been renewed with the approaching dawn. Improprieties among monks, even potentially shocking ones, were the last thing on anyone's mind. As far as anyone knew this might, after all, be Byzantium's last night on earth.

As it turned out, the renewed Saracen offensive was not a harbinger of the end, nor an indication that the Emperor's plans (and ours) were stymied. In fact the opposite was true. Two days later Artabasdos again visited the Praetorium, carrying another gilded tube. The *kouropalates* was quite anxious and animated, and before he gave Michael Camytzes the Emperor's message Artabasdos demanded to tour the dungeons and see for himself the horrors that now dwelled there. If he was repelled by it, he gave no sign of it. When he returned to our office, he said, "I'm pleasantly surprised by what I've seen here today. I dare say we are almost ready. How quickly can you be prepared to begin the transformation of Maslama's surrender envoys, once we deliver them to you?"

Michael, Theophilus and myself exchanged puzzled glances. "I thought that development had been rendered unlikely by the new offensive," said Michael.

"Of course not!" Artabasdos replied. "The Emperor planned it. He's been playing the Saracen commander for a fool." With this, he thrust the gilded message tube into Camytzes's hand.

He opened it and unrolled the message anxiously. Camytzes read it aloud. The Emperor's tone was cheerful, almost jocular. Leo seemed totally untroubled by the Saracens' recent actions, which he was proud to take credit for.

I told Maslama that I'm more than willing to lay down our arms at the earliest opportunity, but that if I did so the churchmen, particularly Patriarch Germanus, would balk, and possibly even try to overthrow me. I suggested that if Maslama mounts a new offensive against the walls, it could convince old Germanus that further resistance is futile, and I could win the churchmen over. As you can see, I've got the Saracen fool eating out of the palm of my hand! How wicked am I?

"What does he say about the peace delegation?" said Theophilus breathlessly. Camytzes continued reading.

Naturally I had to let a few days go by during which I'm supposedly negotiating with the Patriarch. I plan to notify Maslama today that I've received the authority to discuss formal surrender terms. (As if I need authority to do anything! But of course I've lulled the Saracens into thinking I'm merely a puppet of the church, rather than the other way round!) I will suggest that Maslama send a delegation of no fewer than five, but no more than ten, officers who are empowered to speak for him. You'll know if he's accepted if there's a total cease-fire along the walls precisely at sunset today. Assuming Maslama's plenipotentiaries enter the city tomorrow morning, I suggest you be ready to receive the unfortunate envoys tomorrow evening at sundown.

"As soon as you know how many men Maslama is sending," said Camytzes to Artabasdos, "it must be communicated to us. Timing is absolutely crucial. Tomorrow evening we need to be in contact with the palace and the Emperor on a minute-by-minute basis, and we must have all the logistics in place ready to string the corpses up over the walls. We can't risk transforming the Saracens until the very last second. I respectfully suggest, sir, that we establish a network of runners between the palace and this prison to pass messages."

"It will be done," the *kouropalates* replied.

"Tell the Emperor that we'll be ready."

After Artabasdos left, Camytzes stood at the window, looking out at the city and its domes and spires, and the distant puffs of smoke from the walls beyond. "I confess, Brothers," he sighed, "that I have a very strong suspicion that God will condemn me for what we're about to do."

"If there is any condemnation," said Theophilus, "it will be the Emperor's to bear, not ours."

"I guess there's nothing to do but wait," I said.

Wait we did, and it was not in vain. The moment the evening sun passed behind the dome of St. Sofia, all fighting immediately ceased. With no idea of what was happening behind the scenes, collectively Constantinople sucked in its breath, as did we.

The next morning dawned bright and sunny although it was one of the first truly cold mornings of the year. A procession of eight Saracen officers in glittering chain mail, protected from the harsh sun by a brocaded canopy carried by four small turbaned boys, marched solemnly under white flags toward the Third Military Gate. It was said that Maslama had demanded the entrance of his peace delegation through the Golden Gate—the portal through which Byzantine Emperors traditionally marched in triumph when they returned from a victorious campaign—but Leo had forbidden it, stating that the Patriarch's permission to discuss surrender was extremely soft and that he'd likely reverse himself if he thought that the Saracens intended to humiliate us. Alas, the doors of the Third Military Gate were opened and a cadre of Byzantine soldiers escorted the Saracen delegates through the streets that had been carefully cleared and blockaded, lest angry Constantinopolitans take it upon themselves to jeer the Mohammedans.

I didn't know what transpired at the Great Palace. I do know that the eight officers were invited into the *triklinos*, the great reception hall, where a sumptuous luncheon banquet had been prepared for them in the name of Christian hospitality. I don't know whether the Emperor allowed the Saracens to have lunch before they were surrounded and captured, but knowing Leo, I suspect he didn't; why waste a perfectly good meal on them? The envoys were bound hand and foot and set onto the backs of donkeys, facing backwards, to be paraded ignominiously down the Mesē toward the Praetorium.

This time the Emperor ensured there was an ample crowd on

hand. I was part of it, watching the spectacle as the donkeys, led by soldiers, brought their human cargo toward the dungeon. The street was lined on both sides by furious peasants, hurling abuse, insults and garbage at the invaders. Angry shouts of "Go back to where you came from!" and "God will punish you for your heresy!" hung in the chilly air. I watched a woman fling the contents of a chamber pot onto the Saracen first in line, a burly dark-faced man with very sad eyes. His forehead streamed blood from where he'd been hit with a rock, and bits of the shells of rotten eggs clung to his chain mail. Chicken entrails hung from his greasy long hair. He evidenced no reaction as shit and urine splashed into his face and down his front. *These Saracens may be heathens*, I thought, *but they are proud and stout warriors, every bit the equal of our own heroes.* I quietly lamented for the dreadful creature this man would become in a matter of hours.

No amount of caution was spared in the treatment of our prisoners. The Saracens were taken to the prison stables and dismounted one by one, where each of them was laid on a wheeled wooden cart and manacled hand and foot, all the while with no fewer than five swords leveled inches from their throats. The roads between the Praetorium and the Fifth Military Gate, where the bodies would be hung, had already been cleared. Troops were already standing by with the ropes and pulleys that would be employed for the grim purpose. Camytzes had ordered two ghouls to be separated from the shambling population of the dungeons and placed in a cell segregated from the others. One by one, each of the eight Saracens would be wheeled into the cell and the door shut. Once they were bitten, the door would be opened and an infantryman would quickly pierce the Saracen's heart with a sword. Then the corpses were to be wrapped up and transported in haste to the wall at the Fifth Military Gate.

I witnessed the first procedure. The victim was the big sad-eyed Saracen I'd noticed before, and he offered no resistance as he was laid on the cart and the manacles locked. Surprisingly, he spoke Greek. Noticing me as he raised his head from the cart, he said in a heavily accented voice, "I suspect I am about to die. Christian Brother, although we worship different gods, will you bless me?"

"It's sinful to give the sacrament to a heathen," I said. "But I will bless you as best I can." I made the sign of the cross over him and whispered the Lord's prayer. The Saracen's eyes closed; his lips moved and he murmured a little prayer in Arabic. Then Camytzes nodded to the guards, two on each side of the cart, and they began wheeling him toward the doorway that led to the cell of doom.

We remained, Theophilus, Camytzes and I, watching the doorway for some time. The Saracen accepted his fate remarkably well, but even he grew panicked when he saw the ghouls. We couldn't see what was happening beyond the doorway, but I heard him speak in a rush of excited Arabic. Then a blood-curdling scream rang through the dungeon.

"Bring him out," said Camytzes to the guards. They did. The Saracen was missing a hand. Without it, he had been able to draw his bloody stump through the manacle, and thus he had an arm free; but he was wailing in pain and obviously terrified, so he posed little threat. As a guard stabbed him through the heart, I winced and looked away. Theophilus's eyes were closed and he crossed himself.

"Bundle him up," said Camytzes to the two other guards. "Bring in the next one."

"I don't think I can handle it," I said to him, shaking my head.

He patted my shoulder. "There is little need for you to remain, Brothers. There's nothing more for you to do. Take a break. Return to St. Stoudios for supper. When you return here afterwards, the work will be done."

I was grateful for the respite, and I'm sure Theophilus was too. But as we walked through the streets in the lengthening light of dusk, Theophilus voiced what was in my head. "Strangely I don't seem to have much of an appetite." Beyond this statement he was silent and I was glad of it. The last thing I wanted to do was talk to anyone about the dreadful acts with which we were involved.

So, we returned to St. Stoudios, and Rhetorios was his usual kind and welcoming self. The prayer over supper was, predictably, for the deliverance of Constantinople, but the monks gathered around the table had more cause for optimism tonight. "We have enjoyed a complete day without enduring the slings and anger of our enemies," said Rhetorios. "May God favor us by lengthening this fortunate lull into a permanent and lasting peace among nations." We bowed our heads, said amen, and dined, though Theophilus and I ate very little.

Darkness had fallen by the time we started back to the Praetorium. When we were still half a mile from the prison, Theophilus and I began to hear a great commotion from over the walls. The flickering of torchlight was more intense. I started to see fiery projectiles arcing over the parapets in the region of the Golden Gate. Within minutes there were three or four other flash points where active conflict was occurring, and the dreadful smell of burning oil reached our nostrils.

"Well, I guess Camytzes delivered the Saracens back to their brethren," I sighed. "And they're plenty angry about it."

"They have a right to be," said Theophilus. "The Emperor meant to be deliberately insulting."

As we walked up to the Praetorium, I began to notice that things were amiss. The soft orange glow of the windows, from candles and torches in the rooms within, was gone; all the portals were ominously dark. As Theophilus and I neared the heavy iron entry gate, we saw no guards or any other signs of activity. The gate itself had been left ajar. Only one of the two torches hung in brackets flanking the gates was still alight. Instantly fear began to seize my stomach.

"Something's wrong," I said. "There are no guards, no horses— what's happened?"

Theophilus didn't answer, but the cautious way he crept behind me—as if expecting to be attacked at any moment—was reply enough. We proceeded reticently through the gate. The light from a fireball arcing over the wall illuminated the yard in front of the stone prison. In the orange flash I saw the bodies of several guards, torn and broken.

They were little more than twisted skeletons bearing teeth marks and a few pitiful shreds of flesh. Blood pooled in the cracks between the stones on the floor of the courtyard. A knot of ghouls, perhaps as many as ten, were gathered around one of the victims they had not yet finished off. I saw a leg, sheathed in chain mail, being pulled off and flung into the air by one of the ghouls. Another snatched it from midair and began to gnaw ravenously. As soon as they saw—or smelled—Theophilus and me, the group of ghouls began to claw and shamble toward us.

"I think we've got a big problem!" I cried.

Chapter Nine

The Beleaguered Church

"Swords!" Theophilus shouted. The guards who had been overwhelmed by the ghouls had left several weapons littering the floor of the Praetorium courtyard. Within seconds the old monk and I had a sword in each hand, facing down the mass of writhing, blood-streaked demons that ambled toward us.

There was no question that the ghouls we dispatched in the next blood-soaked minutes were from the Praetorium dungeons. I recognized the first ghoul I beheaded—in life he was a notorious thief and cut-purse who'd been transformed about three days ago. By this point Theophilus and I were old hands at destroying ghouls. We slashed, spun, sliced heads and limbs, and soon were as soaked with gore and entrails as the ghouls themselves. Inside of five minutes the Praetorium courtyard was a charnel house of slaughter, and I dreaded once more the return of the pestilence that had bedeviled us since Theophilus and I first walked into Domelium several months before.

"We must find out what happened," said Theophilus, planting a foot on the chest of a slain ghoul in order to withdraw his sword from its head.

"It isn't obvious?" I replied. "The ghouls got loose somehow and overwhelmed the guards." I saw movement in the darkness behind Theophilus. "Behind you!" I cried.

He spun, chopped the ghoul in half, and pierced its head. We could hear moaning and shambling coming from the main doorway of the Praetorium, whose heavy wooden door was ajar; the spikes on it were smeared with blood and bits of flesh. Clearly there were more ghouls inside the prison. I surmised they were finished devouring all the guards and now on the hunt for fresh victims.

"I fear for Michael Camytzes," said Theophilus. "Shouldn't we try to ascertain whether he managed to escape?"

"I hate to say it, but I think he's in there." I motioned to the doorway. "And if he's in there, he obviously didn't make it."

"We should make sure. If he's still alive, we must rescue him. His skills will be desperately needed to contain the outbreak of ghouls that will surely result from this."

Two ghouls staggered from the doorway. Theophilus cut one down, and I the other. One of them made a disturbing gurgling sound as my sword cleaved his throat. We backed away, swords at the ready.

"If Camytzes is alive," I said, "surely he's been bitten and will himself transform in a matter of hours." The groaning sounded from within the Praetorium again. "I wonder how many are left inside there."

"We have to smite them as they come out of the doorway," said Theophilus. "That way they can approach from only one direction."

"No. Picking them off one by one or two by two, we'll be here all night. Eventually we'll get tired and they'll overwhelm us." A ghoul hand shot out of the doorway; I lopped it off. The ghoul it belonged to fell to the stones and a sweep of one of Theophilus's swords decapitated it.

"We have to get out of here, Theophilus," I said. "We must get to the palace and warn the Emperor."

"Surely the alarm has already reached him, or will shortly."

I looked up and saw more fire flickering on the walls. "With the siege going on, the whole city's going to be in chaos in a matter of hours, perhaps minutes. We need heavy troops to prevent the ghouls from fanning out everywhere."

125

"There may be none to spare. Almost all available men are engaged against the Saracens."

"Well, the Emperor's going to have to make a choice then—whether Constantinople falls to the Saracens or the ghouls."

Theophilus slashed another ghoul. "Stables!" he cried. "We need horses."

Cautiously we went around the side of the Praetorium toward the stables. We found there more of what we'd seen in the main courtyard—bloody bones, the skeletonized remains of guards, and a few remaining ghouls that we dispatched easily. The horses, however, were gone. Ghouls had no taste for animal flesh, so the horses must have either run away or been taken by the human survivors. At this, hope sprang in me. *Somebody could have made it out. I hope Camytzes was among them.*

"We'll have to find horses out there in the city," I said. "Isn't there a livery stable somewhere near here?"

"Aye, a few streets over. But surely the ghouls are out there."

"It's a chance we'll have to take. Come on." I tightened my grip on the hilts of my swords, and we started back toward the main courtyard.

Theophilus and I moved west from the Praetorium, and going that direction it was clear that the ghouls had already begun their hellish rampage. From St. Stoudios we'd approached from the east and noticed nothing amiss in the streets near the prison, in the opposite direction we heard a great deal of shouting and commotion in the neighboring streets. Then we began to see bodies. There was a woman lying in the street, her body torn into several pieces. Later we saw two young men, both dead, one of them still clutching a bloody dagger. The bodies had obviously been gnawed by the ghouls, but the ghouls themselves were nowhere to be seen, perhaps having been chased into the nearby streets and alleyways by the local inhabitants. The commotion we heard came from a nearby street, accessible through an alleyway whose walls were streaked with blood.

"The ghouls are in that direction," I said, pointing toward an alleyway.

"We'd best be careful," Theophilus replied. "The citizens don't know what's going on. They're liable to mistake us for ghouls."

"Well, whatever their situation is, they definitely need help—and so do we."

We proceeded boldly into the alley. What we found at the end of it was utterly shocking. Theophilus and I had emerged in a small courtyard in front of a stone church. The floor of the courtyard was littered with corpses. Some were still alive, cleaved and bitten, moaning and shrieking. In the center of the courtyard a huge throng of ghouls, at least fifty of them, shambled and shifted toward a line of Constantinopolitans, some armed with swords and fireplace tools, who were quickly falling back against the line of demons. Occasionally one of the townspeople would stab or strike with a weapon, but more often than not it was a glancing blow. The ghouls kept advancing away from us, but when several of them—ten, perhaps, maybe eleven—caught the scent of Theophilus and me, they turned away from the main group.

"Aim for their heads!" I cried at the townspeople. I leapt into the square, beheading one of the ghouls approaching us. The head with its blank waxy eyes fell to the cobblestones where I cleaved it with one of my swords.

"They can't hear us," Theophilus shouted back. "The ghouls will consume them!"

At that moment, a flash of orange fire seared the air between Theophilus and me. I leaped back, startled, and was astonished to see an arrow with a flaming head embed itself into the back of one of the wounded townspeople, a middle-aged man whose leg had been chewed off. The man screamed and collapsed inches from me. I had only a split second to leap out of the way of another flaming arrow headed right for my head. It impacted on the cobblestones, still smoldering.

"Archers!" cried Theophilus.

There was almost no time to react. A volley of flaming arrows zoomed through the air. Several struck the ghouls we were fighting, but it was clear that whoever was shooting at us wasn't trying to spare us. I looked up at the church across the square. From its arched brick window I could see three flaming arrowheads poking from the darkness. A moment later they were unleashed and I dove out of the way, narrowly avoiding the snapping jaws of another ghoul who in his clumsy lurch impaled himself on one of my swords.

"Troops in the church!" I shouted, withdrawing the sword. "Get to the church, there are troops inside!" A ghoul clawed at me, causing me to drop one of my swords. I brought my other down on his neck. An instant later a flaming arrow embedded itself in the stump of his neck. The corpse immediately slumped.

We raced to the church, shouting all the way. "We're human! We're not ghouls! Let us in, we can help you! Please, let us in!" We pounded on the heavy wooden door, which was decorated with a bronze bas-relief of John the Baptist. It too was smeared with blood.

Six ghouls were about to corner us.

I winced, gritted my teeth and turned on them. I began slashing at them, showering the church's doorway with more blood. A severed arm fell to the dust and continued clawing at me.

Whoever was firing arrows from the church window finally seemed to understand that we were friendly. Several more arrows were fired, these aimed precisely at the ghouls advancing upon us. "Aim for their heads!" said Theophilus. We felled three of the six, and the arrows took out the rest. As the last of the ghoul corpses collapsed, I heard the working of a heavy wooden bolt and the door to the church finally swung open.

We rushed inside. A soldier in chain mail, barely more than a boy, slammed the door shut behind us and drew the heavy bolt to secure it.

The church we found ourselves in was very small, at least by the standards of the grander cathedrals of Constantinople. Its primitive dome rose perhaps thirty feet above the floor, decorated with clumsy mosaics of the saints and the Virgin. The church was so poor and rude that it had no bell tower; its bell hung from the apex of the dome. In the center of the church huddled a crowd of townspeople, perhaps twenty or so. Most were women and children, but there were a few men. All looked dazed and shocked. A small catwalk ringed the church on an upper level, accessible from a flight of rickety wooden stairs. On the catwalk I saw four archers in regular army dress. They were gathered around the window from which they had been firing at us.

"Who is in command here?" I called, my voice booming through the church.

"I am," said one of the archers. The young man who presented himself at the bottom of the stairs was perhaps twenty-five, good-looking, with a neatly trimmed beard and coal-black eyes. "My name is Gregory Panteugenos. Who are you?"

"I'm Stephen Diabetenos of St. Stoudios. This is my colleague Theophilus. We came from the Praetorium."

"You're lucky to have made it," said Panteugenos. "There are dozens of those things out there."

"How did you and your men get here?"

"My commanding officer sent us out to reconnoiter the area of the Chalkē Gate to see if we could use it as an archers' nest if the Saracens broke through the walls. We didn't even get close to Chalkē. We came upon a group of villagers being attacked by those...*things*. We slaughtered a lot of them, but we had to fall back to the church when we realized how many there were." The young archer glanced up at his colleagues on the catwalk. "We're lucky we had our quivers with us."

"Lucky for us too," said Theophilus.

We heard a pounding on the door we'd just come through. I could hear the wail of the beasts and the scrabbling of their dead hands against the wood and bronze. *Dear God*, I thought, *forgive us for bringing this pestilence upon these people! We never should have listened to the Emperor.*

129

"More of them, Sir!" shouted the boy who'd let us in.

"How many?"

One of the archers up above, looking down through the window, answered, "Twelve, maybe fifteen."

"We can't stay here for long," Panteugenos said to me. "We don't have a lot of arrows left, and I'm afraid those monsters will break through the door eventually."

"You're probably right. Is there any other way out of here?"

"Not that I know of, no."

"What kind of weapons do you have with you?"

"Just our swords and whatever arrows we have left. And the swords you two brought."

Theophilus and I exchanged glances. I looked back at the civilians huddled in the church. A woman in plain clothes—the way she was dressed I suspect she was a washerwoman—stepped forward and called, "You must convince the soldiers, Brother, that we have to get out of here! We have to go down!"

"Mind yourself, woman!" shouted one of the troops. "I told you before, there's no cellar here."

I took Panteugenos aside, as I didn't want to be overheard either by his colleagues or the civilians. "Look, Lieutenant," I said softly, "Theophilus and I have just come from the Praetorium. That's the source of the undead ghouls that have begun rampaging through the city. You're right, we can't stay here for long. The ghouls will overwhelm us eventually and we have to get those people out of here."

Panteugenos stared at me and immediately assumed a quizzical look. "You know what these monsters are? You've seen them before?"

"Regrettably, yes. It takes too long to explain and I doubt I'm at liberty anyway. Suffice it to say they are what you must suspect—walking dead, impervious to pain and relentless in their approach. One thing you probably don't know yet is that they multiply. Everyone who's bitten by a ghoul dies, then reanimates and becomes one of them. *That's* the real danger here. Right now I'd estimate there are about five hundred of them fanning out through the city. But by dawn there may be hundreds, even thousands more depending on how many others they've managed to infect."

Panteugenos looked stunned. "Dear God!" he gasped.

"Theophilus and I were on our way to the Great Palace when we got diverted here. I suggest we continue on to the palace. Soon the only safe place in Constantinople will be any place surrounded by large numbers of heavy troops. That's definitely going to be where the Emperor is too." My voice took on a slightly chilly shade as I added, "And I for one intend to have a *word* with the Emperor."

"That's a good idea, but the palace is many leagues away. If the streets are awash in ghouls, or soon will be, how do we get there? There are mostly women and children here."

"Well, we'd better think of something." I glanced around. "There's got to be another exit somewhere."

"I don't think there is. But I admit we haven't checked. We'd only been here a few minutes before you arrived."

I stepped away from the young archer and began examining the church. Theophilus did too. It didn't take long, for there wasn't much to see. The church was little more than a large circular room with an altar. There wasn't even a chamber behind it for the preparation of the sacraments; obviously this was a very poor parish. The only illumination came from candles on wooden stands set on the altar. One side wall had several windows, perhaps eight feet up from the floor, all sheathed in heavy shutters that were bolted closed. As that seemed the only viable option other than the front door, mine and Theophilus's attention naturally focused upon it.

"Do you think we could get the civilians out through one of those windows?" I asked him. "They're elevated, so they're above ground level. Maybe string a rope out leading to the ground, and have the archers fire downwards to take out any ghouls on the ground level long enough to get away?"

131

"I don't think they have enough arrows," Theophilus replied, shaking his head. "An escape that way would be too cumbersome."

"Well, it's either that or the front door. Maybe between you, me and the soldiers we can keep the ghouls away from the door long enough to get the people out one by one."

"Yes, but *then* where do we go? We'd be back out there in the square with ghouls advancing on us from all directions."

We were standing not far from the outspoken washerwoman as we had this conversation. Our voices were low, but she must have heard us, for she spoke up again. "You're looking for a way out?" she said, stepping toward us. "We could try the cistern."

"I beg your pardon?"

Inexplicably, the woman lifted her stained skirt and stamped on the stone floor of the church. It was loud enough to command the attention of everyone in the room. Her footfall, however, did not sound like the typical flat tone of a shoe against solid stone. Indeed there was a curious echo that seemed to reverberate throughout the entire floor of the church.

"There's a cistern under the street. It's what I tried to tell *him* earlier, but he wouldn't listen." She pointed a finger at the guard who had snapped at her.

"A cistern?" said Theophilus.

"Huge one. It was built in the time of Theodosius. The whole neighborhood sits on top of it. This church too. I know, I've lived here all my life. I was baptized in this very room."

One of the male civilians stood up. He wore a green frock. "Don't listen to her!" he shouted. "Pulcheria is a known whore! She's the Devil trying to tempt you!"

"Even if I am a whore it doesn't mean I don't know my own neighborhood!" the woman shot back.

A cistern! This was an intriguing notion. I had heard that Constantinople was riddled with underground reservoirs, some of which had been forgotten and disused for centuries. "A cistern would have to lead to an aqueduct, wouldn't it?" I asked Theophilus.

It was the washerwoman—Pulcheria—who answered. "Of course!" she said. "The cisterns all connect to each other. The whole city is accessible underground. Smugglers dug channels to connect them all centuries ago. Plenty of legitimate merchants use them too. It's much better than traveling on the streets."

I then saw one of the soldiers sidle up to Panteugenos, bow his head and whisper to him. It sounded almost like, *"She's right, Sir,"* but he said it in a very surreptitious way. Given that our very survival could depend on this washerwoman's information I immediately spoke up. "What's that?" I said loudly.

The young archer looked at me, momentarily startled. He glanced at his commander, and said timidly, "Um, she may be right."

"How do you know?" Panteugenos asked him.

"I'd rather not say," replied the soldier, obviously bashful to admit that he'd been to that disreputable part of the city before.

It was the man in the green frock who answered. "Wenches like this fallen woman," he raged, pointing at her, "smuggle whores from the marketplaces to the walls using the underground cisterns! They mean to profit from the lust and vice of the soldiers defending our great city!" He pronounced this sentence as if we were all supposed to find it terribly shocking, but no one did. Perhaps it was the renewed cataract of ghoulish wailing and pounding of undead fists against the church door that rendered his judgment somewhat less than momentous.

"If you know this," I said, stepping closer to the woman, "then you know how and where to get boats that we can use to get these people out of here?"

"I can find boats, yes."

"Can you direct us from here to the Great Palace underground, using the cisterns and channels?"

She nodded. "I believe so."

"It is not enough to believe!" said Theophilus sharply.

Pulcheria corrected herself. "Yes. I can get us there."

"How are we going to break through the floor?" Theophilus asked. "And if we do succeed in that, how do we get these people into the cistern safely?"

I looked around. In the dimness my eyes seized upon the great bronze bell that was fastened in a small wooden frame just under the apex of the dome. A long thick rope, half as thick as a man's thigh, trailed down from it toward the floor. A sudden inspiration seized me.

"You two!" I said, pointing to two of the soldiers. "Go up there and prepare to cut the ropes fastening the church bell. Don't cut them too short—we'll need the ropes." I motioned toward the civilians with my arms. "Stand back! Everybody, stand back, away from the center of the floor."

We began to hear scrabbling and ghoul moaning coming from the shuttered windows as well as the blockaded door.

"We had best make haste!" Theophilus shouted. "They're coming!"

"Stand clear!" shouted one of the soldiers at the apex of the dome. "It's coming down now!"

The other soldier swung his sword. It sliced through the thick taut rope with one swoop. The bell shot straight down, now a huge bronze projectile. The impact of the bell with the stone floor of the church made a *BONGGGGGGGGG!* so loud that it must have been audible all over Constantinople. The bell crashed through the stones of the floor as if they were paper. A moment later we all heard a tremendous splash.

The burst of air from the falling bell blew out the candles on the altar, as well as the torches that some of the archers carried to light their arrows. Plunged into inky darkness, the civilians, especially the children, emitted a great anguished wail. When it died down, we could again hear the moaning of the ghouls and then a loud splintering crack. Suddenly the ghouls were much louder.

"They've broken through the door!" cried Panteugenos.

"I can't see anything!" shouted one of the other soldiers.

The extinguishment of the candles was a disaster greater than any that had befallen us before. The ghouls could smell us; we who were still living beings depended upon our sight. *If we can't see,* I thought, *how are we going to get out of here? There's no time to find a torch or make a fire—those things will be on us in seconds!*

My heart was pounding in my chest. I had only seconds to make a decision. "Everybody who's not armed, drop to the floor!" I shouted. "Stay down as low as you can! Soldiers, if you hear a ghoul or run into anything higher than two feet off the floor, slash at it!"

"I don't know where my men are!" said Panteugenos, off to my right.

"Soldiers, call out your names. Keep shouting your names so we all know where you are. Ghouls can't talk—anything speaking Greek is a living man." I directed my voice toward the ceiling. "You two soldiers, up there! Get the rope and follow the stairs down! We'll start lowering these people down into the cistern. Theophilus, help the women and children crawl along the floor toward the hole."

At once the church was a din of shouting and battle. *"Panteugenos!" "Antiochos!" "Nicetas!" "Zonaras!"* I heard the sound of swords cleaving flesh. The ghouls did not wail when they went down; indeed, they grew silent. Their moaning all seemed to be directed off to my left, toward the door. I could barely see a patch of bluish night beyond the splintered remnants of the door, broken by dark rounded heads of more ghouls spilling in through the opening.

"Over here!" cried Panteugenos. "They're in this direction!"

"Where?" shouted someone else.

"Off, left there! To your left!"

"No, no, it's me, Antiochos!" protested one of the soldiers.

"Antiochos, *Antiochos—*" I heard a sword stabbing into something fleshy. *"Aaaaaauuuughhh!"*

Panteugenos: "Antiochos! *Antiochos!* Are you all right?" A ghoul moaned to my right, between me and Panteugenos's voice. "I think I killed Antiochos!"

"There!" I cried. "A ghoul just came past us! Your left, my right!"

I slashed blindly in the dark, hoping to God that I wasn't stabbing one of our own men. A moment later I heard a thud as a ghoul went down. Another soldier shouted, "Oww, he's got me! He's got my leg, he's got my leg!"

"Zonaras, where are you? *Where are you?*"

"I'm off to your—*auuuughhhh!*"

"Rope!" shouted a soldier behind me. I thought it was Nicetas. "We've got the rope!"

"Down here!" said Theophilus. "I'm standing next to a post. Knot one end of it around the pillar—can you find it?"

I have no idea how long the battle lasted. Probably it was only a few minutes, but it seemed like an eternity. Because of the blackness the archers' craft was useless, which resulted in us being more outnumbered effectively than we were in reality. One piece of luck with which the Lord favored us was that the ghouls did not creep silently. We could tell where they were from the moaning and the shuffling of their feet. At one point I felt the sharp shock of a cold hand grabbing me in the dark. As I'd heard none of our comrades from that direction, I whirled and slashed with my sword. I connected with something and cold blood splashed my face, but the clawing around my arm continued. Evidently a ghoul had grabbed me and I'd severed its arm, but the disembodied hand didn't let go. Ultimately I was able to pry it loose, dash it to the floor and stomp on it. My heart was still hammering. It had been a close shave.

There was much activity off to my right, voices and the sound of shoes on stone and shouted orders, some from Theophilus, some from the archers. Somehow they managed to secure the rope and one of the brave archers, without a clue as to the depth of the hole or the perils contained in it, was the first to descend. I heard him cry out as his body struck the bell that was evidently lodged against the floor of the cistern. I also heard the splash and slosh of water.

"How deep is it?" said Theophilus.

"A few feet," called the archer. His voice echoed in the chamber beneath the church floor. "Waist high on a man."

"Stay there at the end of the rope!" Theophilus commanded. "We'll start sending the children down."

"We've got to get some light," I called out. "A torch, anything."

"Ghouls to your left!" shouted Panteugenos.

And thus the battle continued. The scrambling of the civilians down the hole seemed to take forever. Panteugenos and his two subordinates, Nicetas and Zonaras, held the line against the ghouls somewhere in front of me, stabbing and slashing indiscriminately. "They're gaining!" Panteugenos shouted at me. "We can't hold much longer!"

"Theophilus, how many more do you have to lower down?"

"I don't know. Three, four."

"Well, *hurry!*"

After several terrible minutes, I heard Pulcheria's voice from the pit. "A light! Look, over there! It's a torch! We're saved!"

We're pretty damned far from saved, I thought, lunging at a moaning coming from my left.

In a few moments I began to see a very dim flickering—firelight—coming from the hole. It was so black inside the church that every bit of illumination helped. The moaning of the ghouls had become much louder in the past few minutes. I glanced down at the hole, and was astonished to see my feet merely inches from its edge. When I looked back, I saw the dim outlines of Panteugenos, Nicetas and Zonaras, barely three feet away from a huge throng of ghouls shuffling toward them. The only reason they had not yet been overcome is because the pile of corpses of the ghouls we'd already dispatched—as well as poor Antiochos, who had been torn limb from limb—was an obstacle slowing the progress of the ghouls that sought to get at us by clambering over their inert comrades.

"We can't hold any longer!" I cried. "Everybody who's still left alive, jump into the hole and hope for the best!"

As these words died on my lips, I felt myself pitching backwards. With a sickening, dizzying lurch I fell into the hole, letting go of my sword, and I had only an instant to say a silent prayer to God that He might preserve me. But at this point I thought my luck had just about run out.

Chapter Ten

The Fiery Barricade

I awakened sometime later. My head was splitting and my back was in excruciating agony. My clothes were wet and stank like rank pond water. The light was dim and I heard sloshing all around me. I was lying somewhere but it didn't feel very stable; I kept pitching sickeningly from side to side. By flickering torch light I could see the face of Theophilus bending over me. As I tried to sit up, I realized we were in a small boat. He was seated on a plank and I was lying at its bottom.

"Lie still," he said. "You got quite a knock on the head."

I looked around. The boat was perhaps ten feet long and quite crowded. Gregory Panteugenos, who held the torch, sat on the plank next to Theophilus. Behind him sat many of the children from the church. Walking behind the boat—sloshing through the waist-deep water—were several of the archers and the adult civilians, including Pulcheria. They were hanging on to the rope that the soldiers had cut from the church bell; the rope now trailed behind the boat as a sort of guide line. Our boat was being rowed by a perfectly dreadful-looking man. He had stringy gray hair, one eye and a threadbare, moth-eaten tunic. He smiled at me and I saw he had about three teeth in his head.

"This is Basil," said Theophilus. "It was he who came upon us in this boat when we broke through the floor. We probably owe him our lives."

"I hope you'll remember that when you face the Almighty," said the almost toothless man. "I could use a good word."

"You're still a pimp," said Panteugenos.

"If I hadn't been rowing through the cistern tonight plying my trade and happened upon you," Basil replied, "most of you would be dead now."

I sat up and rubbed my head. There was a lump on the back of it. "How long was I out?" I asked Theophilus.

"An hour, give or take."

"Did the ghouls follow you down through the hole?"

"Aye, some did. We managed to hold them back long enough to make our escape."

"So I take it they're impervious to water."

"Sadly, yes. We don't seem to be able to catch a break."

I looked around at the giant cavern. Under less dire circumstances I might have marveled at it. It was a colossal passageway, perhaps fifty feet wide and many hundreds of feet long. The roof was supported by a forest of stone columns with elegant finials. Many of the pillars were chipped and crumbling, suggesting this part of the cistern had been out of repair for quite a long time. The space was so huge that the dim light of the torch could barely penetrate it and the shadows of the columns danced and leapt like giant dark dragons.

"I'm telling you, Basil," Pulcheria called from behind the boat, "we're going the wrong way. We're headed toward the Aspar Cistern, not the Great Palace."

"Damn you, woman!" shouted the pimp. "I've been working in these cisterns since before you were born. Right now the Mesē is directly above our heads." The one-eyed old man glanced at me. "I know this city better underground than I do above."

"We *have* to get to the palace," I pleaded. "It's absolutely imperative that we reach the Emperor as soon as possible."

"Just pipe down there, young monk. There's still a long way to go."

He kept rowing. "Know the Emperor personally, do you?"

"As a matter of fact I do."

"Well, you can tell him for me that he's a gutless fool. First he lets the Saracens loose upon us, and now these monsters."

"Enough!" said Theophilus sharply.

We continued rowing for quite some time. This particular cistern was immense, far larger than I would have expected. Eventually, however, we neared its end. I saw a crumbling brick wall moving slowly toward us. The water was no longer still. There was a noticeable current drawing the boat. Basil slowed down the rowing by pulling his oars out of the water, but the boat continued to move forward. I noticed a dark shape—the entrance to a much smaller and narrower tunnel bored into the rock—looming ahead.

The almost toothless pimp looked over his shoulder and called to the party following the boat. "We're approaching the tunnel. The water will be moving fast. Make sure everyone's hanging on to a rope."

"You're sure you know where we are?" said Panteugenos.

Basil motioned to the roof. "We're right under the eastern side of the Forum of Constantine. This tunnel leads underneath the plaza. It connects to the catacombs of the Church of St. Euphemia."

"Right across the street from the Great Palace!" said Theophilus breathlessly.

"This passage can be quite dangerous. When we smuggle booze or women through the cisterns, we usually avoid this area because the water moves so fast."

"Well, we don't have a choice," I told him. "Let's go."

Basil began rowing again. The current caught our boat and began to draw it like a giant magnet. Basil warned the men and women walking behind the boat that the bottom of the tunnel was treacherous and irregular. As soon as we entered it, they struggled to keep their footing and their sharp tugs on the guide rope yanked and buffeted the boat several times. I began to see bits of garbage flowing by in the current: bones of animals, frayed bits of fabric and parchment, and the bodies of dead rats. I realized there was no bright dividing line between Constantinople's cisterns—which supplied the drinking water for its citizens—and its sewers.

"I wonder what's happening up there," said Theophilus, a few minutes after we entered the tunnel. His voice echoed eerily against the stone walls.

"I'm sure the ghouls are fanning out through the whole city," I replied.

"I wish Camytzes had survived."

"So do I." I shuddered at the thought of how gruesome his death must have been.

Not long after I began to smell something other than the algae-sodden stink of the water. It was an acrid aroma, like oily smoke. It seemed to be coming from the tunnel ahead of us.

"Do you smell that?" I said. "Something's burning."

Panteugenos seemed to stiffen at the aroma. "Greek fire makes that smell when it burns. It's very distinctive."

"What is Greek fire?"

"It's a weapon. Liquid flame. They squirt it through great siphons and set it alight. It sticks to everything like glue and burns forever. It was used to repel the Saracens in their last siege of the city a century ago. The recipe for it is a state secret."

"There's something ahead!" shouted Basil.

I strained to see. When I squinted, I could barely make out a faint orange glow far ahead of us.

"Something *is* on fire up there!" I said.

Panteugenos rose to his feet, causing the boat to rock. "It *is* Greek fire, I think."

"How could it be burning down here?"

"It's made of oil, so it floats on water. It's impossible to extinguish. When we throw it on an enemy, their first impulse is to douse water on

142

it, but that only spreads the droplets farther and makes the fire worse. Fiendish stuff."

Suddenly a hot breeze began to blow down the tunnel. In addition to the acrid stench of the Greek fire, we were overwhelmed by another and even more awful aroma—the reek of burning human flesh.

All the soldiers in our party—together with myself and Theophilus—tensed as if we were one muscle. No one needed to say it aloud—*Ghouls ahead.*

"Swords!" Panteugenos cried. "Everyone with a sword, come up ahead of the boat! Keep the women and children back!" He turned to Basil. "Stop rowing, we need to slow down."

"I'm *not* rowing," the pimp replied. "The current's drawing us."

"Well, find a way to slow us down!"

The archers, clanking awkwardly in their chain mail, sloshed around the sides of the narrow tunnel to overtake the boat. Theophilus handed me the sword that I'd been using in the church; evidently someone had picked it up. "Move to the front of the boat," Theophilus said. "At least this time we have the advantage of knowing what direction they're coming from."

As the boat continued to drift toward the fiery blockade at the end of the tunnel, Basil extended one of his oars, which scraped the rough stones of the tunnel wall. "Here, use the other oar!" he called to Theophilus. "Try to brace us against the wall." Between the two of them they managed to wedge the oars against two angular crevasses and the boat slowly came to a halt. But holding us there required great effort. Both Basil and Theophilus were straining with all their strength, pushing the oars against the bricks, fighting the current. "You there!" I called to two of the older boys in the boat. "Help them. Try to keep us steady."

Zonaras, one of the archers, shouted, "Here they come!"

Standing in the prow of the boat, sword at the ready, I looked ahead at the glowing disc that marked the end of the tunnel. Against the dancing flames I saw a great mass of dark shambling figures stumbling through the water. A moment later over the rush of the current I could hear their insensate moaning.

Here we go again, I thought, and hastily crossed myself.

There were at least thirty ghouls in the throng approaching us from the far end of the tunnel. The archers, firing from their static positions ahead of the boat, managed to hit a few of them, but an arrow was an inefficient way to bring down a ghoul; unless you hit it directly in the head it will simply keep coming. Swords were the only viable weapon. Panteugenos and I leapt off the prow of the boat into the water and moved toward our attackers. With the current pushing us so powerfully, it was all we could do to keep our footing. The bottom of the tunnel was covered with what felt to me like loose piles of bricks and stone. Trying to maneuver and fight in such conditions was very difficult.

"We have the advantage!" Panteugenos called, his sword flashing in the light of the Greek fire burning in the distance. "The current is pushing the ghouls backwards."

He and a few of the archers formed the vanguard. Panteugenos's sword cleaved the skull of one of the ghouls, who collapsed into the water. I followed the rest of the archers in a surge toward the demons. Once again the dreadful dance repeated itself—swinging swords, the claw and clutch of dead-flesh hands, the terrible kill-or-be-killed urgency that at once sharpened my brain and deadened my senses.

A ghoul lunged at Zonaras. It had once been a man, but its head and arm were on fire. It was close enough to me that I could see its charred jawbone and crooked teeth, burned clean of flesh. Zonaras decapitated it but the body kept coming. He lopped off its arm and it fell into the drink, immediately shedding its coating of Greek fire, which now danced atop the roiling water, still aflame.

A ghoul that was once a woman shot herself at me. Her eye sockets were filled with charred smoldering flesh. I stabbed with my sword directly at her head; it was so burnt that it disintegrated into a shapeless mush of charcoal. I began to see other detritus floating about in the water around us—hands, fingers, bits of severed human scalps with hair still attached, shreds of clothing, a sandal. All were either burning, smoldering or badly singed.

What had happened began to dawn on me—*Someone fought these ghouls before, and they used Greek fire. They squirted it into the tunnel and set it alight to prevent the ghouls from reaching the end of the tunnel.*

"Gregory, to your right!" shouted one of the archers. Panteugenos narrowly missed being bitten by a short stocky wraith that rose up out of the water next to him. He cleaved its head in two and it fell, smearing blood against the wall of the tunnel.

"There are no more coming," said Nicetas.

"Beware of the little pieces in the water!" Zonaras warned. "They're still lethal."

"And under the water too," I added.

Within ten minutes or so we had dispatched all the ghouls at the end of the tunnel. Compared to those others we'd faced they were less of a threat. Many of them were already weakened from their previous battle with whoever lay on the other side of the Greek fire blockade. *The Emperor's troops, perhaps?*

Still holding my sword, I looked around. The heat from the burning oil at the end of the tunnel—maybe forty or fifty feet away—was considerable. The water around us was now dark, fouled with the blood of the ghouls we'd finished off. But there seemed to be many more body parts floating about than could be accounted for by the ghouls we'd just dispatched. We were not the first ghoul slayers to fight here.

"Some help, please!" shouted Theophilus. He and Basil were still straining to hold the boat in place with the oars. Three of the archers moved back to the boat and braced it with their bodies. I soon joined them, handing my sword up to one of the older boys in the front of the boat. The current was quite powerful. Leaning my entire weight against the side of the boat, I felt like I was barely holding on.

"All right," said Panteugenos, wiping blood and sewer water out of his face. "What do we do now? With that fire at the end of the tunnel, we can't move forward."

"We have to!" I insisted.

"Whoever sprayed Greek fire down here did it specifically to prevent any ghouls from reaching the end of the tunnel. They must have changed direction when they smelled us approaching."

"But there have to be more ghouls approaching from the direction we came too," I protested. "And there is no barricade at that end, which means they'll keep coming indefinitely until they overwhelm us. I'm convinced the palace is on the other side of that pool of fire. Our only hope is to get across it somehow."

"It's impossible!"

I thought for a moment. I recalled something that had happened years ago in the art studio at Chenolakkos—I knocked over a candle on a table, which fell onto a beaker of linseed oil, lighting it afire. Like the Greek fire described by Panteugenos, throwing water on it had been useless. The rivulets of burning oil had spread across the table, but when I finally smothered the small fire with a blanket, the wood of the table was unscathed. "You said this stuff, this Greek fire, floats on *top* of the water, right?"

"Yes."

"Then it's possible to swim under it?"

"We have no idea how far the Greek fire stretches. It could be a distance that would take longer to swim under than a man can hold his breath."

Theophilus, listening to us, grunted against the oar and said, "What about the children? Even if a man could swim underwater beneath a mantle of liquid flame, it's too much to ask these children to do that."

In the next tense moments I realized that successfully fighting a plague of ghouls involved much more than swinging a sword. *But our greatest weapon against them is the fact that men with live souls can*

146

think. We had to think very fast. Theophilus's and Basil's strength would soon give out. The boat full of children would then be swept down the tunnel into the conflagration. Perhaps Panteugenos and the other archers could hold the boat in place for a bit longer, but remaining here in the tunnel was not a permanent solution. At any moment I expected to hear the aimless moaning and sloshing of more ghouls coming up behind us. We had not the men or the strength to hold the boat in place *and* fight ghouls coming at us with the current at their backs, as it had been at ours a few minutes before.

"If there are troops on the other side of that barricade," said Panteugenos, "they must have boats. Maybe they can navigate their way through the fire long enough to come back for the children. There's got to be a way."

"In any event," I said, "somebody has to try to swim under that barricade."

We hesitated for only a moment. In the next instant Panteugenos began stripping off his chain mail and I dispatched my monk's cloak. I handed it up to the older boy who had taken my sword.

I stood, in my thin sopping linen undergarment, wiping wet hair out of my face. "Ready?" I said to Panteugenos. He nodded.

"God be with you!" Theophilus shouted.

I took as deep a breath as I could suck in and dove into the murky, blood-fouled water.

Swimming underneath the fiery barricade was one of the strangest experiences of my life—and, given what I'd already been through, that's saying something. The bottom of the tunnel was a ghoulish charnel house of carnage. There were hands, feet, limbs, bones, some still moving and clutching, others dead and silent. The water was so murky and filled with blood, oil and effluvia that I could barely see more than three or four inches in front of me, and my eyes stung horribly all the while. But I knew where the fire was because there was a brilliant yellow-orange blaze above me, illuminating the water in an eerie spectral glow.

My lungs ached. I could feel the heat from the fire crisping my flesh. I was only inches under the water. If I hadn't been immersed, I was certain the thin linen of my undergarment tunic would have burst into flames. I was less swimming than crawling along the irregular bottom of the tunnel. Whenever I felt something grab me—usually a ghoul's severed hand—I thrashed and shook about until it let go.

Still so light up there. The fire must extend a long way.

Gradually the water became clearer. There was less blood here, but now I could see bits of soot and ash raining down from above. The fire was certainly raging at its peak right above me. My lungs were nearly giving out. *I'm not going to make it!* I fought the compelling impulse to surface for air. Just one breath—just one split second with my head above water—that wouldn't kill me, would it?

Yes, it will. I'll surface under a flaming sheen of Greek fire. My face will burn instantly. After that it's all over.

I kept swimming, crawling, stumbling. I could hear my pulse pounding in my ears. *Please, God, let this be over soon,* I prayed. It occurred to me that if I died here at least I could ascend to the Kingdom of Heaven knowing that I fought as a man, and a soldier of Christ, to my very last breath. That was somehow comforting.

Then the water began to grow darker. I still couldn't see what was above me, except it glowed with a dimmer light than before.

I couldn't hold out any longer. I had to take a chance that the Greek fire was no longer directly above me.

My head broke the water, and I gasped. My head wasn't burning. There was a terrible blast of heat on the right side of my face—a flaming pool of the oily stuff was only a few feet away—but I was not on fire.

"Help!" I cried. *"Help, help!"*

I stumbled and splashed out of the water, coughing and sputtering, feeling my flesh sizzle. Instead of the narrow tunnel half-filled with water, I was in what looked like part of a submerged church.

There was a pillar in its center decorated with a mosaic of Christ the Pantocrator. I stumbled toward it, draping myself over it, forcibly expelling the fetid water from my lungs. I looked about. Niches had been carved from the ancient brick walls, and in the eerie hellish firelight in them I could see skeletons, resting in repose, some of them still clutching crosses or with swords at their sides.

This must be the burial catacombs beneath the Church of St. Euphemia! I made it!

"Panteugenos!" I cried. "Panteugenos, where are you?"

A dark shape floated at the edge of the pool of Greek fire. At first I thought it was a ghoul, but I saw it still had a head. It was Panteugenos, half his face burned off, one arm frozen in a desperate clawlike stance. He must not have been able to suppress the temptation to come up for a breath.

I crossed myself and said a little prayer for his soul. There was nothing else I could do for him.

I let go of the pillar and splashed through the water toward the darkened doorway of the catacomb. *"Hey, hello!"* I shouted, my voice echoing on the stone walls. *"Is anybody up there? We need help! There are children trapped down here!"* The doorway was almost pitch-black, and I stumbled. I could feel stone steps beneath me. I began ascending them, but it was difficult. Under my hands and feet I began to feel the shapes of human forms—or at least pieces of them. I felt chain mail slick with a substance I knew must be blood. I touched what felt like an arm, and it was warm; then another extremity, which was cold, definitely ghoul flesh. My foot slipped on something that must have been entrails or possibly brains. Some real human beings were among the dead, suggesting the battle with the ghouls that had taken place here had been a desperate struggle.

"Hello! Hello!" I shouted until my voice gave out. *"Help, we need help!"*

At last I saw a flicker of light above and ahead of me. I heard the clatter of swords and chain mail. Two soldiers in shimmering mail

149

descended toward me.

"Help, we need help!" I cried. "There are people trapped down here—women and children, beyond the Greek fire. We've got to get them out."

The soldiers reached me. I fell into their arms like a limp rag doll. "Who are you?" one of them gasped. "You came from the tunnel?"

I was panting. My breath had nearly given out. "Children...trapped," I gasped. "You have to...get them...*out.*"

My last conscious thought was a comforting one. The soldiers were both wearing purple tunics decorated with gilded crosses over their chain mail. They were members of the Emperor's personal guard.

Chapter Eleven

The View from the Dome

I must have been dreaming of ghouls, because the moment I awakened I lurched, expecting to see one of their hellish blood-streaked visages charging at me. "No!" I cried. Only then did I realize I was not in danger. There were no ghouls around. It occurred to me that the whole thing might have been a dream, but as rational thought kicked in I knew I couldn't get *that* lucky.

I was sitting up in a bed larger and more luxurious than any I'd ever slept in. Its feather-stuffed mattress was gloriously soft and I was draped in silk sheets with brocaded designs. The bedframe was rosewood inlaid with ivory and silver. A large curtain, also brocaded, draped diagonally from the ceiling down to one of the corners of the bedframe. Beyond it I could see walls and floors of stone, several gilded chairs and a silver cross on a large mahogany table. The richness of these surroundings told me immediately that I was in the Great Palace.

My head was still pounding. As I slid out of bed, I realized somebody had smeared a sort of ointment on my back. When I touched it, I felt violent pain and a mantle of blisters. Given the intense heat of the water underneath the Greek fire, the fact that I'd come through the ordeal with nothing more than a blistered back seemed nothing short of miraculous.

There was a chair just off to the side of the bed. Draped across it were clothes—a linen undershirt, a warrior's tunic and a pair of boots.

There was also a silver chamber pot with a gilded rim. As I urinated into it, I marveled that the chamber pot bore intricate bas-relief designs that appeared to illustrate scenes from the *Iliad*. "I definitely *am* in the palace," I said aloud.

So what happened? How much time has passed? What about the ghouls? There were no answers to these questions. As I pulled on the clothes, I noted overcast daylight streaming through the small window high up in the stone wall of the chamber. I then noticed on the other side of the room that a small table had been laid with bread, a glass jar of olive oil and a silver flagon of wine. Realizing only then that I was famished, I fell upon the victuals like a starving animal. I drew up a chair to the table and ate ravenously.

While I was eating, I heard the heavy bolt of the door sliding back. It swung open a moment later and I was astonished to see the Empress enter. She was as beautiful and as charming as ever, and her sea-green eyes seemed almost to twinkle as she met my gaze. Her dress was much simpler than usual, a plain gray tunic, but she was ravishing nonetheless.

"Brother Stephen!" she said, in almost a whisper. "It's very good to see you alive and well. Very good indeed."

I stood up, and we embraced. Under normal circumstances I would never have thought of being familiar with the Emperor's wife under his own roof, but I hadn't appreciated until this moment how the crisis with the ghouls had painted everything with a sort of desperate end-of-the-world quality in which decorum, propriety and genuflection to the Emperor were simply inapplicable. I seized Maria's face between my hands and kissed her deeply.

"It's good to see you," I said when I came up for air. "I almost can't believe I'm alive."

"Your survival was nothing less than a miracle. For a humble iconographer and occasional tanner, Brother Stephen, you have the stout heart of a Grecian *hero*."

"What about the others? Theophilus, Pulcheria, the children—"

Maria put a finger to my lips. "Be calm. They're safe here in the palace. My husband had the clever idea to turn boats upside down and use them as shields against the flames. Several of his men were badly burned, but they brought your friends out alive."

I melted into her arms in a sigh of relief. "Thank God," I whispered. "At least He's still smiling on some of us."

The way Maria hung against me suggested that perhaps her interest in me was more than merely carnal, as it had seemed when she'd come to visit me in my cell. But moving in on the Emperor's wife was the furthest thing from my mind at that moment. *The world is coming to an end, but I'm still alive, and I'm with this woman,* I thought. *There is still hope, however slender it may be.*

The sound of another bolt, from a different door than the one through which the Empress had entered, jarred both of us from our embrace. The door across the room swung open on colossal iron hinges. A stocky chubby man in chain mail and purple boots stood there, casually cracking pistachio nuts. Next to him stood an unpleasant-looking bald fellow and a tall swarthy man with a ratlike visage. The Emperor's narrow slitted brown eyes fixed directly on me. I let go of the Empress instantly. For a brief moment I was as afraid of him as I was of the ghouls.

Fine thing! I thought. *If we manage to survive the ghoul holocaust, the Emperor will probably have me executed for philandering with his wife.*

If he was upset at having witnessed our embrace, Leo said nothing of it. He cracked a nut, popped its meat into his mouth and said, "Brother Stephen! Your presence is requested for a strategy meeting." He brushed pistachio shells off his uniform. "That is, if you're not too *busy.*"

"Of course not, Sire." I backed away from Maria.

"My dear, why don't you go look in on our daughter?" said the Emperor to his wife, with an edge of frostiness to his voice. "I've seen to it that her chamber is heavily guarded, but you know how skittish she is. With these ghouls running loose, she's bound to need some reassurance from time to time."

Maria said nothing, but she nodded deferentially. So we parted, Maria through the door from which she'd come, and me into the hallway where I found myself flanked by the eunuch Eutropius and the *kouropalates* Artabasdos. The Emperor casually extended his hand, which was full of nuts. "Want a pistachio?" he said, with a hint of a smile on his face.

I shook my head. The iciness of this man amazed me. With his capital besieged by Saracens and infested with undead ghouls, he was completely unflappable. I guessed there wasn't a crisis on Earth that could cause him to break a sweat.

We were soon joined by a cadre of sword-wielding guards, who led us deep through the broad colonnaded corridors and windowless candle-lit passageways of the Great Palace. I didn't dare ask where we were going. Eventually we found ourselves in a large hallway with marble stairs leading to a set of gilded doors decorated with giant crosses. The stone of the walls was a purplish rose color, exactly the hue that the great church of St. Sofia seemed to glow in the light of sunset. I'd heard that there was a secret passageway between the Great Palace and the Church of the Holy Wisdom, but why we would be going to St. Sofia at a moment like this baffled me.

Is the Emperor giving up? I thought. *Maybe he's decided the situation is hopeless, and he's bringing us there so the Patriarch can administer our last rites.* Or perhaps the Emperor had decided that St. Sofia—which had survived many earthquakes in the two centuries since Justinian built it—was the safest redoubt against the ghouls.

As we began climbing the stairs toward the golden doors, I noticed a curious thing—the walls of this alcove were draped. Large sheets of plain flaxen cloth, like painters' drop cloths, shrouded them, but in a crack between two such draperies I saw a silver of a fabulous mosaic, glittering with tiny tiles inlaid in gold and lapis. The Emperor, still leaving a trail of pistachio shells behind him, seemed to read my mind. He motioned to the walls and said, "If you're wondering why these are hidden, it's because they contain graven images of the Lord and saints, which is blasphemous idolatry utterly forbidden by scripture. I ordered them shrouded from my sight until such time as I can employ a team of artisans to tear them down. It would've been my first directive as Emperor—until Maslama and the Saracens so rudely placed themselves at the head of the priority list."

"And it would seem the ghouls have supplanted them," I remarked.

The Emperor chuckled. "Indeed. It gives me pleasure to think it vexes the Saracens that they're no longer the center of attention."

We reached the landing at the top of the stairs. Two guards opened the great gilded doors. A moment later I stepped out into the most astounding grandeur I had ever seen.

The great cathedral of St. Sofia was staggering in its scope. The dome was so high above our heads it seemed the vault of Heaven itself, ringed in a halo of arched windows that glowed with a holy brilliance. The porphyry columns, capped with carved finials that looked like nothing so much as frills of stone lace, marched in endless rows around the central nave. Huge chandeliers—they were colossal rings of iron, as far across in diameter as a man is tall, studded with candles— hung from chains large enough to anchor the largest ship. The altar was a blaze of gold, the Patriarch's empty throne a grander and more splendid seat than I imagined even the Emperor himself possessed. The room was so large and so quiet that the slightest whisper seemed to echo forever. I recalled hearing that when he dedicated St. Sofia, the Emperor Justinian was supposed to have said, *"Solomon, I have surpassed thee!"* At this moment I didn't doubt it.

The great church was empty except for three men, who, when we entered through the Emperor's secret doorway, were merely dots in the distance. As we approached, I saw that two of the men were in military dress and one the robes of a monk. One of them was the elder Camytzes. The monk was Theophilus, who seemed none the worse for our ordeal in the cistern and the catacombs. The third man had his back to me but he looked familiar. When he turned around, my heart nearly stopped cold from the shock.

"Michael!" I shouted.

"Brother Stephen!" The younger Camytzes broke into a broad grin. We met and he embraced me heartily. "I was very pleased when they told me you survived."

"I'm stunned. How did you manage to escape the Praetorium?"

"I was the first one out," he explained. "When the ghouls broke loose from the dungeon, I knew somebody had to ride immediately to warn the Emperor. I fully intended to return with a cadre of troops to subdue the Praetorium, but it was already too late." His face fell. "I lost many comrades there."

I patted Michael's shoulder. Gabriel Camytzes extended his hand, and we shook reticently. "It is agreeable to see you," the old man admitted.

The Emperor cleared his throat loudly. We all turned to look at him. As he shucked another pistachio nut, he said, "I have two suggestions. Number one--let's spend the few remaining hours of our lives fellating each other and gushing about how wonderful it is for everyone to have survived the ghouls long enough to permit this happy reunion. Number two—let's go up to the dome, scope out the situation and figure out how the hell we're going to defeat this evil before we're reduced to the last pitiful island of humanity awash in a sea of undead, brain-eating demons. Does anyone wish to argue in favor of suggestion number one?"

He did not wait for an answer. The Emperor brushed shell bits off his hands and began striding toward the Patriarch's altar. Artabasdos, Eutropius, the Camytzes, Theophilus and I followed. The guards remained.

There was a small door hidden in the elegant gilded panels of the altar. It was incorporated into the wall so completely that no one would have known to look for it unless they already knew it was there. The

Emperor manipulated a small hidden latch and the secret door swung open to admit him. "I hope you're all in shape," he sighed, and ducked inside. We followed.

The door concealed a tiny narrow staircase barely three feet wide, dimly lit from a skylight hundreds of feet above. After fifty or so such steps, the staircase reached a landing, and then a farther flight of stairs, parallel to the first one, led still higher. The Emperor barely paused on the landing but the rest of us were panting like beasts. Gabriel Camytzes had to brace himself against the wall to catch his breath.

"Come on!" the Emperor goaded us from above. "This is no time to rest. The ghouls aren't resting, why should we?"

Four flights later the stairway changed. It became even narrower, and its walls were curved. I realized this staircase occupied the tiny space between the inner and outer walls of the cathedral's great dome. The dome itself was braced with heavy timbers that I guessed must have dated from the church's original construction. Some of them had graffiti carved into them, Greek initials of builders or tourists who may have been dead a hundred years or more. One such beam brushed my head as we continued to ascend into the dome of St. Sofia.

Hundreds of stairs wound their way in zigzag layers ascending the dome. In some places they ascended through near-total darkness. Eventually a square hazy light loomed ahead. It was a hatchway barely large enough to admit a man, and the only access to it was a rickety wooden ladder. The Emperor, chubby and large-statured as he was, had to suck in his breath (and his gut) in order to squeeze through the hatch. Michael Camytzes was next, and I followed. In the darkness below I could hear the wheezing breaths of the elder Camytzes, the eunuch Eutropius, Theophilus and the *kouropalates* Artabasdos. It seemed a great effort for all of them. An ascent to the top of the dome of St. Sofia was certainly not for the faint of heart.

We found ourselves on a tiny circular catwalk, barely eighteen inches wide, surrounding the gilded onion-shaped finial at the top of the dome. There was no railing preventing us from toppling over and

157

sliding down the curved exterior of the dome to our deaths. The little catwalk became even more crowded and precarious when the elder Camytzes and the Emperor's two adjutants finally reached the top and joined us there.

If the Emperor had even been winded on the long ascent up the dome, he gave no sign of it. Shading his eyes from the sun, he looked off to the east, and his breathing was entirely normal. By contrast, I was panting and I paused to wipe sweat from my brow with the sleeve of my tunic.

"Take a good look, gentlemen," said the Emperor. "Unless we miraculously sprout wings and take flight, this is as good a vantage point on the whole of Constantinople as we're likely to have in our present circumstances."

Looking out across the city, I was struck by the same sense of awe I felt when I had first laid eyes on the capital. It truly was magnificent. The domes of churches, the Column of Justinian, and the tops of various other majestic monuments gave the city the look of a rich child's gilded toy. Along the top of the Hippodrome I could see a golden smudge that I knew was the sculpture of four horses, covered in gold leaf, adorning the entrance to the Emperor's box. Even at a distance the Land Walls looked stout and hardy, the towers impregnable redoubts against the wickedness of the Saracens. For a few precious seconds I might have been able to believe that nothing was wrong and that Byzantium's awe-inspiring first city was forever secure in its glory. But that illusion disintegrated quickly enough.

The air above Constantinople was quite hazy. Several columns of black smoke lumbered languidly into the stratosphere from fires in various quarters. A large building, obviously a church of some type, was in flames perhaps half a mile from St. Sofia. There was a much larger fire on the far side of the city where it appeared many buildings were burning. Closer to the great cathedral, I could see into the streets. They were littered with corpses. I could also see a dead horse and a broken-down, half-burnt wagon. In one of the gardens near St. Sofia there were small gray figures moving about. Squinting to see them more clearly, I shuddered to realize they were ghouls, wandering aimlessly in search of fresh human meat.

"*Droungarios* and Captain Camytzes," said the Emperor calmly, "may I ask for your respective military assessments of the situation, based on what you can see from here?"

"Each one of those smoke plumes," Michael replied, "probably represents the site of a major battle against the ghouls. Look, you can see that closest one over there, right where the Mesē begins—there are carts piled up and some other junk that was set on fire. Soldiers or townspeople probably made that as a barricade to block off the streets and contain the ghouls in a specific area."

"It wouldn't have been soldiers," the Emperor replied. "Last night I ordered all our troops to retreat to the inner walls and barricade themselves inside the towers. I gave specific instructions to all commanders not to engage the ghouls *or* the Saracens unless they were in imminent danger of being overrun."

Gabriel Camytzes seemed surprised by this. "Sire?" he said, with an incredulous tone in his voice. "May I ask—" He stopped himself, most likely when he realized he was about to question his sovereign's judgment—something he had once admonished his son and myself for having done.

"May you ask *why?*" said Leo, finishing his thought for him.

It was Artabasdos who answered, "We must keep the army intact until we can determine how best to combat the ghouls. Whatever we decide here today, it's going to take thousands of heavy troops to get Constantinople back under control. It won't do to have our men getting slaughtered in pointless battles until we can come up with some sort of unified strategy."

"And what of the Saracens?" asked Gabriel.

"I wouldn't worry about them," the Emperor replied. He pointed off to the east toward the land walls. "That's where they're all camped, there beyond the walls. See all the plumes of smoke coming from that area? That means they're fighting the ghouls too. And the fact that they

159

haven't mounted a massive coordinated attack against us, despite my troops having disengaged, means the Saracens have got as big or an even bigger problem with ghouls on their side of the wall as we do on ours."

"Maybe they figure that you've drawn back your forces to mass for an attack against *them*," Michael suggested.

"With what?" Leo shrugged. "If I had the strength to do that, wouldn't I have done it already? No—the ghouls are running rampant through the Saracens' lines. I'm convinced of that. Maslama can't renew his attack against us until he exterminates the ghouls in his own camp, and you can see from all the smoke over there that the effort isn't going particularly well. Brothers Theophilus and Stephen, I tip my crown to you. Your plan to introduce the ghouls into the Saracens' camp seems to have worked brilliantly."

"At the cost of losing our *own* city," I scoffed.

"How dare you!" blasted Eutropius.

Leo held up a hand. "It's all right. Brother Stephen's criticism isn't entirely baseless. It is...*possible* that I may have miscalculated the danger that the ghouls posed to our own people."

I nearly fainted away right then and there. In a fleeting moment I realized this was as close as I would ever get to hearing the Emperor admit that he was wrong.

"The city is not yet lost," said Artabasdos.

I wasn't the only one in a spiteful mood. At Artabasdos's hopeful comment I heard Michael Camytzes grunt. Shaking his head, he said, "With all due respect, *Kouropalates*, take a look at what's going on out there. How many plumes of smoke do you see? Fifteen? Eighteen? Each one represents a battle with the ghouls, probably a hopeless one. Look, over there—the entire Jewish quarter is on fire. Look at all the corpses in the streets that we can see from this vantage point alone. I wouldn't be surprised if half the civilian population of Constantinople is dead. And the ghouls have been on the loose for little more than a full day. What are things going to be like in two days, or three? Have we even a chance of surviving this?"

"Not half," said the Emperor.

"Sire?"

"You said half the civilian population of Constantinople is dead. I don't believe it's that many."

Camytzes looked a bit taken aback. "Well, whatever the toll, Sire," he sputtered, "it must be extremely—"

"What would *you* do?" Leo interrupted.

"Excuse me?"

"Let's say you're a civilian, a completely ordinary schmoe off the street here in Constantinople. Your church, workshop or home is besieged by legions of flesh-eating ghouls. There are no troops in the streets because your Emperor, in his infinite wisdom, has withdrawn all his forces to the towers, which means no one is going to come rescue you. How would you deal with the situation and protect your wife and children?"

Camytzes's mouth opened and closed several times but no sound emerged. Instantly the Emperor's expression soured. "Never mind, you're a soldier," he grunted. "Your answer would no doubt be influenced by your military experience. *You*, Brother Stephen—if you were in that situation, how would you respond?"

I felt very put on the spot. "Well, I would..." The Emperor's eyes seemed to burn into my soul. I finally thought of something rational. "I'd probably band together with others in my neighborhood and do the best I could to defend our families against the ghouls, with whatever weapons were at hand."

This answer seemed to please Leo. "*Aha!*" he cried, stabbing a chubby finger toward me. "You would do *precisely* that. And the evidence we see here bears out that most of the good citizens of Constantinople would be like-minded. Having no weapons to speak of, they piled carts and furniture in the streets and lit them afire to drive the ghouls this way and that. Surely they would not—*could* not—mount a coordinated offensive to reclaim their city. Only cadres of well-

161

armed troops could do that. What, then, would the people do? Well, the answer is obvious--once they realized they couldn't defeat the ghouls themselves, they'd hole up in their houses, churches and other defensible structures and wait for help to arrive. *That* is why the ghouls have free reign of the streets now. They're lurching around out there looking for fresh victims, while everyone who's still left alive is hunkered down under cover, desperately hoping that I'll send troops to rescue them. I credit the people of Constantinople with more resilience and fortitude, Captain Camytzes, than you seem to. I don't think half of them are dead. A distressing number are, to be sure, but not half. There's still quite a wellspring of talent and courage remaining in those streets to be tapped, gentlemen. Combine that with the force of an army that I was prudent enough to preserve from destruction, and we have in our hands the seeds of victory not only against the ghouls, but against Maslama as well."

Gabriel Camytzes was the only one of us brave enough to speak up in the wake of the Emperor's rousing—but wholly unsatisfying—oration. "But, Sire," he said, "how can we possibly retake the city with all of these ghouls running wild in the streets? We have, what—ten, fifteen thousand troops, and no hope of gaining any more? The ghouls' numbers are increasing geometrically. With nearly every casualty they take, they gain yet another of their kind to swell their numbers. As more and more victims reanimate, our forces are further outnumbered, and our chances of regaining Constantinople become ever more remote. Not to mention the fact that sending our troops through the streets of the city to fight ghouls necessarily means abandoning the defense of the walls against the Saracens. *We haven't enough men*, Sire. We should be thinking in terms of evacuating our essential people and withdrawing to some place where we can regroup with fresh troops from the themes. In my view, that's the only sensible course of action."

Leo looked off toward the east. A new plume of smoke had just begun to rise from some street within a few blocks of St. Sofia. I couldn't see what caused it, but I could imagine what was happening down there—the terrible lurching and moaning of the ghouls, the screams of their victims, the desperate panic of the survivors trying something—anything—to stem the monsters' inexorable advance.

"We shall have to make peace with Maslama," said the Emperor. "That much seems certain."

"What will you offer him for peace?" inquired Artabasdos of his liege.

"If you were Maslama, what would you want more than anything else right now?"

"To take Constantinople, of course."

"Are you sure about that?" The Emperor was smiling, and it struck me as woefully inappropriate. "Wouldn't you rather have the same thing that *we're* hoping in the back of our minds to receive—that is, some sort of magic deliverance from the pestilence of the ghouls?"

The Emperor Leo left this question hanging in the air. He pushed past me—not an easy task given his girth and the narrowness of the catwalk—and mounted the top step of the small wooden ladder leading back down into the narrow passageway. The rest of us did not need to be told—the reconnoitering atop Byzantium's grandest cathedral was over. As we started back down the stairs, I had the sense that Leo's cool self-assurance was not necessarily a bluff. Yes, he was arrogant; yes, he was self-obsessed, conceited and vain, and the conclusion that he was utterly without scruples lay beneath these realizations. But I suspected that he might just have an idea on how to reclaim our city from the ghouls. Since I had none, I was more than willing to give our eccentric ruler the benefit of the doubt.

Chapter Twelve

The Saracens

The Emperor led us down the steps of the dome, through the cavernous main room of St. Sofia and back down the shrouded hallway that led to the Great Palace. No one spoke. As the guards opened the heavy bolts of door after door in front of our party, it seemed the Emperor was leading us ever deeper into the compound.

At the top of another stone staircase we emerged into a large sunny room with arched windows. I guessed it was some sort of military conference room. The walls were hung with maps of the Empire, some of them woven into elaborate tapestries. There was a large central table surrounded by armchairs with gilded armrests and feet carved like the talons of eagles. But this was no ordinary table. It was more like a large rectangular wooden chest, ten or twelve feet long. The *kouropalates* strode over to a fixture on the wall which looked to be some sort of winch. As he manipulated its wooden crank, the top of the conference table split into two halves which swung upward and outward like the doors of a wardrobe chest. With the creaking of ropes and pulleys, something hidden inside the table began to rise out of it.

The large table concealed a stunningly detailed scale model of the city. When it had risen into place, Artabasdos secured the winch and the Emperor sat casually down at the head of the miniature Constantinople, the lord pondering over his domain. I bent down to examine the model. Every building was reproduced with exact precision. The Palace was complete with miniature gardens and stables. The Forum of Constantine was a neat circle with a needle protruding from its center. The land and sea walls marched in jagged impenetrable rows around the perimeter of the capital. There were small paper flags of various colors sticking up out of many towers on the land wall side, and I surmised that these represented military units.

"Brother Stephen," said the Emperor, after we were all seated around the table. "What is it that these ghouls want?"

"Human flesh, Sire," I replied.

"Would you say they're good at detecting human flesh? I understand that when you came through the cistern, you and Panteugenos's archers did battle with numerous ghouls who sloshed through the sewers to get to you. At the palace we too observed the phenomenon of ghouls massing in one direction or another, moving toward the greatest concentration of live human beings. It seemed they could see or smell their desired prey through walls and across great distances. Would you agree with that?"

"I would, Sire."

Leo stroked his chin. He was staring at the model but I couldn't tell exactly what he was looking at. Finally he said, "The ghouls, mindless and thoughtless as they are, appear to be driven by convenience. They pursue only the prey that's easiest for them to reach. Say you have a group of ten ghouls on a street. You, Brother Stephen, and you, Brother Theophilus, are standing at opposite ends of the street equidistant from the pack of ghouls. You, Brother Theophilus, take ten steps backwards, meaning that Brother Stephen is now ten feet closer to the ghouls than you are. I would expect to see the ghouls turn *en masse* toward Stephen and away from you. Does that stand to reason?"

"I don't know if it's capable of being reduced to such a simple formula," said Theophilus, the first time he'd spoken during our entire interview with the Emperor.

165

"Well, why shouldn't it be? The ghouls are incapable of rational thought. Their senses exist only for the purpose of finding fresh human meat to consume. Since they can't think, they would have no reason to choose to pursue you, who's farther away, as opposed to Stephen, who's closer and more accessible. Granted, it would make sense if there were, say, *two* humans twenty feet away as opposed to *one* human ten feet away, that the pack might reverse direction and head for the greater concentration of potential prey even though it might be farther away, or they might still opt to pursue the closer prey—but if we concern ourselves with questions of that nature, we'll soon be debating how many angels can dance on the head of a pin. The point I'm making is, we can be reasonably certain that ghouls will always pursue the greater mass of people that's closer to them and easiest to reach, correct?"

Artabasdos said, "What have you in mind, my liege?"

The Emperor rose slightly from his chair and began to make gestures in the air over the model, his fingers evidently representing lines of troops that might well exist only in his head.

"We send our troops out into the city. They go street by street, house by house, herding the people who are still left alive to a predetermined evacuation route. Our troops engage the ghouls only as much as necessary to protect the civilians to the greatest extent possible. We bring the mass of Constantinople's survivors to one of the main gates in the walls and escort them outside. Then we seal all the gates, thus locking the ghouls inside the city."

"The casualties would be frightful," said Gabriel Camytzes.

"There will be heavy casualties no matter what we do. We give the troops strict orders to leave behind all the dead, all the wounded. *Only* able-bodied soldiers and civilians who haven't been bitten by ghouls will be permitted into the sanctuary beyond the walls. We keep the survivors penned up there, surrounded by a row of siege towers."

"But the survivors will be beleaguered by masses of ghouls just the same as they would be anywhere else," Theophilus protested.

The Emperor replied, "Not if we deploy a counterweight."

I was puzzled. "A *what?*"

"A counterweight. We need a large mass of human beings which outnumbers our troops and the surviving civilians, and is closer to the ghouls as the crow flies. We also need to make sure this mass is physically separated from the ghouls. If we kept this mass, for instance, concentrated up here, in the Blachernae Quarter, with the city walls between themselves and the ghouls—and if that mass is closer to the ghouls than the body of civilians and our own troops that are proceeding with the evacuation—the majority of the ghouls will be attracted to the Blachernae Quarter, away from where the evacuation is taking place. There may be some stragglers still attracted to the evacuation, but our troops can deal with them as they approach. It's a classic diversion tactic. Split our forces, tempt the enemy into following a decoy that they can't reach, while ferrying the vulnerable portion of your host to relative safety."

"Where will we get such a large mass of human beings?" asked Michael Camytzes. "And how do we get them outside the city walls?"

"We already have it," the Emperor replied. "And it's already outside the walls."

The rest of us seemed to get it at the same moment. I said, "We're going to use Maslama's army as the counterweight."

"Precisely!" The Emperor's eyes flickered with the contemplation of impending glory. "Right now the Saracen troops are fighting pitched battles with the ghouls out there beyond the walls. Once the Mohammedans have eradicated them, Maslama will certainly draw his surviving troops back into a concentrated body. When I make peace with him this afternoon, I'll suggest that he amass his forces up here near the Golden Horn. Then I'll release our troops from the wall towers into the city to round up our civilians. Maslama keeps the ghouls relatively concentrated up in this northwest corner of the city, while we get our people out down here in the southwest corner, perhaps through the Golden Gate. Then Maslama brings his troops the long way around the western side of the city to link up with our forces, and together with the Saracens we form a solid cordon of soldiers that will march the mass of Constantinople's surviving civilians several miles to the west—far enough away so the ghouls can't smell them anymore—while the ghouls themselves remain locked safely inside the city."

Eutropius looked chagrined. "With all due respect, Your Majesty," he said, "I'm not certain that abandoning our capital to the ghouls is any less viable an option that simply surrendering to the Saracens. Either way the Empire will be lost."

"And the ghouls will get out eventually," Gabriel Camytzes cautioned. "As strong as the walls and gates are, the ghouls will eventually overrun them. Given enough time and left to their own devices they could probably climb over the walls."

Artabasdos spoke next. "And what's to say that Maslama won't take advantage of the situation? You're talking about delivering the entire remaining civilian population of Constantinople directly into his hands. Even if we succeed in evacuating Constantinople, Maslama can then exact any ransom he wants from us—including the unconditional surrender of the Byzantine Empire—by merely threatening to order his troops to turn their swords on the civilians."

Leo sat back in his chair, casually crossed one leg over the other, and raised a hand as if batting the criticisms out of the air like gnats. "Gentlemen, calm yourselves. I certainly have no intention of permanently abandoning Constantinople. I agree that would be an act of madness, and in any event we must endeavor to destroy the ghouls instead of simply penning them up. There is another part of my plan." He pointed at me. "Brother Stephen said he believed that ghouls will gravitate toward human flesh wherever it is. I think he's right. When Maslama marches our people away from the city, beyond the range of the ghouls' sensitivity, there will be a small handful of humans—maybe even just one or two—remaining alive inside the walls. They'll be together in one specific place, an area with a perimeter large enough to accommodate tens of thousands of ghouls. Say, maybe—" the Emperor tapped the building on the model, "—the Hippodrome."

It made sense to me. "All the ghouls in the city will converge on the last remaining prey."

"Then we can destroy them."

"With what?" Gabriel Camytzes asked.

The Emperor shrugged as if this question was trivial. "I was thinking of Greek fire. But I'm open to suggestions."

"How do we deploy it?"

"While we're evacuating our people, we line the Hippodrome with drums of Greek fire, all connected together with fuses. Enough to incinerate the entire lot of them. The human bait in the center will light the master fuse at the appropriate time. The Greek fire ignites the greatest fireball in the history of the world, and poof—the ghouls are sent back to Hell *en masse* with a minimum of Byzantine casualties."

"You mean the human bait," said Theophilus.

"Not necessarily," said Leo. "In order for this to work, the bait has to be kept alive at the center of the Hippodrome long enough for the evacuation to take place and the ghouls to congregate around them. We construct a small impregnable bunker in the very center of the arena. If it's strong enough to keep the ghouls out for a period of days, it *might* be strong enough to protect the occupants from the intense blast of the Greek fire going off. It's a long shot, but at least it's a chance."

I didn't think it sounded like very much of one. *Somebody's going to have to volunteer for a suicide mission,* I thought. *But since we're all going to die anyway, does it matter?*

"I'm still concerned about the Saracens," said Artabasdos. "Even if you can get Maslama to agree to help us, once the ghouls are destroyed, he stands to lose nothing by holding our people for ransom, or perhaps simply massacring them. Constantinople will be his for the taking, empty of people and undefended by Byzantine troops. He couldn't dream of an easier or more complete victory."

"I have an idea or two about that," replied the Emperor. "But leave that up to me. What do we need to put this plan into motion?"

169

"Lots of troops," said Gabriel Camytzes.

"Then you'll be in charge of coordinating them," the Emperor decreed.

"We'll need a lot of Greek fire," said Gabriel's son.

"You have my express order to commandeer every drop of it you can possibly find. Start by visiting the troops in the wall towers and requisitioning their stocks."

"We need bricklayers and stonemasons to build the bunker for the bait," said Eutropius.

"Get on it, then."

"First and foremost," Artabasdos spoke up, "we need a truce with Maslama, don't we? Without his cooperation this plan can go nowhere."

"Exactly right." I was completely unprepared when the Emperor motioned to Theophilus and myself. "We'll send the two monks to secure that."

"What?" I gasped.

"Who else would you have me send? *I* certainly can't go. After we double-crossed him last time, Maslama certainly won't trust any of the usual envoys, including Eutropius or Artabasdos. But he'd think twice before slaughtering two helpless monks traveling under a flag of truce."

"Your Majesty," I protested, "I'm certainly not a diplomat—"

"You need not be. All you have to do is carry my message to Maslama and bring his reply back to me. Brother Stephen, we all must do our parts. God has chosen us to deliver our people from evil. The Byzantine Empire is out there waiting for us to save it, if we can." The Emperor stepped over to me and patted my shoulder. "Besides, after all the ghouls you and Theophilus have destroyed, negotiating with Maslama should be child's play by comparison."

Four hours later Theophilus and I found ourselves in a small boat drifting through the Water Gate of Bucoleon Harbor toward the Sea of

Marmara that was filled with the Saracens' blockading ships. A large white flag, marked with a message hastily scrawled in Arabic, hung from a pole lashed to the front of the boat. Because the Emperor could spare none of his guards to escort us into the Saracen lines, Nicetas and Zonaras had volunteered to accompany us. They wore their armor but brought no weapons. They rowed the boat slowly and cautiously. The rolled-up parchment containing the Emperor's message to the Saracen commander was hidden in my cassock. I swallowed hard as I realized this piece of paper was the only thing standing between me and swift execution by a Saracen scimitar, or perhaps a lifetime of slavery under their yoke.

"Which ship should we steer toward?" Nicetas asked me.

"I've no idea. They all look the same to me."

It was late afternoon now, the sun poised to begin its descent toward the hazy smoke-filled horizon. From the viewpoint of the water, Constantinople did not seem to be in visible distress. Many of the fires on our side of the wall, whose smoke plumes we'd observed from the dome of St. Sofia, were now out. With the tall sturdy Sea Walls blocking our view of the streets the carnage that must have filled them was invisible to us. Artabasdos and the Emperor had decided to send their white-flag envoy by boat because reaching the Land Walls on the other side of the capital would have meant a long bloody trek through streets we presumed were largely controlled by the ghouls. Theophilus and I had already made that journey once. Time, Leo impressed upon us, was of the essence. The longer it took to reach Maslama and gain his assent to the Emperor's plan, the more people would die and the greater the numbers of the ghouls that would eventually have to be exterminated.

"Their ships are awfully quiet," said Zonaras, noticing, as I had, that there was very little activity on or around them. Their green crescent banners fluttered in the wind and we could see a few dark dots of men on deck, but the ships themselves were motionless. "Why aren't they taking part in the battle against the ghouls?"

"Probably not much they can do from out here," Nicetas replied. "I

171

could see why they might want to deploy a few ships along the shoreline to help, but they'd want to keep the blockade in place in case our forces tried to evacuate the city by sea."

Theophilus, shading his eyes from the sun, suddenly pointed. "Look, there!" he cried.

A small boat, lowered from one of the Saracen ships, was rowing toward us. Several figures, their helmets and chain mail glinting in the sun, were on board. In a few moments we started to hear the shouting of the Saracens' gruff voices. I saw a puff of smoke rise from the boat, then another—there were archers aboard, lighting their arrows, no doubt aiming at us.

"Stop rowing!" I told the soldiers. "Everybody, put your hands up. Let them come to us."

Our boat bobbed and drifted in the choppy waters. One of the Saracens shouted something but it was in Arabic and thus unintelligible to me.

The Emperor had made Theophilus and I memorize a few Arabic words; this was how we found out it was true he was fluent in that tongue. Theophilus cried through cupped hands, *"Hoodna! Hoodna!"* (*Truce!*)

The Saracen boat neared. There were six or seven archers, their bows ready to let loose. One gray-haired man in chain mail and a green turban seemed to be the leader. He kept shouting back at us but whatever it was I couldn't understand. I held my hands up. I dreaded the thought of seeing one of those flaming arrows arcing toward me. Somehow the idea of being killed by the Saracens while on a mission of truce seemed more cosmically tragic than being torn to death by the ghouls or burned alive down in the cistern.

"Hoodna!" shouted Theophilus again.

Finally the gray-haired man hollered something in Greek, though it was heavily accented. *"What is plan?"*

"What?"

The boat was now about twenty feet away. "Your flag," said the gray-haired man, pointing to the banner on our bow. "It say, 'Truce, Emperor has plan to destroy devils.' What is plan?"

So that's what it means. The Emperor had painted it himself.

I cupped my hands and cried, "We're allowed to tell only Maslama himself!"

"No more Greek tricks!" shouted the gray-haired man. "Your Emperor—liar!"

"This isn't a trick, I swear. We're unarmed. I bear a personal message from the Emperor to your commander."

The gray-haired man looked back at the men in his boat. There followed an animated conversation in Arabic between him and another man who stood behind the archers. During the brief exchange, the smoldering tips of the arrows never wavered in their aim. The Saracens' boat rose and fell on the water, but the archers compensated perfectly. These were well-trained men of war.

If I were the Saracen commander, I thought, *I wouldn't trust us either. How many times has Leo double-crossed them since the siege began? And they must be even madder now, knowing that we introduced the pestilence of the ghouls into their lines.*

Finally the gray-haired man looked over at us. "Okay," he shouted. "But any trick, you all die."

They came alongside us, threw a rope onto our boat and the gray-haired man, accompanied by two fierce-eyed Saracen warriors, clambered aboard. They frisked Theophilus and myself. Finding no swords or daggers, the gray-haired man motioned to the two of us and then to his own boat. He put his hand out in front of Nicetas and Zonaras. "Soldiers—no come," he said. I nodded, and then Theophilus and I began to transfer awkwardly to the enemy's boat. My heart was pounding. As soon as I sat down in the prow of their boat, one of the warriors drew a long curved dagger and held it at my throat. I made a point to keep my hands folded and in view.

"We'll wait for you by the Bucoleon Gate," Nicetas called to us as the Saracens began to row away from the truce boat.

"Good luck!" Zonaras added. "God be with you."

So, with knives to our necks, the Saracens brought us toward the shore beyond the Land Walls. As we drew closer, I started to smell the acrid reek of burning flesh. *Perhaps their battles with the ghouls have been as desperate and bloody as ours,* I thought. Even sitting there in the boat, though, part of me was amazed and sobered to be face-to-face with our enemies. As fearsome as they seemed to us, as blasphemous and offensive as our patriarchs thundered that infidel Mohammedanism was in the sight of God, these men surrounding us were people like any other. The soldier holding the knife to my throat looked to be younger than I was. I wondered how many of his friends had already been food for the ghouls.

"So," said a voice, in Arabic-accented Greek, "the treacherous lying swinish butcher who calls himself the Emperor sends two men of God, one young and one old, to tempt me with his latest trick. What makes him think this will be more successful than any of his other swindles?"

I could not see Maslama. The moment we reached the shore another cadre of Saracen troops surrounded us. Theophilus and I had been blindfolded and our hands bound behind us. The Saracens had led us roughly along a jumbled and chaotic path that led deep into their camp. I presumed they blindfolded us so we could gain no intelligence on their defenses.

My nose and my ears told me much, however. The smell of burning flesh was intense, and at one point we walked so close to a pit of burning corpses that I could feel the heat against my face and hear the crackling of the flames. *They must be burning the ghouls they've killed.* I heard the squeak of wooden cart wheels and the scraping of metal— definitely sword blades—on sharpening stones. *They're keeping their weapons sharp and at the ready.* Distantly I could hear the clang of swords and the shout of Arabic voices. *There are still battles with the ghouls going on somewhere in their camp.* In several places I also heard the low hum of somber voices, which I imagined to be Saracens saying rites over their own dead. I had seen nothing but I'd be able to report to the Emperor that his surmises about the Saracens' troubles with the ghouls seemed to be true.

So now we were in a tent of some kind. I could sense there were several men around, and they seemed to defer to the voice that had spoken to me. I also smelled incense and some sort of food, a spicy aroma that tempted me since I'd had little to eat all day.

"If you are Lord Maslama," I finally spoke up, "I have a message for you from the Emperor. It's in the front of my cassock, rolled up in a parchment."

"And if I do not wish to read it?" replied the Saracen commander. "My eyes have been seared one too many times with your Emperor's insulting lies. They cannot take much more."

"The Emperor desperately needs your help," said Theophilus. "We have a common enemy now. Neither of us can defeat it alone. Please, at least read the Emperor's proposal."

"And what makes you think we cannot defeat the *alksala* on our own?" I did not know this word he used, but I guessed it must have been the Arabic word for *ghouls* or *demons*. "We have swords. We have stout warriors. The *alksala* will prove but to be a temporary annoyance. Once they're vanquished, we will go on to take the city."

Theophilus again surprised me with his penchant for bold and blunt speaking. "I think not," he retorted. "Last night the Emperor directed all of his soldiers to stand down and remain battened up in their defensive towers. No Byzantine sword or arrow has drawn Saracen blood for an entire night and day. If the ghouls were so minor a problem, you would have seized the chance to attack, and you could have taken the city already."

Maslama gave as good as he got. "Perhaps I am staying my hand because I suspect that your withdrawal was merely a trick, and the silence was intended to lure me into a Byzantine trap! I know your Emperor well. He has no honor. He hung the bodies of my emissaries of peace over the walls on ropes, and made *alksala* of them. One of them was the younger brother of my wife. He was like a son to me. When he became one of the *alksala,* I had to crush his head with the butt of my sword. A man who would do such a thing to an enemy—an honorable enemy—will stoop to any form of treachery. It was your Emperor who conceived of unleashing this evil as a means to destroy us. Like the djinn that, once released from its bottle, cannot be placed back inside, let your Emperor live with the consequences of his fiendish invention. I will offer him no assistance."

I thought of something to say but held my tongue. *No—if I say that, they will execute me for sure.* But in the next few moments of silence I realized our diplomatic mission was over unless I spoke up.

"It was not the Emperor's idea to do this terrible thing," I finally said. "It was mine."

The next few moments were silent, and then Maslama said something in Arabic to one of his adjutants. There was a brief conversation. He gave an order. I sensed someone coming around behind me, and a moment later the blindfold was snatched off my face. The warrior took off Theophilus's blindfold too, and we beheld our captors.

The tent was posh. It was made of brocaded fabric and decorated with banners spangled with gilded Arabic writing, probably quotes from the Quran. Maslama sat on a pile of rugs. He was about forty with dark flinty eyes, a goatee and a very straight prominent nose. He was eating something—dates, by the look of them—from an ornate silver dish. There was something inviting about his eyes. He did not seem like a monster or even much like an infidel. I recalled what Michael had said about the Saracens as the siege began, that they were people just like us, with art and culture and love of their God equal to ours. Perhaps he was right.

"It was *your* idea?" said the Saracen commander skeptically. "You are a warrior merely disguised as a monk, then?"

"No, Sir. I really am a monk. I paint icons. My friend Theophilus and I were on our way to Constantinople from Mt. Olympus when we happened upon the ghouls just by chance. One thing led to another, and the Emperor found out about it. He ordered us to think of a way we could use the ghouls as a weapon against you. The plan to turn your peace emissaries into ghouls and hang them over the walls was my idea. It was an evil one. I should have refused to help the Emperor. Don't blame him. He was just doing his duty to defend Byzantium. In the sight of God, the responsibility for all of this havoc is mine. If offering my life to you as payment for what your army has suffered means you'll be more disposed to read the Emperor's proposal, I'll do it without hesitation. I'm not sure how I could live with myself after all this is over anyway."

Maslama chewed another date. He studied me up and down. His reply wasn't what I expected. "You paint icons?"

"Yes, Sir, I do."

"Are you not aware that making graven images of Allah is idolatry, a mortal sin forbidden by your own scripture?"

"Sir, there are many Byzantines who hold that view. The Emperor, in fact, is one of them. If you were to take Constantinople, you'd find that he had begun in earnest the project of ridding the Empire of graven images. That project was interrupted when you attacked."

Maslama chomped two more dates and then set the silver dish on the low table in front of him. He said something to one of his aides, a tall burly man with eyes that stared in slightly different directions. The two men held a brief conversation in Arabic. Then at last Maslama rose from his sitting position and approached me. He gave an order to the guard behind me, who began to untie my hands.

"Give me your Emperor's message," said Maslama. "If you're telling the truth, I will know it from the Emperor's words. If the vitriol of his lies burns away my eyes, you will die."

I reached into my cassock, took out the parchment and handed it to Maslama. His flinty eyes burned into mine. I tried to match the sincerity of his gaze, as if to tell him with my eyes, *Please, know that this is the truth.* He seemed a wise man, but our situation was so extreme that it was easy for the judgment of men to be clouded by emotion. I thought of the young man he'd spoken of, his wife's younger brother. Perhaps he had been the sad-eyed fellow who I'd watched be transformed into a ghoul. I shuddered to think of it.

Maslama unrolled the parchment and read it. He turned away from me, still reading. When he was done, he passed the note to the burly adjutant. He read it too and they conversed. Only then did Maslama turn back to me.

"You are prepared to disclose," he said, "the strength, armaments and exact positions of *all* of your troops defending the walls of Constantinople?"

Theophilus answered, "Yes, we are."

"We must not merely be *told* of this intelligence. One of my men must *see* it with his own eyes. You must admit one of my commanders into your redoubts and demonstrate to him that there is no deception."

"I believe the Emperor would be fully prepared to do that," I replied.

"Very well. The Emperor will have his reply."

Theophilus and I both nearly crumpled from relief.

Maslama patted my shoulder. "It is a brave man who ventures into the lion's den to offer peace to an enemy who has been grievously offended," he told me. "We're of different faiths, young Byzantine monk, but I admire courage, even among infidels. Perhaps you will return to your Emperor and tell him that we Saracens are not so barbarous as he may think."

"I believe that to be true, Sir."

A bare hint of a smile was visible at the corners of Maslama's mouth. I said a silent prayer. *Thank you, God, for letting wisdom carry the day.* We were still very far from victory over the ghouls, but there was now at least a glimmer of its possibility, shining up at us like a gemstone on the bottom of a river of blood.

Chapter Thirteen

The War Room

The preparations for the execution of the Emperor's plan took three days, and they were three of the most hellish days in the long violent history of Constantinople.

Our troops began fanning out into the streets the morning after Theophilus and I returned to Constantinople through the Bucoleon Gate with Maslama's reply. All night there had been frenzied activity along the walls. The Saracens had made a large cordoned camp just off the Golden Gate in the southwest corner of the city, ringed by siege towers kept constantly illuminated with torches. The idea was that our troops would begin the cleanup operation near the Blachernae Quarter, herding the civilians down one end of the large peninsula on which Constantinople was built, then back again along the southern edge and eventually to the Golden Gate. Since we had no idea how many ghouls there were—estimates ranged anywhere from ten to fifty thousand—the number of our men who would lose their lives in this dangerous process could not be predicted. But it would certainly be frightful. Perhaps only a handful of civilians and troops might survive the attrition and eventually make it to the Saracens' camp, in which case the whole operation would be something of a Pyrrhic victory. Nevertheless, destroying the ghouls was necessary regardless of how many Constantinopolitans died in the process. We were all committed now, Maslama's forces just the same as ours.

I stayed in the Great Palace for those three days, but between the prickly burns on my back and my apprehension about the operation I slept little. I spent much time in the conference room where the Emperor, Artabasdos and Eutropius pored over dispatches and tracked the progress of the battle on the model of the city. The Emperor had literally camped out in this room, retiring every few hours for a catnap on the tented bed his servants had installed in the corner. He seemed curiously cheerful and animated, almost as if he was having fun. Perhaps he'd always fancied himself as a master strategist directing a great battle such as this. The fact that he was playing with the lives of tens of thousands of real people on his little model didn't seem to faze him.

On Thursday morning the dispatches coming in began to take an alarming tone. Artabasdos awakened the Emperor with one, said to be from a cavalry captain near the Church of Christ Pantepoptes. The Emperor read it aloud. "Several hundred civilians trapped in the church. Force of two thousand men now surrounded by ghouls on three sides. We cannot reach the civilians without suffering casualties that would mean the decimation of our force. Please advise." The Emperor, eating biscuits from a gilded plate, calmly set the parchment down on the table next to him. "Well?"

"We can't afford to lose two thousand troops," said Artabasdos.

"But we can't abandon those civilians either," I pleaded.

The Emperor tore off a piece of bread and dipped it in olive oil. "Send a message to Maslama," he said calmly. "See if he can spare a phalanx or two from the counterweight to relieve our men and get those civilians to safety." He looked at me, smiled and winked. "It's rather handy having a backup army at our disposal, isn't it?"

I napped for two hours in the midafternoon. When I awakened and returned to the conference room, the news had come that the troops had reached Christ Pantepoptes Church, but when they opened its doors, they found the entire population within had been transformed into ghouls. The Byzantines, and the Saracens that had come to relieve them, were now engaged in a desperate retreat to the Mesē, surrounding a throng of nearly three thousand terrified civilians.

In the meantime there was word from the Camytzes. Gabriel, in charge of doling out reinforcements from the wall towers, reported that he was already running low on troops; Michael, in charge of transporting the vital Greek fire to the Hippodrome, said that he'd already had to detonate a few barrels of the precious stuff to stave off advances by waves of ghouls.

"Well, I don't know what else to tell them," sighed the Emperor, staring at the forest of paper flags on the model. Red flags represented our troops, green Maslama's, and gray large groups of ghouls. For hours the gray flags had been multiplying as more and more of the fiends were reported in all areas of the city. "They're just going to have to fight to the last man. We dare not shave off more of Maslama's troops from the counterweight. We're stretching things thin as it is."

"The counterweight isn't working," I protested. "Look at all the ghouls down here by the Forum of Bovis. They should be gravitating toward the Blachernae Quarter, but they're not."

The Emperor stroked his chin. "Why isn't the counterweight having any effect?"

"I don't know."

We waited. In the early evening the Empress made a brief appearance. "Anna's things are packed and she's ready to go," Maria reported to her husband. "Do you wish to say goodbye to her?"

The Emperor, crunching pistachio nuts as usual, brushed her off with a casual wave of his hand. "Tell her Daddy loves her and have a good trip," he said casually. "There's too much to do here to leave now."

"It's only the last time you may actually see your daughter *alive*," gushed Maria.

Where is he sending Anna? And how is she getting out of the city? I supposed it was now possible for people to come and go by sea, since Maslama's ships had at least loosened the blockade; but I figured the whereabouts of Leo's daughter was none of my business, so I kept my mouth shut.

"Give her my love," was all the Emperor said.

Maria glanced at me, an annoyed expression on her face. She grunted, drew her skirts up around her and breezed out of the room.

I remained as long as I could. I spent long hours sitting in silence, watching the Emperor and his aides move the flags around the map. Occasionally I got up and looked out the window. There wasn't much to see besides the increasing clouds of smoke drifting over the city. I wondered what poor sap the Emperor would order to serve as the human bait, to await their fiery death in the bunker at the bottom of the Hippodrome. *So much horror behind us, but so much still to come. I pray God this is over soon.*

Toward sunset I was standing at the window, looking out onto the streets below the palace. It had been a while since I'd seen anything, but this evening I peered into the street and beheld the hideous sight of two ghouls munching on the severed bottom half of a human being. I grimaced and turned away. *That must be going on all over the city,* I thought.

The image gave me a sudden epiphany. "I think I know why the counterweight isn't working," I said, leaning over the model table.

Leo, a green flag in his hand, looked up at me. "Do tell."

"The ghouls haven't run out of food yet. They're still consuming all the victims they've killed since the outbreak. I just saw two ghouls down there in the street dragging body parts behind them. If they're still eating the people they've already killed, they won't be tempted to find new sources of food until they've stripped everybody else to the bone. And with more and more bodies piling up in the streets from this fighting, they don't have to move very far to find food. As long as they're still eating, the smell of the counterweight won't tempt them."

For the first time in the entire venture Leo looked vexed. He grimaced, stared at the flag in his hand, and finally put it down on the edge of the model table. "I didn't even think of that." He thought for a moment and looked up again. "How long do you think it would take for the ghouls to strip every cadaver in the city of its flesh?"

"I haven't a clue, Sire. We don't know how many casualties there really are. It could be weeks before the counterweight has the effect we want it to."

"*Weeks?* We have days at most. The truce with Maslama is very fragile, and we'd be ill-advised to leave our civilians in his care one second longer than we have to."

I was almost tempted to retort angrily to the Emperor, W*ell, what do you expect me to do about it? It's not like I'm just making this up!* But I tempered my words. "I doubt, Sire, that the ghouls will understand that rationale."

The Emperor was silent for a few moments. Then he got up out of his chair and paced toward the windows, chin in hand. Finally he said, "Artabasdos, we're going to need a corpse detail. Pick some men. Not soldiers—we can't spare any. Use workers. No, better yet—slaves. Promise them their freedom and full citizenship if they help us. Provide them with a couple of big carts. Give them orders to round up every single corpse they can find and throw it on the carts. We haven't the time to burn or bury them, so we'll just have to dump them in the Bosporus. And all the corpses must be beheaded or else we'll have even more problems to deal with. Impress upon them that we need the streets as empty as possible of corpses. It's crucial to our plan."

The *kouropalates* wore a grave expression. "That will be ultra-hazardous duty," he remarked.

"Aye. But I don't see that we have a choice. It's either that or we hunker down for weeks waiting for the ghouls to finish the job for us."

I winced, just thinking of the horror the corpse detail would experience. *They're going to have to literally tear bodies out of the hands of the ghouls,* I thought with a shudder. *Probably many of the people on that crew will wind up being ghouls themselves.* Once more I damned the pestilence of the ghouls. Every time you thought of a move against them, some other and more terrible consequence that you hadn't thought of before loomed up as still another obstacle. I wondered if we would ever be rid of them.

Thinking this, I was suddenly quite disgusted with the whole thing. "Sire, I think I may retire for a while," I sighed.

The Emperor had resumed his seat at the map table. "Very well," he said casually, reaching for more flags. "Rest up. You'll need your strength soon enough."

It was only after I had walked out of the conference room and started down the steps toward the palace quarters that I realized what he'd said. *I'll need my strength? What for?* I paused in mid-step, wondering if the Emperor had something else in mind for me. Just as quickly I put the thought out of my mind. There was no need to throw yet another worry on top of my already crushing burdens. If Leo did have some special mission planned for me, I'd know it soon enough, and there would be nothing I could do about it.

"Brother Stephen."

I turned. I had just reached the door of my chamber and was about to open it when the voice diverted my attention. The Empress was standing at the end of the hallway, her face and the silk veil over her hair softly backlit in the dancing fire of a nearby torch. In the dimness all I could see of her besides her silhouette was the glinting of the brocade threads in her dress.

"I'm sorry, Your Majesty," I replied. "I'm *very* tired."

She moved forward. She didn't touch me, but she stood very close. "We didn't get a chance to really *talk* earlier."

"This crisis with the ghouls has consumed the bulk of everybody's attention."

"I'd like to ask you something, if I may. In *private*."

Maria looked up at me with her deep inviting eyes as she said this. With a twitch of her head, she motioned toward my door. *Please, no, not another seduction*, I protested silently, but how can you say no to an Empress? Finally I grasped the door handle and pushed open the door. I stepped inside and the Empress followed, her silky dress billowing.

The room was even dimmer than the hallway. The dusky light coming through the window was fading. Some servants had lit candles earlier, but by now they had dripped away to almost nothing. Maria stood before me, a dark shape with a charged and exciting aura.

She is beautiful and alluring, I thought. *I'm tired and sick of everything, but if she did want to seduce me now, perhaps it wouldn't be so bad.*

"What's your question?" I asked her.

"I was wondering about the icon. Where is it now?"

I shrugged. "I guess it's still in my cell at St. Stoudios. I haven't been back there since the ghouls got loose."

"Do you suppose it survived?"

"I don't see why not, unless the monastery itself was burned or otherwise damaged. We have no way of knowing."

"I hope it's all right. I think we need the intercession of the Virgin more now than we ever did."

"I won't argue with that."

She turned away from me, toward one of the candles. Her face was momentarily illuminated, just her chin and the end of her nose. It looked as if her features were carved from the finest marble.

"I fear what will happen if we do survive the ghouls," she sighed. "Let us suppose my husband's plan to defeat them succeeds, and by some miracle we manage to avoid being captured by the Saracens. Leo has become a *fanatic* about icons. He probably hasn't said anything to you about it, but he believes God sent us the plague of ghouls to punish Byzantium for idolatry. This crisis will make him even more determined to rid our lands of the sin he thinks we all committed. He'll tear the Empire apart over it. There could even be a civil war."

I could scarcely believe this. "Over icons?" I scoffed. "I can't believe he'd push it that far. They're just pictures. They can't substitute for the true worship of God. They were never intended to."

"My husband doesn't see such subtleties. To him everything is black-and-white."

"I think you're worrying unnecessarily. Anyway, why bother thinking about that now? The ghouls are still running wild out there. Haven't we enough to worry about without compounding our troubles by speculating on what might happen down the road?"

"But you see, I *have* thought about what might happen down the road. I've been struggling many months to think of what I would do if it came down to a choice between my husband and my beliefs. When the ghoul outbreak started, I felt almost—well, I hate to say it—*relieved*. But if we do come through this, that ugly choice will still be out there. Only it'll be worse, because Leo will be even more hell-fired to rid the Empire of icons."

The word *relieved* communicated perfectly what was on the Empress's mind. *She thought he might be killed,* I realized. *She expected him to die fighting the ghouls and she'd be absolved of having to split up with him over the icon issue. Now she's afraid he'll survive!*

I reached forward and touched her shoulder. "If you don't want to be with him," I said, "then *don't*. You have a choice. God gave us free will for a reason."

"Oh, Stephen, be reasonable. Do you know what happens to empresses who fall out of favor? They get packed off to nunneries. If I refuse to give up icons, I could see Leo doing just that. I'll end my days on the Isle of Lesbos, maybe, or perhaps even farther away. I'll never have my own life."

I was at a loss for words. "Well," I sighed, "there's not much I can do about that."

She looked up at me again. I sensed there was some dark political machination swirling around in her head. I wanted nothing of it, but on the other hand I felt it was my duty to be there for her. This wasn't the first time she'd sought me out as a confidante.

"Perhaps there is," she said softly. "I'm not entirely helpless in this situation, and neither are you. If something were to happen to the Emperor, we'd be looking at a whole new game. If, say, I remarried—and, more particularly, if I remarried someone who was firmly in favor of icons—then this whole nasty civil war business could be avoided."

My first reaction was fear. "Stop it!" I whispered harshly. "If you're talking about some kind of plot against your husband, I can't be a part of it. I don't even want to *know* about it. He could have me blinded, or thrown in a dungeon or tortured to death—"

"No, no. Nothing like that. I'm not planning to poison him or something. Do you take me for a conspirator? I'm just saying that things could *change*. The situation could change. If he died in battle, for instance, fighting the ghouls—"

"I can't listen to this. I can't even believe you're *thinking* about things like that. Whatever's happening behind the scenes, keep me out of it. *Please.* Keep me out of it."

"You're already in it, I'm afraid. If I were to confess to Leo what happened between us..."

I clapped my hands over my ears. "I'm not listening!" I cried.

At last she relented. "All right. All right. I was just thinking out loud." She paused, and then moved toward the door. "Anyway—I just wanted you to think about it. That's all I ask. Think."

I felt like I'd missed something. "Think about *what?* Joining some palace coup to murder your husband?"

"No, I told you that wasn't the plan," Maria grunted. With her hand on the door handle, she shook her head in apparent exasperation. "You monks are awfully *dense* sometimes." With this, she opened the door, swept out into the hallway and closed the door behind her. The puff of air from the door caused the thin flames of the dying candles to dance.

What the hell? I was thoroughly puzzled. If Maria hadn't been hinting at some sort of plot, whatever it was she had in mind was lost on me.

It was only after I sat down on the edge of my bed and began to pull off my boots did certain of her words come back to me.

"If, say, I remarried—and more particularly, if I remarried someone firmly in favor of icons..."

I gasped out loud.

If Leo dies and she remarries, her second husband becomes the next Emperor. And if she wants to prevent a split over icons by firmly embracing them, who could she count on to do that more reliably than a former iconographer?

I looked down at my hands. They were shaking.

A few months ago I'd been a simple monk, an artist at a third-rate monastery in the sticks. Tonight I had just been offered the crown of Byzantium.

I was so exhausted that I slept all the way through the evening and the night. When I awakened it was daybreak on the third day of the battle. Peering through the window while fastening my tunic I saw much less smoke hanging over the city. Indeed, things looked almost normal, and I dared to hope that we might be making progress against the ghouls.

Could it be? Has God seen fit to redeem us? Are our troops scoring victories against the demons?

I bounded up the steps to the war room two at a time. The guards outside the door knew me well enough by now; they moved aside and one of them swung open the thick heavy door to admit me. I was surprised to find the room as silent as a tomb. Chairs were scattered haphazardly about and the stone floor was strewn with parchments. Every table in the room save for the map table was piled with dirty plates and drinking vessels. In a corner I saw Artabasdos slumbering silently on a couch. Eutropius was slumped in a chair. I saw two more adjutants lying on a blanket in the corner. The drapes over the Emperor's camp bed were drawn. As I approached it quietly, I heard very faintly the grating of his snoring. One big knobby toe stuck out of the crack between the brocaded drapes.

Looks like they were up all night, I thought. *I must have missed the climax of the battle.*

I turned toward the map table. I had no idea how old the last intelligence on the ghouls was, but as I looked over the map my dare of a hope blossomed into something more.

A cluster of red flags littered the southwestern corner of the city, near the Golden Gate. A smaller grouping, encircled by the green of Maslama's forces, was on the other side of the wall. A line of red flags led between them, indicating that the evacuation of the civilians and our troops had begun.

The bulk of the green flags were concentrated outside the wall near the Blachernae Quarter. On the other side of the wall, gathered together in the far corner of the city, was a great mass of gray. There were a few other gray flags in various other locales—it looked like the ghoul infestation of the Church of Christ Pantepoptes was still a problem—but it was obvious that the counterweight had finally begun to work. The ghouls were, at last, congregating where we wanted them.

"God be praised," I whispered.

I heard a sudden snort from the Emperor's camp bed. The big hairy toe withdrew, and there was a brief rustling as Leo stirred and composed himself. A moment later the curtains parted. A very strange-looking head poked out between them. Without any crown or helmet, the Emperor looked strange. Twin curtains of long dark curly hair hung on either side of his face. His beard was more scraggly and unkempt than usual. His eyes were bloodshot and sleepy. It took a moment for him to recognize me.

"Oh, Stephen," he said. He stuck a fat-fingered hand out of the drapes and pointed at one of the end tables. "Would you bring me my pistachios please? They're in the silver dish over there on that table."

I fetched them, stepped over and handed them to him. He set the dish on the floor, took a few pistachios in his hands and began to crack the shells open.

"I saw the map," I said breathlessly. "It looks like we had a breakthrough."

"Ghouls in full retreat," replied the Emperor, before tossing two nutmeats into his mouth. "That corpse detail made all the difference. The sons of bitches finally started to smell the counterweight. Now with the Hippodrome area cleared, Michael Camytzes can set the Greek fire canisters and rig the fuses. The bricklayers have already started building the bunker on the floor of the arena."

"That's terrific news. Now what?"

The Emperor crunched more nuts. "Now we put the human bait in position at the Hippodrome. I have decided there will be two. No sense risking more than that, and we need to keep the bunker small if it's going to be finished in time for this to work. See, the damn thing is, in order to make the bunker impregnable from the literally thousands of ghouls that'll eventually converge on it, there can't be any doors or windows. The bricklayers are going to have to literally build the bunker around the occupants—wall them up alive."

"Like a mausoleum." I swallowed hard. "That's grisly."

The Emperor smiled. "Ah, well," he shrugged, "most of the other emperors are buried in the rotunda over at the Church of the Holy Apostles. My tomb will be a novelty, a tourist attraction. When they rebuild the Hippodrome they'll probably turn the bunker into a monument. I think that's rather neat—cheering crowds with chariot races orbiting my last resting place for the rest of eternity." He casually spat a fragment of nutshell onto the floor.

My eyes widened. *"You're* going to be the bait?" I gasped.

"Of course." He motioned to the sleeping figures around the room. "Do you think I'd let any of these pathetic yes-men soak up all the glory? Besides, it makes me look selfless. In centuries to come the bards will sing that I refused to put any of my subjects into more danger than I was willing to face myself."

I was aghast. "Sire, we can't spare you," I said. "The Empire needs you. Once the ghouls are dead we still have to make sure Maslama retreats like he agreed. Who can negotiate with him if not you?"

"Don't you worry about Maslama. And be careful that you don't look *too* eager to see me dead. After all, I might just survive!" At this Leo laughed and winked at me, but I didn't think it was very funny.

He's planning to bring Maria into the bunker with him, I thought grimly. *She doesn't even know about it yet, I'll bet.* In light of this revelation, the fact that she'd hinted that I should marry her and become Emperor seemed positively macabre. It made sense, though, that Leo wouldn't want to tell her until the last minute.

"So that's why you sent your daughter out of the city," I said softly. "To make sure she survived to carry on the dynasty once you and the Empress are gone."

Crunching another pistachio, Leo regarded me with a cocked eyebrow. "The Empress?" he said, puzzled. "What makes you think *she* has anything to do with this?"

"You said there'll be two people in the bunker. I can only assume you want the Empress to die by your side."

The Emperor laughed again, loudly enough that he caused Artabasdos and Eutropius to stir. "Oh, my!" Leo snorted. "You *do* have quite an imagination, don't you, Brother Stephen? The Empress isn't coming with me into the bunker. *You* are."

Chapter Fourteen

The Bunker

In the small private chapel just down the hall from the Emperor's bedchamber, Theophilus blessed me and recited the last rites. Dressed again in my cassock—I wanted to die a monk and an iconographer, not a warrior—I knelt, received communion, and listened to Theophilus mumble the ancient Latin words that would herald my entry into Heaven. I knelt there, my knees on a velvet pillow, staring up at an ornate gilded cross on the Emperor's private altar, and I felt completely dazed.

I can't believe this is happening. This makes no sense at all. Why does the Emperor want me to accompany him? He didn't tell me, and I dare not even ask—it's my place merely to obey—but it'd sure be nice to know what possessed him to think that I was the guy for the job.

Another part of me said, *He's punishing me. He knows I slept with his wife, and he wants me to die in retribution. If he can't have her, maybe he figures he'll make sure I won't either once he's gone.*

"Stephen?" Theophilus was tapping my shoulder. *"Stephen!"*

I jarred myself back to reality. "Oh...yes?"

"We're finished, Brother."

I rose and bowed my head. "Thanks."

Theophilus clasped my hand. "I have no doubt that the Lord will receive you as one of His own," said the old monk. "And I want to say, it's been an honor and a privilege to serve God—and to fight evil—by your side."

Our handclasp turned into an embrace. "It's an honor for me too," I said, feeling tears welling up. "If you do make it back to Chenolakkos, tell everyone there goodbye for me."

"I'll do that."

I parted from my good friend and fellow ghoul-fighter. "Oh, there's one more thing," I whispered, after glancing over my shoulder to make sure none of the Emperor's lackeys were listening. "In my cell at St. Stoudios, under my sleeping pallet, you'll find an icon I was working on. It was commissioned by the Empress. If St. Stoudios hasn't been totally destroyed, please go back for it. Have someone finish it— Gennadios, perhaps, if he's still alive. Make sure it's delivered safely to the Empress. I don't know whether icons will still be forbidden after tomorrow, but if they are, be sure to take care that no one finds out she has it."

"You have my word on it," said Theophilus.

We exited the chapel. In the hallway, lit by a sunbeam slanting through a half-moon window in the great porphyry wall, Empress Maria stood there. She wasn't wasting any time. She was already clothed in mourning black. With the ebony veil across the bottom half of her face she looked eerily like a Saracen, save for her intense sea-green eyes. Theophilus glanced at me and then at her. He patted my shoulder. "I'll leave you two alone," he said, and tactfully drew himself away into the corridor.

"I heard that you didn't even protest," said Maria, after she unfastened her half-veil. "Eutropius said that when my husband told you that you were going into the Hippodrome to face the ghouls, you just said, 'Yes, Sire' and that was that."

"What point would there have been in arguing? I've known the Emperor only a fraction of the time you have, but even I know that once he's made up his mind it's impossible to change it."

"That is true enough."

"I wish I knew why he wanted me, though. I mean, I figured it was to punish me. Maybe he knows about...well, you know what. Maybe he's angry."

Maria shook her head. "No. It's not that." She looked down, and then began reaching into her black dress. "I think I *do* know the reason. There's something you should know before you die, but I can't tell it to you here. I wouldn't want Leo to know either, but if you don't make it out of that bunker, I suppose it won't make any difference whether he knows or not." The Empress drew out a small parchment, folded in thirds and sealed in wax. The seal was a royal one—the emblem of the Empress of Byzantium.

She placed the letter surreptitiously into the sleeve of my cassock.

"Promise me you won't open it until the very last moment," she said. "Right before you trigger the Greek fire. If that is your last action on earth, let the opening of this parchment be your *second* to last."

I nodded. Choking back tears, I employed one of the Emperor's own not-very-funny jokes. "Don't be so hasty to see me dead," I told her. "We might just survive."

She embraced me. She was in tears now too.

"God be with you, Brother Stephen," she said as we parted, her chin quivering.

"And with you." I kissed her forehead.

I think one of us wanted to say *I love you*, but that was too heavy a burden for such a moment to bear.

The Empress turned one way down the corridor, and I the other.

There was a secret passageway that led from the Great Palace to the Hippodrome, but it had been decided that we would not use it. In fact, I heard from Eutropius that bricklayers were feverishly bricking it up to prevent any ghouls from wandering into the palace complex, and also to shield the royal buildings from the inevitable blast of fire that would result when we triggered the incendiaries. Thus the Emperor and I would be traveling to the Hippodrome through the streets.

Leo had a special armored carriage that he used to travel to and fro in hostile conditions. It was little more than a large wooden box on wheels with iron-sheathed sides. The royal standard flew on a short pole from above it. At shortly after noon, amidst a cadre of soldiers in the garden of the Great Palace, two guards swung open the heavy doors and we clambered into the little wagon, I in my simple monk's cassock, the Emperor fidgeting in his finest military tunic, purple cloak and matching boots.

Artabasdos paused at the rear of the wagon. "May God watch over you, my liege," he said, making the sign of the cross on his forehead and shoulders.

"Oh, stop being so dramatic," the Emperor grunted. "Close the doors, let's get this damn thing moving."

Artabasdos shut the doors of the wagon. I heard a heavy bolt drawing across them. The Emperor laid back on one of the velvet settees built into the sides of the wagon and casually reached for his drawstring suede bag of pistachio nuts.

As I'd climbed into the wagon, I had noticed it was packed with provisions. Much of the floor between the two settees was piled with small wooden boxes as well as several amphorae that I assumed contained wine or olive oil. Hanging from a hook overhead—swinging as the wagon jiggled and swayed—was a cage containing six pigeons. Their cooing was strangely calming.

"What is all this stuff for?" I asked the Emperor.

"We're going to be in the bunker for two or three days," he replied. "After they seal us in we have to wait for Maslama to draw both the counterweight and our army away from the walls of the city. It'll also take some time for the ghouls to smell us and converge on the bunker. I had my stewards stock plenty of bread, some olive oil, dates, and of course some nuts for me. I even brought some books. Do you like Plutarch? If the classics bore you, I think there's a Bible in one of these boxes. I told them to pack it, but the palace domestic staff is notoriously forgetful. Then again the moaning of tens of thousands of ghouls might be such a racket that concentrating on scripture is impossible."

"And the pigeons? Do you plan to dine on fresh squabs?"

Leo chuckled. "I wish, as I do love squab. No, they're homing pigeons. For messages. I made sure the bunker was designed with a small chimney, large enough to give us some air and let the pigeons in and out, but too small for a ghoul to climb through. So far as we've been able to observe the ghouls ignore all forms of animal life so the pigeons should have no problem. I've asked Artabasdos to keep me updated on the mop-up operations, and of course your friend Camytzes will alert us when he believes all the ghouls are in the Hippodrome and ready to be ignited, because without windows we won't be able to see for ourselves."

I nodded. "Clever."

The Emperor crunched another nut, and then he turned around and peered out the narrow slit, barricaded by heavy bars, that served as one of the battle wagon's windows. "I think we're moving out of the palace complex," he said. "I'm curious about the extent of the destruction."

I was curious too, so I took up position at my own window. Once we passed out of the Great Palace gates, the wagon rumbled through the open streets of Constantinople. At first there was very little to see. The houses, churches and shops were empty and dark, and there was no sign of life in the streets. But there were subtler signs of the disaster. When we reached the Milion, we passed an alleyway in which I could see the burnt remnants of a barricade that had been erected against the ghouls, and several buildings in this area had scorched windows and collapsed roofs. Puddles of blood stood in the streets. I saw weapons—a discarded sword, many arrows, a crushed shield, even an abandoned trebuchet, its timbers splashed and smeared with blood. But there were no bodies nor parts of bodies. The corpse detail had done their grisly job with efficiency.

The Emperor didn't seem distressed. "On the whole, it's not as bad as I thought," he commented. "We'll have to pull down some buildings here and there, but I bet we can have Constantinople as good as new in six months. Eight months tops. I'll tell the Patriarch to pressure the churches to give generously for rebuilding funds."

Are buildings all he's concerned about? "How many dead, do you think?" I asked.

"No way of knowing," he shrugged. "The size of the ghoul army is estimated at between fifteen and twenty thousand. Surviving corpse detail guesses they dumped about ten thousand into the Bosporus. So that's thirty there. But those numbers could be wildly overestimated. We won't know until this is over."

The wagon approached a street from which a large column of smoke rose toward the sky. We drew to a halt before one of the secondary entrances to the Hippodrome, and another cadre of guards surrounded us. The reason for the smoke was evident—the street outside the great horse-racing arena had been turned into a makeshift brick foundry. Men, stripped to the waist and sweating profusely, moved large smoking bricks with metal tongs, shuttling them in and out of large earthenware ovens set up on blocks. Soot-smeared stokers tended the fires beneath the ovens. A line of workers had formed a bucket brigade to ferry vessels of cool water to douse the still-hot bricks; others mixed huge vats of mortar. Flatbed carts filled with bricks, drawn by exhausted horses with foamy mouths and sweat-glistening flanks, rolled back and forth between the foundry and the Hippodrome.

Two guards unbolted and swung open the doors of the battle wagon. "Well, here we go," said the Emperor, clambering over me to exit the carriage.

I followed. The guards bowed to the Emperor. A bedraggled-looking man in a sweat-stained tunic approached. It was Michael Camytzes. He bowed to the Emperor dutifully, but he seemed especially happy to see me.

"Brother Stephen," he smiled. "The ghouls haven't yet been able to smite you."

"Nor you," I replied.

"We have no time to lose," said the Emperor. "Captain Camytzes, will you be so good as to escort us to the small brick oven in which Brother Stephen and I will likely meet our ends?"

"This way, Sire."

We followed Camytzes through the gate and into the Hippodrome. Even the grandeur of Constantinople that I'd witnessed thus far couldn't prepare me for the moment where we stepped through the archway into the grand arena itself. St. Sofia had been impressive, but *this* was truly the marvel of the ages.

The arena was an immensely long U-shaped track surrounded on all sides by vast terraced risers of marble. In the center of the arena was a long row of fountains crowned with majestic statues—horsemen, cherubim, and sculptures of the great heroes of Byzantium perched atop lofty columns. The very center was marked with an obelisk, no doubt taken from one of the many Roman sacks of Egypt. Around the entire perimeter of the Hippodrome marched a majestic row of stone columns, often punctuated with grand arches, gables, staircases and gates. The sheer size of the place was daunting. The men working feverishly at the center of the arena seemed to be tiny ants dwarfed by the enormity of masonry. As my eyes moved along the rim of the great building, I beheld more splendor—great towers, glinting statues, and crowning the apex of the rounded side, the four gilded horses that stood watch over the imperial entrance.

The signs of the coming battle with the ghouls, however, were everywhere in evidence. The perimeter of the arena floor was lined with dozens of earthenware vats. Ropes smeared with an oily black substance—pitch, maybe, or perhaps Greek fire itself—drooped between them, some dripping the foul-smelling stuff onto the sandy floor of the track. Another row of such vats had been established midway between the center of the arena and its edge. In the center of the great space, just under the obelisk, a boxy shape of masonry, sheathed in wooden scaffolding, was taking shape. Bricklayers buzzed about it like bees around a hive. A pit of dread grew in my stomach when I realized I had just laid eyes on my own tomb.

But it's not totally certain that we'll die, I tried to reassure myself. *It's at least possible that we'll survive.*

If he was impressed, the Emperor, true to form, made no big show of it. "Not bad for the work of forty-eight hours," he said as we continued walking toward the bunker.

"We've had hundreds of men working around the clock," Camytzes replied. "In the early stages we had to deploy a perimeter of troops to ward off ghoul attacks, and the occasional stray one will still wander close to the Hippodrome and have to be slaughtered. But since most of the ghouls have concentrated in the Blachernae Quarter we've been able to make much better progress."

We reached the bunker. It was a very plain box made of bland-looking tan bricks, perhaps fourteen feet on a side. There were no doors, windows or portals of any kind. A wooden ladder had been erected on one side by which I guessed we would make our entrance. The bunker was ugly. In marked contrast to the grandeur of the rest of the Hippodrome, no artistry had gone into the design of this structure. It was a utilitarian wart sprouting in the midst of a garden of splendor.

"How long do you think we're going to have to be inside of this thing?" I asked Camytzes.

"Well, it will take about twelve hours for the mortar to set. We don't want it melting when the Greek fire goes off, so we have to be sure it's cured. After that, who knows?"

The Emperor, stoic as always, did give one indication that what he was seeing and hearing was disturbing to him. I saw his left cheek bulge out as if he had stuck his tongue into it. Still, he voiced no protest. A moment later he said, "Do you think we have any realistic chance of surviving this?"

"Actually, Sire, I do," Camytzes replied. "Come over here."

He took us around the side of the bunker. One of the bricks like those used to build the bunker—it was perhaps two feet long by a foot high and a foot wide—had been suspended on sawhorses over a small pit in the sand. The pit was filled with flames and I knew instantly it was Greek fire because it smelled exactly like the watery catacombs through which we'd made our escape across the city. Camytzes gingerly approached the brick. Its bottom was thoroughly blackened and the flames had painted ghostly ebony streamers up its sides, but the top surface was unmarred.

"We decided to test the bricks using this little demonstration," said Camytzes. "They're specially designed to dissipate heat. The fire has been burning underneath this block for over twelve hours. Go ahead, touch the top."

The Emperor crept closer. He put out his hand but couldn't seem to bring himself to touch the block. His hand withdrew, and then he finally made contact with it. He looked up at me. I joined him and set my index finger on the top of the stone surface. It felt warm, but not so warm as to burn my skin. It was about as warm as a hot bath.

"Ingenious," the Emperor remarked.

"Depending on how long the fire burns," Camytzes explained, "it will no doubt be very warm inside the bunker. And it could be quite some time before the Greek fire burns itself out and we're able to dismantle the bunker to rescue you. But you may well survive."

"But you don't know for sure."

"No, Sire. There's no way to know."

I looked back at the gate through which we'd entered. Several of the Emperor's guards were approaching, hauling the provisions from the battle wagon.

"Well, I guess it's time for us to take our places," the Emperor sighed. He patted Camytzes's shoulder. "Good work, Captain. If anything should happen to us, I've left word for Artabasdos that you're to be promoted. Any position you want in the Byzantine army or bureaucracy is yours for the asking. We need good men like you."

"Thank you, Sire. There is one thing."

"Yes?"

"The village of Domelium—the place where we first came upon the ghouls—lies in my father's lands. With their village destroyed, the townspeople are destitute. They can't pay their rents to my father. I respectfully ask that you forgive the taxes due to the Empire on Domelium, at least until the people can rebuild their homes and regain their livelihoods. I would much rather see the people of Domelium given a fair chance to put their lives back together than to occupy an office that would benefit only myself."

Without even pausing the Emperor replied, "Taxes on the village of Domelium are hereby rescinded until further notice. Send word to Eutropius. He'll get it straightened out."

"Thank you, Sire."

The Emperor looked at me. "All right, let's do this," he grunted, and approached the ladder, that seemed to me for a moment like Jacob's ladder leading to Heaven.

The interior of the bunker was barely twelve feet square. When packed with our provisions, two chairs, the pigeon cage and the two of us, it was dreadfully cramped and claustrophobic. The only free space inside the bunker where a person could stand upright was just to the side of our chairs, and it was only big enough for one person to stand at a time. I didn't relish spending the next several days literally inches away from the Emperor. I hadn't noticed it before but in close proximity his body odor was extremely disagreeable, and he continually breathed the aroma of stale pistachios into my face. He farted and the stench lingered in the tiny room for nearly an hour.

The palace courtiers had provided us each with an elegant silver chamber pot in which to relieve ourselves, but when not in use they had to be stowed under our chairs with only a thin cloth laid over them to provide whatever minimal restraint was possible on the smell of their contents. As much as a hero that he might turn out to be for Byzantium, watching—and hearing—Emperor Leo III, God's Vice-Regent on Earth, urinating and defecating six inches away from me was a trying experience. At least the Emperor had the decency to acknowledge the hardship. "Sorry, Brother," he said when he was done, stashing the stinking chamber pot under his chair. "I had too much olive oil with breakfast. Olive oil always makes my bowels loose and runny. But don't worry, all the pistachios I eat will prove an effective antidote."

Adding to the misery of being trapped in the bunker was the trial of the construction work going on above us. After we were safely inside, the bricklayers began laying the bunker's roof and chimney, and at one point Leo and I were obliged to cower under an animal hide to protect us from dollops of fresh mortar that splattered down from above. There was also the matter of the pigeons' shit; the birds squirted endless blots of whitish effluvia out of their cage which soon dotted and streaked the plain tan walls. As the ceiling took shape—only a small hole a foot square communicated with the outside world—the inside of the bunker was plunged into darkness. Among the Emperor's provisions was a small oil lamp which we soon lit. It helped, but it was too dark to read. Thus the Emperor and I had to entertain each other by talking.

"Okay, I've got an idea," said Leo, brushing pistachio shells off his tunic. "I'll think of an animal. You can ask me twenty questions, only answerable with yes or no. From my answers you guess what animal I'm thinking of. Go!"

The workmen finished the bunker long after darkness had fallen in the world outside our little stinking universe. The square hole in the ceiling led up into a chimney nearly ten feet tall, and through it I could see a tiny patch of deep blue sky and a few stars. The bricks were so thick we could see very little of what was happening outside, so we were unprepared to hear Camytzes's voice booming down the shaft. "Helloooooooooooo! Your majesty and Brother Stephen, how fare you?"

"We're fine," the Emperor shouted up through the chimney.

"It's cramped, but we're making do," I said.

"We're finished with the bunker," Camytzes called down. "We're now going to lower the master fuse down to you. It's covered in pitch. Try not to get it on your hands."

"Aye," said the Emperor. "We're ready."

A few minutes later Camytzes lowered a long snake of rope, with a thick stone block tied to its end, into the bunker. The rope was smeared with a sticky black goo. The smell of pitch was added to the already rich mixture of burning lamp oil, pigeon shit, the contents of our chamber pots and the Emperor's farts. Leo secured the fuse on the opposite corner of the bunker from where our lamp hung. "It won't do to have *this* go up accidentally," he said.

"Do you have the fuse?" Camytzes shouted.

"We've got it!" I said.

There was a brief pause. Then Camytzes said, "Well, that's it, then."

"Pull your men out of the Hippodrome, Captain," the Emperor ordered. "And start withdrawing all the soldiers and workmen from Constantinople. When your father assures Artabasdos that everyone is safe and all the gates of the city are securely locked, the *kouropalates* will give the word to Maslama to begin the retreat from the walls."

"Aye, Sire."

"Good luck!" I cried.

"Same to you," said Camytzes. "God be with you both."

"God be with us all," said the Emperor.

We did not hear Camytzes's voice again.

"Well," the Emperor sighed, "I guess that's that."

"It's going to be a long wait."

"Indeed it is."

And so it was. I was surprised that I managed to sleep a little. The Emperor did too; I heard him snoring loudly next to me. In the morning we were both awakened by a pigeon flapping its way down the chimney. A tiny spot of dawn filtered down from the long shaft and pooled on the sandy floor of the bunker next to my foot. The pigeon descended, perching on the top of the cage. There was a parchment clipped to one of its feet. Leo got up on his knees on the chair and took the parchment.

"Well!" he exclaimed after reading it. "Not such bad news." He handed the paper to me.

All troops withdrawn from the city. Golden Gate and all other exterior wall gates firmly bolted. I have exchanged messages with Maslama and the Saracen army has begun its march. Hippodrome gates and doors left wide open. Ghouls should start converging on your position sometime in the next few hours. Please advise us periodically of your condition.

Artabasdos

The Emperor sent a reply, reporting that we were well. It was at least comforting to have some contact with the outside world. Hearing nothing from inside the bunker was quite eerie and made me feel as if we two were the only people left on earth.

The day wore on. After a while the Emperor engaged me in a debate on theology. "What's your view on the divinity of Christ?" he said. "Do you think that the Father, the Son and the Holy Spirit are coequal or hierarchical?"

This debate consumed several hours, during which the Emperor showed glimpses of his rigid theology against icons. I didn't argue with him—if we did get out of here, I had no desire to be condemned as a heretic—but it was very clear that Leo was inalterably opposed to graven images of any kind. Evidently he had gotten this idea, strangely enough, from the Saracens. "Their views on graven images are exactly the ones we should adopt," he said firmly. "Unfortunately the association of these views with Mohammedanism is going to make it a hard sell to the people of Byzantium. Nonetheless, if we do survive and peace with the Caliph is secured, abolition of icons will become my first priority."

Toward sunset another pigeon fluttered down the chimney. This time it was I who caught it and took the parchment from its leg. The note was in a different hand than the last one.

Bulk of Byzantine and Saracen armies now two miles from Constantinople walls and continuing to retreat. We have conducted a preliminary count—18,900 civilians currently under the protection of Saracen forces. We retain force of 9,000 infantry, 2,000 cavalry, approximately 1,500 naval personnel. Saracen army reliably counted at 70,000+. Their casualties from the ghouls fewer than ours. No ghouls have been seen outside of city walls.

G. Camytzes

"Only nineteen thousand civilians," said the Emperor after reading the note.

"So few."

"If we'd delayed any longer, there would have been even fewer. Those nineteen thousand will be the seed of Constantinople's renaissance. They're the very future of our empire."

At long last I gave voice to a question that had been floating around in my mind. "Sire, can I ask you something about the civilians?" I said.

"Sure," he shrugged, reaching for his bag of pistachios.

"You just said they're vital to our future. We've risked all to protect them. Clearly that's the right course, but just how is it that you can trust Maslama with them? I mean, it seems to me that Artabasdos was right. If we deliver all the people of Constantinople into the hands of the Saracens, what's stopping Maslama from taking them hostage or even slaughtering them?"

The Emperor crunched a nut between his molars. "That's a very good question," he replied. "And in fact it was the very key to this entire plan. The answer has to do with my daughter."

"Anna?"

"Yes."

"I thought you sent her out of the city to safety."

He nodded. "I did. I had some guards ferry her in a small boat across the Golden Horn to Galata, where the Saracen fleet had stood down. From there a small cadre of troops escorted her to the Bulgarian frontier. She reached it yesterday morning, just before they put us down here in the bunker."

I was horrified. *"Bulgaria!"* I gasped. "They're our enemies, aren't they?"

"Indeed they are. Khan Tervel knows nothing of the ghouls, but he figures whoever is left holding Constantinople—us or the Saracens—will be so weakened by the battle for it that they'll be easy pickings for him."

"So why send your own daughter into the enemy's hands?"

Leo bore a hint of a smile on his face as he answered, "Tervel doesn't know it, but he's unwittingly become the guarantor of the safety of Constantinople's civilians. I told Maslama that I sent Anna to the Bulgarians. I also told him that I gave Eutropius a small vial of fast-acting poison earmarked for Maria. If the Saracens harm a hair on the head of a single one of the civilians of Constantinople, Eutropius's poison goes into my wife's drink. She'll be dead in three minutes. If by some miracle you and I make it out of this bunker alive, and I find out that the civilians have been harmed, I vowed to Maslama that I would commit suicide by the same means. So I've got Maslama boxed in."

"I don't get it," I said, shaking my head.

"Well, it has to do with the succession. I have Anna, but I have no sons. Under Byzantine law the crown can't pass to a woman so long as there's a man around—*any* man—with a viable claim on the throne. If I die in here and Maria's still alive, the succession passes to her. She'll almost certainly marry again and her second husband will become the next Emperor of Byzantium. But if both Maria *and* I are dead, the succession passes to Anna. If she's a hostage of Khan Tervel and he finds out that Maria and I are dead, he'll marry Anna and *he* becomes the next Emperor. He'll gain the entire Empire as Anna's dowry, which means he'll have conquered Byzantium without unsheathing his sword. But there's one catch. Tervel's a pagan. In order for the marriage and his succession to be legitimate in the eyes of the Patriarch and the Pope, Tervel will have to convert to Christianity before he takes his wedding vows. Whichever way it comes out, I've guaranteed that the next emperor of Byzantium will be a Christian."

I began to perceive a glimmer of the Emperor's strategy but I still didn't quite understand. "But how will that prevent Maslama from harming the civilians or using them as hostages to convince the next emperor to surrender Constantinople?"

"Think of it this way. Let's say the ghouls are destroyed and you and I survive. If Maslama keeps his word that the civilians won't be harmed, they'll just be repatriated back into Constantinople and the siege is over. If, on the other hand, Maslama double-crosses us and marches into Constantinople, Eutropius ices Maria with the poison and I commit suicide. Tervel converts to Christianity, marries Anna and becomes the next Emperor. Even if Maslama is in actual possession of Constantinople at that time, Tervel will undoubtedly march down here with the Bulgarian army to conquer it and place himself on the throne. If I don't get out of here and Maslama double-crosses us, Maria again dies by poison and Tervel converts and marries Anna. If I die and Maslama keeps his word, Maria marries a fellow Christian and we carry on from there. See? I've fixed things so it doesn't matter whether I survive, and the Empire continues on under the rule of a Christian emperor no matter what happens. Maslama knows this. So what are his choices? He can either keep his word on the civilians and let them go when this is all over, in which case he'll deal with either me or Maria's second husband, and he can withdraw and live to fight another day. Or he can break his word on the civilians and end up pissing away the entire Saracen army fighting a bloody war with Tervel over the smoking ruins of Constantinople—which is a war he knows he'd probably lose anyway. You met the guy. You know he's not stupid. Which of those alternatives do you think he's going to choose?"

I stared at Leo, my mind reeling. "Wow," I finally said. "That's really—"

"Brilliant?" The Emperor smiled. "Why, yes it is, if I say so myself."

"You saved the Empire."

"I would *never* have let Byzantium go, Stephen. If I have to swallow poison, order the death of my own wife, or sell my daughter in marriage to a barbarian heathen she doesn't love in order to save the Empire, I'll do it in a heartbeat. God has called upon me to save Byzantium. I mean to do it, and I have."

I've underestimated Leo, I think. He's not the mercenary I thought he was. He's ruthless for sure, but he does care about something—the integrity of the Empire.

"So why am I here?" I asked him. "You never explained that either."

"You remember how I said that if I don't make it out of here, the Empress will marry again and her next husband will become Emperor?"

"Yeah."

"No offense, but I'd rather not have her next husband be you."

My stomach sank. *Oh, God! He knows! He knows everything! Lord, forgive me! Forgive me this dreadful sin!* My mouth opened and closed. Finally I said, "Sire, I—please, if you—I don't know what you're thinking, but—"

"Oh, come now, there's no reason to deny it." Leo tossed a nutmeat into his mouth. "And don't start groveling, please. We're way past the point where that will do any good. Frankly I'm glad *somebody* is boning Maria. I find the task somewhat disagreeable myself. As a matter of fact, I prefer to have sex with men, but that's neither here nor there. No—the reason I'd rather not have you marry her is not because you ravished her, but because you're an iconographer. If you're out of the picture, at least there's a chance that Maria *might* marry someone who can find it in their heart to carry on my campaign against idolatry. It's a faint hope, I admit, but a valiant one. Alas, as clever as I am in guaranteeing that the next Emperor of Byzantium will be a Christian, I can't quite ensure that the next emperor will also be an iconoclast. But if we roast in this little box together, Brother Stephen, at least the next emperor won't be a former icon painter. It's nothing personal!"

He munched his pistachios casually and mindlessly, sitting across from me in this tiny brick box that would soon be besieged by ghouls. As my mind reeled at Leo's machinations, I began to realize that, even if my death was soon at hand, God was answering the prayers of the people of Byzantium. This strange, ugly, smelly, little fat man with his fetid breath and green-stained fingers was indeed the unlikely savior of all of Christendom. He had his faults, but at this moment I doubted that we could have done better.

Chapter Fifteen

The Ball of Fire

In the morning we began to hear the ghouls. I awakened in my chair, my back aching and my legs almost numb, and in the inky darkness—our little oil lamp had gone out during the night—I heard a strange sound drifting down the chimney. At first it didn't sound like the ghouls at all, but rather the wind, and I wondered if it was a storm; then with a start I understood it was a multitude of voices, if they could be called that, warbling and groaning mindlessly in a vast and cacophonous chorus.

I shook the Emperor. "Sire! I think they're here!"

He snorted. "Hm? Erk? Moog?" I heard him rustling in the dark. He farted again. "What say you, Brother Stephen?"

"The ghouls. I think they're coming."

Leo listened. "I think you're right." He rummaged about in the dark for the flint, which he used to relight the oil lamp. Then he reached for the parchment and quill. "We'd better send a message to Camytzes and the others. I don't know if they have any way of telling how many ghouls are in the Hippodrome, but maybe somebody can advise us when they think we should light the fuse."

As the Emperor scratched his message on one of the parchments, I began to hear another sound—a kind of scraping noise, very distant and muffled. I realized it was the ghouls scrabbling with their hands against the outside of the bunker. The walls were so thick that the sound was barely audible. It was eerie imagining them out there, clawing and swaying in mindless obedience to their desires for our brains, smelling us through two feet of solid masonry.

Leo showed me his note before he attached it to the leg of one of our pigeons.

We cannot hear much and can obviously see nothing, but from their moans and the scraping of their fingers we believe the ghouls have converged upon the bunker. Please let us know when you advise us to light the fuse.

Basileus Imperator of Rome and Constantinople,
God's Vice-Regent on Earth, His Majesty Leo III.

The pigeon flapped and fluttered its way up the chimney, perhaps terrified to leave our little haven. No birds returned for many hours. In the meantime, the moaning of the ghouls increased by a factor of ten. Their wailing was eerie and unnerving. It caused the hair on the back of my neck to stand on end. "I wonder how many thousands of them are out there," I said. It had been at least an hour since my last conversation with the Emperor.

"All of them, if God smiles upon us," Leo replied.

"I fear that God has done precious little smiling lately, Sire."

After what seemed like an impossibly long time a pigeon appeared at the top of the chimney and swooped down into the darkness. "Aha!" the Emperor cried. Eagerly he pried the parchment from the band around the pigeon's foot.

We recommend you wait approximately eight hours to light the fuse. Artabasdos, Eutropius and I agree that we should allow sufficient time for all the ghouls of the city to find their way to the Hippodrome. Though we understand the waiting must be excruciating, we must maximize the chances of incinerating all the demons at once.

Michael Camytzes

"We have no way to tell how much time passes in here," the Emperor grunted. "And with the city deserted, no one is manning the church bells anymore, so we can't mark time by listening for them."

"It's daylight up above," I said, peering up the dark chimney. "Maybe we'll wait until sundown."

At that moment a second pigeon appeared. "What, hey?" said the Emperor. It floated down to us and again the Emperor was the first to read the message. His expression brightened. With almost a smug look on his face he handed the parchment to me. "It seems Maslama came to precisely the calculation that I predicted he would," he said.

Civilians now safely encamped nine miles from walls of Constantinople. Maslama's men have been distributing bread and blankets, also fresh milk for the children. Many of our commanders including myself impressed with generosity and honor of the Saracens. In my presence Maslama swore upon the Quran that all civilians will be given safe conduct back into Constantinople after annihilation of ghouls.

Artabasdos

The Emperor wrote on the backside of this message—

Please give Maslama my regards, as well as my personal assurance that once ghouls are destroyed there will be no hostile actions against any Saracens so long as they retreat from Byzantine territory immediately. Brother Stephen and I will light the fuse at sundown. All people of Constantinople are to offer prayer for their own deliverance when they see the great fireball rising from the city. It shall serve as a reminder of the awesome power of God against the enemies of righteousness.

Basileus Imperator of Rome and Constantinople,
God's Vice-Regent on Earth, His Majesty Leo III.

"Well, I suppose it's all over," the Emperor remarked after we had sent the pigeon on its way. "We made peace with the Saracens, the deliverance of our city is guaranteed, and Byzantium is saved. Tervel might even be persuaded to send my daughter back when he realizes he has nothing to gain by holding her. Not bad for being only a few months on the throne, wouldn't you say?"

"There's still the matter of the ghouls," I replied. "Suppose the Greek fire doesn't work? Or it does work, but we don't manage to smite them all?"

"We may never know. Notwithstanding the younger Camytzes's clever demonstration of the heat resistance of these stones, I have a sneaking suspicion that once we light this thing up we'll be baked like loaves of bread in an oven."

"I kind of think so too," I sighed.

The Emperor paused a moment. Then he reached inside his tunic and took out a small glass vial with a cork stopper. "I didn't tell anyone about this," he said, "because if we die here I want to go down in history unbesmirched by any hint of cowardice. It's the same stuff I gave Eutropius to use on Maria if Maslama had double-crossed us. If the heat and the pain are too unbearable and there seems to be no hope left, I'll swallow half of it. You can take the other half. It's very quick, so they tell me."

"Suicide is a mortal sin," I said. "I wouldn't dash my chances of reaching Heaven at the last moment of my life."

Leo chortled. "You make your living as an idolater, you lay with my wife, and you bred an army of undead brain-eating ghouls to slay your

213

fellow man. Do you really think, Brother Stephen, that swallowing a few drops of poison is going to make that much difference with the Almighty in our present circumstances?"

I took the vial from him. The liquid inside was colorless and looked like water.

"All right," I finally agreed.

I handed the vial back to Leo. He put it on the floor under his chair, next to the chamber pot. He craned his neck to peer up the chimney. "Not much longer, then," he said.

I recalled the letter that Maria had given me. *I suppose now is the time, isn't it?* Reaching into my cassock for it I said, "Sire, there's one more thing. Before I left the palace your wife gave me a letter that she specified I was to open it only just before we triggered the Greek fire. She bade that I keep it secret, but considering that you already know everything..." My voice trailed off and I offered the sealed envelope to him.

Leo looked down at it, but then drew his hand away. "No thanks," he replied. "I think I already know what it says."

"I am profoundly sorry, Your Majesty, for violating the sanctity of your marital bed."

The Emperor rolled his eyes. "Don't start with that. Just open it."

With my pulse quickening I stuck my thumb under the flap of the parchment and broke the Empress's seal. Her handwriting was clear and bold. The letter was not long, but my eyes grew wide as I gazed upon it.

Stephen, my love:

If this is to be the hour of your death, I want you to know that I love you and care for you deeply. While I will mourn your passing, all is not lost. I am with child. I will cherish your son or daughter forever, knowing that your blood beats within their veins. Go to God with satisfaction and joy.

Love, Maria

"Congratulations," smiled the Emperor. He couldn't even see the writing on the parchment but he'd correctly guessed the message.

I was nearly speechless. My mouth opened and closed. "I...I don't know what..."

"You'd better hope it's a boy. If it is, he has at least a chance of sitting on the throne of Byzantium someday. If it's a girl—well, the Empire can always use one more nun!" Leo laughed, and I detected in his laughter a slight ring of bitterness, which was as close as he ever came to reproaching me. It was shame enough. I folded the letter and put it back in my cassock.

He did not announce that the time had come upon us to do our duty, but it was obvious that it had. Leo reached casually for the end of the pitch-smeared fuse. "It may not make much difference," he said, handing the end of the fuse to me, "but I think as the Emperor that I should be the one to light the wick. Do you want to pray or anything beforehand?"

I shrugged. "Honestly, I don't know what good it would do now."

There was a moment of silence as the Emperor took the oil lamp from the cord on which it hung. Well, not *silence*—the moaning of the ghouls outside was as strong as ever, but it was now so steady and relentless that it had faded to the level of ambient noise. I held the end of the wick out to him. He held the small flame of the oil lamp an inch or so from the fuse.

"God bless the Byzantine Empire!" cried the Emperor. He touched the flame to the end of the wick. As it blazed to fiery life, I let go instantly, but my fingers were still slightly singed. A knot of fire lengthened into a glowing line, crawling quickly up the rope, showering sparks and cinders down on us.

And now, we probably die, I thought, as I watched the fire dance its way up the chimney. As the flame moved past the pigeon cage, the terrified birds—we had seven now—squawked and flapped furiously.

The flame reached the top of the chimney and flashed brightly as it reached the top of the rope. It would be seconds now before the fire traveled down the length of the fuse to the Greek fire canisters surrounding the bunker. I crossed myself. Both of us were transfixed by the sight of the flame blazing out of sight. My heart pounded as we awaited the explosion—the roar of fire, the hot blast and the screech of the ghouls in their final destruction.

We waited.

And nothing happened.

The Emperor, peering up the chimney, stood up from his chair. "What the hell?" he grumbled.

"The fuse must have gone out!" I gasped. "Somewhere up there outside the bunker."

For the first time ever I saw the Emperor angry. His jaw hardened, his eyes blazed with consternation and he cried, "The bastards! The fucking ghouls—they must have cut the fuse somehow out there."

"How could they do that?" I asked. "They can't think."

"It was probably an accident. The fuse was out there in the open. *Idiots!* Why didn't Camytzes rig a backup? *How fucking hard was that to figure out?*"

"What are we going to do?"

Leo stood on his chair, peering up the chimney, as if standing closer to the portal would somehow help. "The idiots—the *idiots!* There shouldn't have been *one* fuse. There should have been ten or twelve of them!"

Railing against what should have been done didn't strike me as productive in figuring out how to proceed. "We've got to reconnect the fuse somehow," I said. "Figure out where it broke, and light the remainder. Either that or we come up with some way to trigger the

Greek fire ourselves."

"And how do you propose to do that? There's not even a door or a window in this bunker. What, we're going to disassemble the bricks with our bare hands? Good luck!"

He climbed down from his chair. He was fuming with rage and frustration. Finally I reached for the pigeon cage. "We have to tell Camytzes and Artabasdos. Maybe they can figure out some way to relight the fuse."

"How? They're nine miles away. We're the only two people left in Constantinople who aren't undead."

I took a parchment and the quill and penned a short note.

We triggered the fuse but it didn't ignite the Greek fire. We suspect the rope broke somewhere outside the bunker where we can't reach it. Please advise.

Brother Stephen

Just as I finished the note the Emperor tore it out of my hands. "No pun intended, but we need to light a *fire* under these assholes," he muttered. Underneath my note he scrawled—

You morons better figure out how to light up the Hippodrome, and fast! Otherwise someone's head will roll for this!

YOUR VERY PISSED OFF EMPEROR.

He attached the parchment to the leg of one of the pigeons and flung it up the chimney. "Now we'll probably have to wait all night for a response," he grunted.

He wasn't far wrong. After the pigeon departed there was nothing for the two of us to do but wait. We'd been sealed in the bunker for two stifling, cramped, butt-numbing, foul-smelling, ego-bruising nights. Being forced to wait even longer was more excruciating than ever. The wailing of the ghouls was an endless torment. I thought I could now actually feel them pressing against the walls of the bunker. One ghoul in particular must have been especially ravenous for our flesh, for I could feel very faintly through the bricks a rhythmic thud like a body flinging itself against the side of the bunker repeatedly.

I could sense the Emperor was nearly going stir-crazy. He could not sit still and fidgeted endlessly in his chair. Ultimately he couldn't take it any longer. He stood on his chair, clawing his hair, pounding impotently against the brick walls. "God, please let this be *over!*" he wailed. "At this point I don't even mind if we *do* bake to death in here. I just want this to be over with. Please, God, strike the Hippodrome with lightning or something! *I want to get out of here!*"

By contrast, I was very melancholy. I sat in my chair, chin in my hand, mulling all that had gone wrong. *I guess we aren't going to defeat the ghouls after all,* I thought dejectedly. *Maybe we were wrong to believe that we could. Maybe God is teaching us a lesson about pride and hubris. Maybe tinkering with death and evil, trying to shape it to our ends, has poisoned Him against us once and for all.*

I had the disturbing image of the ghouls of Constantinople breaking out of their prison and fanning out across the world. There would be no way to contain them. In a few years—or even months—the entire earth could be nothing but a charnel house of flesh-eating monsters, and mankind would exist only so long as it could supply food to the demons. God would want nothing to do with such a world.

Dawn came and there was no reply to our pigeon. After a long silence, I finally gave voice to my suspicions. "What if they gave up?" I asked the Emperor. "Suppose Artabasdos and Eutropius and the others got our note and decided there was no way to set off the incendiaries. Suppose they decided to take the suggestion that you rejected—to close the gates of Constantinople and abandon it to the ghouls forever. Why would they bother to tell us if they'd done that? They wouldn't want to panic us, after all."

"It could be worse than that," said the Emperor. "There could have been a coup. Maybe Artabasdos took the throne as soon as they walled us up in here. I wouldn't put it past the old bastard to double-cross me."

I thought ominously of the vial of poison under his chair. "When do you think—" *It's a sin!* screamed part of me, but another part protested, *It doesn't matter anymore, does it?* "When do you think we're past the point of no return? I mean, when do you think there's no hope?"

"Honestly," sighed the Emperor, "I think it was about six hours ago. Maybe there's still hope. I suppose Artabasdos and the others could be scrambling to come to some kind of decision. I could see maybe some sort of harebrained scheme to surround the Hippodrome with catapults and lob flaming projectiles over the walls in the hopes that one might light the fuse accidentally. But that's pretty farfetched. It would take a lot of men to do that, and any large force of men they send into the city is going to divert the ghouls away from us and scatter them all over again. No—if I were Artabasdos, I don't think I'd really have any—"

A sudden flapping at the top of the chimney stopped his words in midsentence. We both sprang up, colliding with each other in the small space, reaching into the air for the pigeon that was now fluttering down the chimney.

"Grab it! Get it!" shouted the Emperor.

I literally snatched the pigeon out of the air. The Emperor, scrambling for the parchment tied to its leg, nearly tore the poor bird apart. "It's from Michael Camytzes," he said breathlessly, once he'd unfolded the paper. He read the note to me.

Received your news about the broken fuse. There is no option we can think of except to send a single man into the Hippodrome to try and trigger the Greek fire by any means possible. It must be one man because any more would risk drawing the ghouls away from the bunker.

"Thank God!" I gasped.

"They're using their heads," said the Emperor. "There's more."

He read it, and my face grew white.

There can be no question about this man returning from this mission. I doubt even that there will remain of him anything left to bury. If I may make one further request of the Emperor, it is that the church in the town of Domelium be reconstructed. I would like to have a memorial stone erected there. I will not lie beneath it, but I want it known for all time that I have given my life in the service of my people, my village, and my God.

Michael Camytzes

"Hell, I'll build him the grandest cathedral in Byzantium if he pulls this off," said the Emperor.

I was devastated. "Michael," I whispered. I sat down heavily. *No, not Michael! Please—anyone but him! He's been so brave and so valiant throughout this turmoil. Byzantium needs warriors like him. How can he think to sacrifice himself?*

"He's probably already on his way here. Let's hope he's bringing plenty of fire arrows with him. He's only going to have one chance at this, so he'd better make it count."

"He was my friend."

The Emperor patted my shoulder. "I'm sorry." This was the first time I'd ever heard him express sympathy for a single one of the ghouls' multitudinous victims. "He was a good man."

"He *is* a good man." I felt tears coming to my eyes.

Leo sat back down in his chair. He reached for the edge of the animal hide that we had used to protect ourselves from the dripping of the mortar. "We have no way of knowing when this thing is going to

220

light up," he said. "We'd better be prepared for it at any moment." He began to pull the hide up over our heads. It wouldn't be much protection against the heat, but it might keep any flaming cinders or other debris off of us.

And so we spent the last hours of our imprisonment cowered together in the darkness under an animal hide, listening to the wailing of the ghouls, the scraping and scrabbling of their claws against the bricks, and wondering how much longer it would be before Michael Camytzes brought about our hellish deliverance. I had never in my life felt more helpless. When you become a monk, supposedly you abandon yourself entirely to God, but until this terrible night I hadn't really known what that truly meant. Now I thought I understood. Crouching there in the dark bunker inside the Hippodrome, even though I was inches away from the most powerful man in the world, all of his power was meaningless. God would rap his gavel on this exact spot, and the outcome of our great battle could be affected only by Him.

And Michael Camytzes.

At just after dawn on the Day of St. Gregory the Wonder-Worker, Bishop of Neo-Caesaria, in the year Anno Mundi 6226, the greatest explosion ever known in the history of the world since the fire of Creation blossomed into the morning sky above the city of Constantinople.

The colossal fireball erupted into the air without warning. The Byzantine Army and the surviving civilians of the city, camped amidst the Saracens nine miles west of the city, watched the flash rise into the reddish sky like a huge fiery mushroom. The Patriarch had assured them that seeing a great holy fire over Constantinople meant that God was personally intervening to smite the ghouls once and for all. Oddly enough the Saracens were praying for the same thing. Two peoples prayed to their different gods for the same result, hoping that the fire in the sky would bring the renewal of the world. Ironically I was told later that the fireball blossomed just as the muezzins were calling the Mohammedan faithful in the Saracens' camp to prayer. Maslama was reported to have clapped his hands and said, "Allah has smiled upon the world this day."

It happened inside the bunker without warning too. The first thing we heard was a loud *wumph!* and then the Emperor and I, our food and amphorae, the chamber pots, the pigeon cage and the terrified squawking birds were rocked by a shock wave that dashed us about in our tiny bunker like dice shaken in a cup. Instantly I was nearly deaf from the roar of the explosion. I could see a shower of sparks falling across the edge of the animal hide that protected us. Only then did we begin to feel the wave of intense heat. It felt like all the air had been sucked out of my lungs. I remained there on the floor of the bunker, gasping for breath, trying not to touch anything, for the walls of the bunker and any object inside of it made of metal, porcelain or masonry was now so hot that it would have burned the skin off my body to have come in contact with it.

Because I was deafened by the explosion of the Greek fire, I couldn't hear the ghouls die. But I imagined them—hordes of screaming, wailing demons, splashed with flaming oil, seething and writhing together in one panicked mass, flesh melting off their bones and the bones themselves crumbling into charred and blackened dust. The initial ignition of the incendiaries was only partial. A few minutes after the first explosion there was a second, most likely the outer ring of Greek fire canisters going up; it was less powerful but certainly increased the heat inside the bunker.

And Michael is dead, I thought. I wondered how he had detonated the canisters. Perhaps he shot one of the fuses with a flaming arrow. Maybe he fought his way through legions of ghouls, slashing frantically with his sword, until he reached a fuse, and maybe he lit it directly. Perhaps he had died only feet away from us, separated by the thick wall of masonry whose construction he had commanded. However he did it, the plans seemed to have worked.

Over the whole course of my life I never knew anything as close to

Hell as I did inside that bunker while the ghouls burned outside. Leo and I remained on the floor of the brick oven, covered by the thick tanned hide, too afraid even to move. There was a small gap between the edge of the hide and the floor and through it I could see sparks, bits of charcoal and other flaming debris raining down. At one point I saw one of the pigeons, its feathers blackened and smoking, fall dead to the floor, twitch twice and then lie still. In the explosion, the chamber pots had overturned. There was a puddle of piss on the floor inches away from me, and as the heat mounted, I watched it boil away in a cloud of foul-smelling steam. I wondered how long it would be before our own skin and hair simply burst into flame.

I don't know how long the intense heat lasted. After a while it became difficult to breathe. The fire had sucked most of the oxygen out of the bunker, and there was very little filtering down to us from the chimney. The reddish-orange light of the flames had begun to fade slightly by the time I became dizzy. *So maybe this is how it's going to end*, I thought. *We don't burn to death, but rather suffocate.*

As I thought this, I felt the Emperor move next to me for the first time since the conflagration began. Shifting under the hide, I opened a crack of light that illuminated his face in hell-fire orange. He looked strange and desperate. His face and head were covered with sweat. The ends of his long hair had begun to singe, smoking faintly. I could see blistered flesh on the ends of his fingers and the backs of his hands. His mouth opened and closed, but if he was talking, I couldn't make out his words.

Do I look like that too? I wondered.

The motion was his arm. He was reaching for something—the vial of poison.

With his burned fingers, he managed to grasp it. But his hand shook terribly. *Yes, it's time for this*, I thought. *God forgive me, but we're not going to make it. We're cooking to death and suffocating. We might as well end the torment now.* As I saw the Emperor's quaking fingers pull the stopper from the vial of poison, I said a silent prayer for my unborn child in Maria's womb, and for the departed soul of Michael

Camytzes. I hoped the church would make him a saint.

Leo pulled the stopper from the vial, but then the glass vessel slipped from his fingers. It fell to the floor of the bunker, leaking the poison onto the stones. The Emperor laid his head down on the ground and stuck out his tongue. His hideous visage was like some sort of gargoyle. I realized he was trying to lick the poison from the floor. He failed. The pool of poison began to boil and steam away in the heat. My last coherent thought before I lost consciousness was to try to inhale as much of the steam as possible. We had lost the poison itself, but maybe the steam would kill us if we were lucky.

Chapter Sixteen

Corpronymous

The next thing I remembered was a strange plinking sound, like metal against stone. It was pitch-black and my head was spinning. *How is it we're still alive?* I wondered. My entire body was raw and desiccated. My skin felt like leather. I raised my head up off the stone floor. I could see light coming through the crack between the edge of the animal hide and the floor. It wasn't the dim light of the bunker's oil lamp, nor the hellish orange glow of the flames shining down through the chimney. It was daylight.

"There they are!" I heard a voice shout.

"Are they alive?"

Plink! Plink! Plink! I saw chunks of stone land on the floor. I felt pebbles striking the animal hide that covered me. I opened my mouth and tried to shout, but my voice was gone. Slowly I began to rouse myself. Being able to take a full deep breath was one of the sweetest experiences of my life.

"One of them is moving!" cried one of our rescuers.

"Is it the Emperor?"

The Emperor. As I struggled to crawl out from under the hide, I was aware of an inert figure next to me. Leo hadn't moved and I could not hear him breathing. *Did he suffocate? Did he manage to take enough of the poison to kill himself?* I looked down at him, his body partially covered by the animal skin; I could see one hairy foot protruding from it. His purple boots were split, their leather blistered and singed. I knew for sure he was dead.

I looked up. Several Byzantine soldiers were busy smashing through the bricks with crowbars and picks. Chunks of stone continued to rain down onto me. But I could see the blue sky of day— and I could *not* see any ghouls.

"At least one of them is alive!" shouted one of the men. With a sudden fury of crowbars the soldiers smashed through the partial hole they had made in the bunker and enlarged the opening so a man could slip through. The soldier clambered down into the bunker, his chain mail scraping against the stone walls. He was almost frantic. "Sire! Sire! Your Majesty! Can you hear me?"

I was still unable to speak. I reached up my hand toward the soldier, but he completely ignored me. Indeed, he squeezed past me so ·he could attend the Emperor, pulling at the heavy animal hide to uncover his body.

"We'll need a hook and a sling down here!" shouted the soldier to his comrades. "And have the surgeon stand by!"

Finally an arm grabbed me and began to haul me up toward the hole. I was barely strong enough to hold on. The stab of bright sunlight into my eyes was almost painful. I nearly lost consciousness again, but I was coherent enough to think—*It worked. We must have destroyed the ghouls. God indeed has saved us.*

As my eyes adjusted to the sunlight, I found the Hippodrome one of the strangest and most nightmarish scenes I'd ever laid eyes upon.

The entire arena seemed to be completely covered in what looked at first like gnarled black rosebushes. There were mounds upon mounds of stringy, thorny blackish things, some in towering piles, and so many of them piled up on the bunker itself that the bricks of the structure were barely visible. When I saw that some of the burnt rosebushes seemed to have hands, feet and even heads, I realized that these stinking black mounds were all that remained of the ghouls. I was being hauled bodily across the shoulders of two Byzantine soldiers, and their mail-clad legs crunched and snapped through the piles of burnt ghoul bodies that were impossible to avoid because they stretched in every direction.

The soldiers were carrying me to a horse-drawn cart not far from the bunker. A sort of pathway had been literally shoveled through the layers of ghoul carcasses to make way for the cart and the cadre of soldiers who were busy dismantling the bunker. Across the arena I saw several more carts, and a platoon of soldiers shoveling and flinging burnt ghoul corpses into them. All the grand marble statues and fountains of the Hippodrome were now totally invisible, buried beneath mountains of ghouls. The grand white columns supporting the perimeter of the arena were uniformly black. Even the great gilded horses atop the Emperor's viewing box were charred and singed. The heat of the fire had been so intense that it had partially melted the horses, whose legs and hindquarters were now formless lumpy masses of melted and re-solidified metal.

There were many people gathered around the cart onto which the soldiers lifted me. I saw Eutropius, the *kouropalates* Artabasdos, Theophilus, Nicetas and even Gabriel Camytzes. As they laid me on the cart—one of the soldiers put a pillow under my head—another figure, robed in blue, appeared. Bits of charcoal and fluttery remnants of the ghouls' burnt clothes and skin swirled about the Empress Maria as she approached. She rushed toward the cart, seized my head and planted a kiss upon it.

"You *survived!*" she gushed. "Dear God in *Heaven*, I can't believe you made it!"

I finally had the strength to speak. "The...Emperor," I croaked. "I don't think he—"

"They're bringing him out now!" Artabasdos cried.

The soldiers hauled out the Emperor's limp body in a canvas sling. I raised my head off the pillow and could see only a fat black lump silhouetted against the sky. Maria looked over, wailed in anguish and

227

buried her head against my chest.

"Dear God," Eutropius whispered.

Four soldiers carried the Emperor to the cart and gently laid him next to me. At first I wondered, with his singed hair, blistered fingers and charcoal-smeared face, how he had come through the ordeal so much worse than I had. Then I realized—*That's the kind of shape I'm in too.* My whole body was one vast repository of pain.

Maria rushed around the side of the cart and clutched her husband's hand. "Leo! Leo! Can you hear me? Give me a sign. *Please!*"

Artabasdos came up next to her. As she began sobbing, he put his arm around her. "I'm very sorry, Your Majesty," he said softly.

Theophilus approached the cart too. He took my hand.

"Michael?" I whispered, hoping against hope. Maybe by some miracle he had managed to survive.

Theophilus shook his head. His old wrinkled face registered an expression of sorrow.

Eutropius leaned over the Emperor's body, listening for any signs of life. When the eunuch straightened up, his blank visage communicated everything. He looked over at the Empress, still sobbing, and then bowed deeply before her.

"Your Majesty," he said. "You are the new ruler of Byzantium. What are your orders?"

At that moment the Emperor's mouth dropped open and a sudden ugly hacking sound emerged.

It was like a sudden electric shock. Everyone crowded around Leo again, Maria frantically squeezing his hand, Eutropius and Artabasdos shaking him. "Your Majesty! *Your Majesty!* Can you hear me?"

The Emperor's body shifted on the cart next to me. He squirmed; then his loins issued a long, deep, wet-sounding fart. He opened his eyes.

"*Pistachios,*" said the Emperor, in a labored and anguished gasp. "*Somebody bring me my pistachios!*"

The day after the soldiers hauled us out of the pitted bunker the people began to return to Constantinople. In a driving autumn rain our army marched the thousands of civilians who had survived the ghoul catastrophe back to the city to reclaim their homes, businesses and churches—or what was left of them. In the meantime the Saracens began to pack up their camp and prepare for the long march back to their own lands.

The torrential rains were something of a baptism. The gutters of Constantinople ran with blood, cinders and soot, especially from the Hippodrome. The rain washed off the layers of filth and tragedy that had settled upon the city during the ghoul rampages, leaving our great Christian capital clean and unblemished, ready to shine again as the jewel in God's own empire.

The people returned humble and pious. The next day after the march was Sunday, and nearly every church in Constantinople was full of parishioners giving thanks for their deliverance. The Emperor was still too ill to appear in the gallery of St. Sofia—as was I—but the Patriarch himself led the congregation in a lengthy series of prayers and thanksgivings to praise God for having delivered us from the greatest evil Byzantium had yet faced. The siege towers and twinkling nighttime fires against the Walls of Theodosius were gone. So too were the Saracen ships; one could look out onto the Bosporus, the Marmara and the Golden Horn and see instead the distant sails of Byzantine trade ships returning to bring the city much-needed grain, lumber and other materials to fuel its inevitable resurrection.

The Saracens didn't attack, but they did linger for an uncomfortably long time beyond the walls. After a few days their presence became concerning. As I convalesced in the Great Palace, I heard rumors that Maslama had broken his word and was preparing to renew the siege. As it turned out, however, he and his army remained because he demanded a personal meeting with the Emperor before departing, and Leo was still too sick to see him. When the weather cleared the audience finally happened, Leo was carried to the meeting on a litter. I wasn't there, but Artabasdos was. He said that the two commanders met alone in Maslama's command tent for nearly an hour, and when he was carried out, the Emperor was tight-lipped about whatever had gone on inside. "You can be assured, however," the Emperor reportedly told Artabasdos, "that the Saracens will be marching away no later than dawn tomorrow morning." And they did, heading back to the south in a long train of clinking armor and fluttering green banners. They left nearly ten thousand of their own dead, many of them ghouls, which they had burned. They dumped the ashes into the Sea of Marmara.

Two weeks or so after the Great Deliverance, as the people of Constantinople had begun to call it, the Emperor held an intimate banquet at the Great Palace to bid farewell and thanks to those of us who were instrumental in defeating the ghouls. The long table draped in brocaded cloth was mounded with gilded plates of plenty—roast duck, roast chickens, beef, tureens of steaming sauces, colossal wheels of cheese, mountainous loaves of bread, and endless silver flagons of the finest wine. It was one of the greatest feasts of my life. I sat next to Theophilus on one side and Gabriel Camytzes on the other. The elder Camytzes had insisted that an empty chair be placed at the table to symbolize the absence of his son.

After we'd eaten quite a lot and the Emperor began the toasts, he raised his jewel-encrusted goblet to the fallen hero. "Every man, woman and child in the Byzantine Empire, from me on down to the rudest peasant, owes a debt of gratitude to Michael Camytzes—truly one of the greatest, bravest and most selfless men our country has ever produced. He gave his life without hesitation to destroy the ghouls, and we'll forever remember him. I want you all to know that not only do I intend to respect his last wishes regarding the reconstruction of the church in his home village of Domelium, but I've ordered the finest architects, craftsmen and stonemasons to rebuild the church as a grand cathedral. It shall be called the Church of St. Michael the Martyr. May God bless him and all his kin!"

"Hear hear!" We all raised our goblets.

The Emperor led us in many more toasts—to the elder Camytzes, to the military commanders of the various cadres, the builders of the bunker, to Maslama and the Saracens for keeping their word, and to me for my ingenuity and bravery. I felt somewhat uncomfortable with all the accolades. *It's good that we're leaving and going back to our homes and monasteries*, I thought during the toast. *I'm just a simple monk, and I should get back to the cloister.*

At the end of the toasts, however, the Emperor gave a strange little speech. Raising his goblet one more time he said, "In concluding this evening of celebration, I must say a few words to you about how we'll look back on this incident. Some of you may recall that I had a meeting with Maslama shortly before the Saracens marched away. I was somewhat concerned with how our recent travails will go down in the history books. It's not just my own vanity and my desire to be remembered as the savior of Byzantium—which, of course, I am. But while I was convalescing the Patriarch came to my chambers to bless my recovery, and I asked him to say a prayer for the Saracens. He startled me by refusing. The Saracens, being infidel Mohammedans, are eternally damned in the eyes of God. It would be blasphemy, said the Patriarch, to admit that they're capable of Christian virtues such as honor, piety and dignity in the eyes of the Lord. When I asked him how it would look, then, that I cooperated with Maslama during the siege, and that he and I had worked out a deal for the deliverance of our city from the ghouls, the Patriarch replied, 'It will be looked upon as rank blasphemy, an abomination to God, and it is right that it be so, for it is.'"

The banquet room was silent. Theophilus glanced at me uneasily. *I certainly don't agree with that*, I thought, but I couldn't say it; the Patriarch was the head of our church and the leader of our faith, and it would be heresy to disagree with him publicly, especially in front of the Emperor.

"As you know," the Emperor continued, "my office is a secular one, and under Byzantine law I'm bound by the ecclesiastical authority of

231

the Patriarch of Constantinople. Therefore, his word on the subject is final and beyond dispute. As it turns out, Maslama had a similar problem. He sent a message to me stating that he couldn't very well march back to Baghdad and tell his brother the Caliph that he voluntarily abandoned the almost certain conquest of Constantinople, electing instead to help the hated Byzantines save the very city the Saracens wanted to conquer. Furthermore, it is heresy in his faith, as it is in ours, to suggest that the ghouls—which the Patriarch believes are a punishment from God—afflicted Christians and Muslims equally, because that would suggest that the two faiths are coequal in the eyes of God. Naturally *that* can't be. So, Maslama and I came to an accord that I believe solves the very thorny religious questions raised by the ghoul plague.

"At our brief summit meeting Maslama and I agreed that we would tell our respective chroniclers to record that a great clash occurred between the armies of Byzantium and those of the Saracens. The Saracens besieged Constantinople. We held fast. Decimated by hunger, disease and cold—after all, Maslama has to explain to the Caliph why ten thousand of his men didn't return—the Saracens abandoned the siege and withdrew. There is to be no mention of ghouls. Let me repeat that—*the infestation of ghouls never happened.* From this day forward no one is to speak of ghouls, of corpses, of fireballs or anything of the kind. We owe the deliverance of the city to the intercession of the Virgin Mary. Even the very word 'ghoul' is to be banished from the Greek language for all time. This is my decree. Anyone who violates it will suffer the ultimate penalty."

The Emperor looked around the room, making eye contact with each and every one of us present. The last person he looked at was his wife. She nodded obediently.

Leo's expression brightened. He sat down, set his goblet on the table and then clapped his hands. "Bring forth the desserts!"

And so, our history was written.

The next day I returned to the Monastery of St. Stoudios, which was a curious pastiche of ruin and triumph. The courtyard where we'd battled the ghouls before was ruined, and every monk who could lift a spade or carry a potted tree was set to work trying to restore the gardens to their former glory. The infirmary was a gloomy chamber of gore and carnage. Brownish bloodstains splattered the walls, most of the wooden bedsteads were broken and the tile floor was littered with bones, shattered glass and crockery, and stained shreds of clothes. Our chapel was also a shambles. It seemed that a large group of ghouls had congregated inside of it during the siege. On the second day after my arrival my friend Henoch, cleaning up the debris in the chapel, made a horrifying discovery—the skeleton of a little girl, bits of rotting flesh still clinging to her blackened bones, was wedged behind the altar. This type of thing was hardly unique in our monastery; such dreadful surprises were turning up all over Constantinople, and they probably would be for years to come.

I supervised the cleanup efforts. Rhetorios, the former *hegoumenos*, had regrettably been killed by ghouls—one of the tens of thousands of sad losses with which the city was grappling—and his replacement had not yet been selected. Those of us who had survived didn't think much of rules and hierarchies, for we were all laboring as hard as our bodies would permit just to make the monastery livable again and to erase all traces of the horrors that had occurred there. We had charred and gnawed bones to bury, bloodstains to scrape and cleanse from walls, larders to restock with grain and fowl, the garden to repair, and our infirmary to set in order so it could again serve the poor and destitute of the city. This was a full-time job. Although I'd returned to my little cell and found it had been relatively unscathed during the ghoul siege, I gave little thought to the Empress's secret icon, which was right where I'd left it under my sleeping pallet. *Worry about that later*, I told myself. *There's still so much to do. Everybody in Constantinople will be very busy for the foreseeable future.*

We were working so hard that I'd hardly noticed Christmas was almost upon us. The first snow of the season, which fell on December 18, surprised me. That night after vespers—with great effort we'd been able to restore our chapel such that it was usable—Henoch and Gennadios approached me. "Brother Stephen," said Gennadios, "the great holiday marking Christ's birth is almost here, and it is not proper that we have no *hegoumenos* to lead the congregation in Christmas prayer. The time has come to select one."

"I agree," I said. "Who do you have in mind?"

"There is talk among the monks," said Henoch. "No other name is mentioned as often as yours."

I almost collapsed from shock. "That can't be. I'm far too young to be *hegoumenos*. I have no seniority. I doubt the Patriarch would confirm me."

"You are a hero, Brother Stephen," Gennadios said. "Your bravery in fighting the ghouls is known far and wide. You also have a rapport with the Emperor, which would be of no small value to this institution. Theophilus similarly commands the respect and admiration of the monks, but as you know he's returned to his own cloister at Chenolakkos. Please, Brother—let us put your name forward."

"I'm flattered," I said, "and if you want to do that, I guess I can't stop you. But you're wasting your time. The Patriarch has to approve the appointment, and he certainly won't choose a twenty-one-year-old misfit from the boondocks to be the head of the most important monastery in Constantinople."

"The Lord will provide," Henoch shrugged.

He did. Two days before Christmas a parchment arrived from St. Sofia, spangled with the gaudy seals of the Patriarch. The monks of St. Stoudios had voted almost unanimously for my selection as *hegoumenos*, and the Patriarch approved it glowingly. The next day I found myself leading Christmas Eve vespers, wearing a brand-new robe and the cross on a golden chain that was the insignia of the head of a monastic order. I was the youngest *hegoumenos* in the whole of the Byzantine Empire.

It was not until after the services were over, and I retired to my new expansive quarters in lieu of the rude cell where I'd once lived, that I finally turned my attention back to the Empress's secret icon. Since I now occupied the *hegoumenos*'s private apartments, I felt far more secure than I had in my cell. It was late and the snow was falling gently outside my arched window, but I lit the candles, washed my brushes and again engaged in the pleasing ritual of mixing my paints. I took the shroud off the icon and stared at it for a while. The arms of the Virgin Mary, outstretched to the people of Constantinople, were broad and inviting. The Virgin's eyes—I'd made them sea-green, like Maria's—were suitably sad and plaintive. But something was missing.

"It doesn't look right," I whispered to the picture. "Something about the background."

I examined my work up close. I had begun to paint the small figures of the Saracen troops, teeming against the walls of the city in their chain mail and spiked helmets. On impulse, I took a small brush and took onto it a dollop of white paint. I mixed it with black, forming an ashy-gray color, and painted over one of the faces of the Saracen troops. Then, using a smaller brush, I edged the soldier's eyes and mouth with bright crimson blood. In a few minutes I had painted over many of the Saracens in this manner, covering up their chain mail and helmets with hair, torn clothes and bare gray flesh. This was what was wrong—the Saracens should be ghouls.

But if the mere word "ghoul" is now forbidden, I thought as I painted, *surely the image of one must also be.* This gave me pause, but then I considered that since the entire icon itself was heresy, and to be kept secret, it made little difference. The icon might as well portray the truth accurately. The Virgin Mary had indeed delivered Constantinople, but not from the Saracens—she, and the Emperor, had rescued us from the minions of the Devil.

The following August, the Empress Maria gave birth to a healthy baby boy. Anna had by now returned from Bulgaria and was again betrothed to Artabasdos. Anna's younger brother was born in the porphyry bedchamber of the Great Palace, and since he was born during his father's reign, he was known as *porphyrogennetos*—born in the purple—the highest purity a Byzantine heir could possess. The Emperor Leo doted and fawned over the son that no one knew was not his. Maria certainly said nothing, nor did I, but I thought it interesting that the invitation I received to attend the child's official baptism in St. Sofia was written by the Emperor himself. It was an intensely hot day, but in my long wool robes and sporting my new flowing beard, I took my place among the churchmen upon the altar of St. Sofia and prepared to see my son for the first time in the flesh.

He was a fidgety and vexatious little child. Maria brought him to the Patriarch in brocaded swaddling clothes, and his indignant wail seemed to fill the grand space of St. Sofia. The Emperor, in full regalia, wearing his crown of gilded laurels and for once without pistachio nuts in his hand, knelt on the porphyry disk set into the floor on which he'd been coronated. Patriarch Germanus took the baby, and I, on tiptoes, peered over his shoulder to see its face. The baby's eyes were squinted shut, but I could see that his features rather resembled mine. I couldn't help but grin slightly.

Murmuring in Latin, the Patriarch brought my baby to the edge of the marble font. He set the child on the edge of the font and dipped a golden cup into the holy water.

"I baptize thee Constantine Leo Konon the Porphyrogennetos," said the Patriarch, dripping the holy water over my son's head. "Blessed be the Father, the Son and the Holy—"

The Patriarch suddenly recoiled. There was something bobbing in the baptismal font—a gooey tannish-brown ooze. From its color and stench it was instantly recognizable as the fecal matter of a newborn baby. My son had taken a shit in the holy water.

"Er, the Holy Spirit," said the Patriarch. Holding the baby at arm's length, he quickly handed him back to his mother. As she took him, she glanced at me. She too was suppressing a smile. Our eyes locked for only an instant, but it was enough; we were connected now, and we always would be.

Leo III remained on the throne of Byzantium for another twenty-three years. In the years following the siege of Constantinople and the restoration of peace, he launched an assault against the veneration of icons which nearly tore the Empire apart. At the time of his death in June 741, at the age of fifty-six, he was revered by many of his subjects and hated by many more. The controversy regarding icons raged for another century and claimed many lives.

The Empress Maria survived her husband, but spent her final years in a convent on the Island of Lesbos. She remained firmly—though quietly—devoted to icons until the end of her life.

Constantine attained the throne in his own right in 741 upon his father's death. He was officially designated Constantine V, but was nicknamed "Corpronymous"—"he who is named for shit"—as a result of the embarrassing incident at his baptism. He allegedly invoked the death penalty against anyone who referred to him by that name in his presence. Constantine V Corpronymous reigned for thirty-four tumultuous years and carried on his father's campaign against icons. He died in September 775 while on a military campaign against the Bulgarians.

Artabasdos, the kouropalates under Leo III, married Leo's daughter Anna. Shortly after Constantine V came to the throne, Artabasdos launched a revolt against him and attempted to take the throne for himself. Artabasdos was a believer in icons. His revolt failed, and Constantine had Artabasdos and his sons blinded and imprisoned at the Monastery of Chora. Anna followed him into exile and died there too, years later.

Stephen Diabetenos remained the hegoumenos of the Monastery of St. Stoudios well into the reign of his own son. He was removed from his position for refusing to support the Emperor's persecution of those who still worshiped icons. He returned to Chenolakkos a common monk, and died there in 770. His remains were placed in the same ossuary as Theophilus who had died there peacefully fifty years before.

Maslama returned to Saracen lands and led many military expeditions over the years, some against Byzantine forces, though much of his later career was spent campaigning against the Khazars. He eventually fell out of favor with the Caliph, retired from public life and died in Syria in 738.

Khan Tervel continued to connive and scheme to take over Byzantium, though he was never able to mount an all-out military effort to conquer it. At one point he supported a rival of Leo, hoping to incite a rebellion, but this was unsuccessful. The date of his death is not known.

No history books mention the role of undead ghouls in the Saracen siege of 717. According to all historical accounts, the Saracens were thwarted by lack of supplies and the harsh winter. Although the Muslim world under various rulers long coveted Constantinople, none were successful at subduing it until Ottoman Sultan Mehmet II finally conquered the city on May 29, 1453. On that day, the Byzantine Empire ceased to exist.

About the Author

At the age of seven Sean Munger learned to type on a 1948 Remington Rand portable typewriter, and his earliest stories involved monsters, aliens and time travel. Since then he's regarded books as time machines, able to transport the reader to fantastic worlds both real and imagined. He takes trips to both kinds of worlds frequently.

The son of a military family, Sean lived all over the United States before settling in the Pacific Northwest. Before attending law school he worked as a retail clerk, a go-fer for a professional sports team and briefly was a staff writer for a short-lived horror series on cable TV in the Midwest. He was a practicing attorney for twelve years before returning to his two first loves, history and writing. He now studies and teaches history at a large university in the Northwest.

Sean has been a dedicated fan of heavy metal music for most of his life. In addition to writing historical short stories and zombie novels, he has written for several metal-related publications, both digital and print. He was formerly a Western columnist for Painkiller Magazine, the largest heavy metal magazine in China.

Sean loves to hear from his readers. You can interact with him on his website, http://seanmunger.com, or through his Twitter account, http://twitter.com/Sean_Munger.

SAMHAIN
PUBLISHING

It's all about the story...

Romance

HORROR

www.samhainpublishing.com

CPSIA information can be obtained at www.ICGtesting.com
Printed in the USA
LVOW051504130213

319909LV00006B/596/P